PRAISE FOR JASON HEWITT'S
THE DYNAMITE ROOM

Long-listed for the Desmond Elliott Prize

"With its unshowy, confident prose, this novel is accomplished, resonant, and surprising, and poses some delicately handled questions about whether redemption is possible, and at what point a good heart becomes forever besmirched."

—Jill Dawson, *The Guardian*

"In this fine balance of taut suspense and tragedy, Hewitt has created an emotionally charged character study in which he explores the loneliness, fear, hope, and shame that war visits on ordinary people. Mystery and general-fiction book groups will enjoy dissecting these characters and their nuanced story; highly recommended...to readers of character-driven historical fiction."

—Christine Tran, *Booklist*

"Hidden in a boarded-up house, the soldier keeps the girl hostage, their two stories slowly emerging in tandem as the bond between them grows. There are no happy endings with this book. But, as Hewitt movingly evokes, both are lost, just trying to find their way home." —Sam Baker, *Harper's Bazaar* (UK)

"*The Dynamite Room* explores what can happen to a good person swept up in a bad cause, and how the maelstrom of war sears its youngest victims. The themes of the novel run closely to those of another recent work, *All the Light We Cannot See,* by Anthony Doerr....Hewitt poses some profound questions: What if the wolf who comes to the door has the soul of a musician? What if he is self-aware enough to have retained his sense of right and wrong?" —Tom Young, *Washington Independent Review of Books*

"Suspenseful and powerful. A novel of great humanity that exposes the absurd contradictions of war."

—Samantha Harvey, author of *The Wilderness*

"A claustrophobic psychological thriller, as powerfully visualized as a screenplay.... Hewitt handles this complicated narrative with assurance, juggling the reader's sympathies while adding crumbs of information, all the while pitting Heiden's tarnished ideals against Lydia's vulnerability. A sense of theatricality pervades the contemporary scenes—small cast, stifling domestic setting—but these are usefully crafted in the closing pages to deliver a jolting finale. An unusual, intricate drama delivered with accomplishment."

—*Kirkus Reviews*

"Hewitt weaves a spellbinding tale to linger over and savor, looping back and drawing us forward to a conclusion that is equally heartbreaking and beautiful.... This gripping first novel is a book for the ages, so engaging and well-written I did not want it to end. Very highly recommended." —Historical Novel Society

"Well-crafted and engrossing.... Hewitt artfully explores family and identity, and how war changes the lives of both soldiers and civilians."

—*Publishers Weekly*

"A gripping tale.... *The Dynamite Room* is, in a word, dynamite.... Hewitt's debut novel is likely to stay with you for a long time." —Fran Wood, NJ.com

THE
DYNAMITE
ROOM

A NOVEL

JASON HEWITT

BACK BAY BOOKS
Little, Brown and Company
New York Boston London

Back Bay Books / Little, Brown and Company
Hachette Book Group
1290 Avenue of the Americas
New York, NY 10104
littlebrown.com

First North American edition published in hardcover by Little, Brown and Company, March 2015
First Back Bay paperback edition, June 2016
Originally published in Great Britain by Simon & Schuster UK Ltd., March 2014

Back Bay Books is an imprint of Little, Brown and Company, a divisin of Hachette Book Group. The Back Bay Books name and logo are trademarks of Hachette Book Group, Inc.

The publisher is not responsible for websites (or their content) that are not owned by the publisher.

The Hachette Speakers Bureau provides a wide range of authors for speaking events. To find out more, go to hachettespeakersbureau.com or call (866) 376-6591.

ISBN 978-0-316-32765-7 (hc) / 978-0-316-32766-4 (pb)
LCCN 2014956720

10 9 8 7 6 5 4 3 2 1

RRD-C

Printed in the United States of America

To my parents

THURSDAY

SHE WAS THE only person to get off the train, and as it pulled out again, leaving her on the empty platform, she watched the receding line of carriages tail into the distance; the dried leaves, caught in a flurry of air, chased after them down the track. She walked out through the gates, into the sunshine, and onto the road, but there didn't seem to be anyone about. The station shop was shut. She wandered back onto the platform and prized her last two pennies out of her secret pocket so that she could buy a bar of Fry's chocolate from the vending machine, but that was empty as well. She wondered where everyone was. The station name that swung from the awning was gone; just hooks poked out where it had once been. She'd heard about this on Mrs. Duggan's wireless: all across the country, towns and villages were losing their identities and road signs were being taken down. Her mother had written about it too in one of her letters. Six letters, one for every week she'd been away, and all of them folded and folded again until they were small enough to keep safe and secret.

It was a short walk into the village across the Suffolk flatlands, and she struggled along the lane, her heavy suitcase bumping against her leg and the box for her gas mask swinging from her shoulders. The sun blazed over the top of the hedgerow. The first sight or sound of an airplane and she'd have to scramble into the ditch; she'd be an easy target for them on such an open road. It surprised her that there was nothing in the road to stop them from trying to land on it—railway sleepers, rotten tree trunks, old bedsteads or mangled bicycles. All over Sutton Heath antiglider ditches had been hand dug to stop the Jerries landing. But the road winding through the fields ahead of her was empty in the heat haze, and everything was roasted dry. Ivy coiled its way out of the brambles, and there were poppies out and blackberries too that were formed but not yet ripe. The sun shone through loops in the top half of the hedge, casting her a shadow-companion that stepped in time along the ditch, and the air coming in off the salt flats was thick and humid. She wiped the sweat from her face and her hand on her dress. There was no sign of anyone. The only sound was the scrunch of her sandals on the lane and the heavy puff of her breath.

She needed to decide what she was going to say. Her intention had been to think about it on the train, but it was so noisy with all the servicemen heading this way that she'd hardly been able to think at all; and besides, they had wanted to talk and joke with her, the only schoolgirl in the carriage. They bundled into her compartment, full of high spirits, sitting on each other and asking her questions that she'd rather not answer: what had she been doing all summer, what was her name, did she have any older sisters, any friends, were they pretty like her, and where was she going anyway, all on her own.

She wasn't on her own, she had told them. Her mother was powdering her nose.

Oh, her ma's powdering her nose! one of them said, mocking her perhaps, for he was red faced and seemed a little drunk. He combed his fingers through his hair, stood up, and saluted. *Better make ourselves ship-shape for the lady then, lads.*

But her mother never did come back; it was just something she had said in the hope that they'd leave her alone.

She tried to focus her thoughts, scanning the hedgerows for crickets and grasshoppers. Sometimes, if you clapped your hands loudly enough, five or six would leap up. Alfie and Eddie used to catch them in fishing nets, sweeping the nets through the air as the little creatures catapulted themselves out of the grass.

She stopped and put the suitcase down, readjusted the box for her gas mask, and tried carrying the case with the other hand. Its cracked handle pinched at her fingers. She tipped her head back and looked at the vastness of the sky, so deep and blue. A top-notch day for flying, Alfie would say, but there were no planes, nor any birds. Even the sky was empty.

It had become something of a national obsession, sky gazing. If she could see a plane, she told herself, everything was all right and it was just her being silly. She clambered up onto the verge to get a better look across the marsh, then looked up and down the lane and listened, trying to hear a car somewhere—if not on this road, then another nearby, or a tractor in a field. Perhaps an army officer on a motorbike. Or the sound of a voice, the Local Defence Volunteers on drill somewhere, the sudden bark of an order. Or a dog. Even the bark of a dog would do. There had to be someone somewhere. The strange, empty silence was making her uneasy. She could feel a tightening in her chest. She would not let herself cry.

She picked up the case again and carried on, walking faster now. A wind blew out from across the lagoons and reed beds, stirring the grasses along the verge. Gorse seeds chased across the lane. And then a sudden sob erupted from inside her because she was so hot and tired now, and she hated this stillness; she thought she might choke on it. Where was everybody?

Maybe it had happened. She had heard people talking about

it. She had heard the warnings on the BBC Home Service. She fumbled at her gas mask box, struggling to open it. That was why there wasn't anyone about. That was why there weren't any cars, any planes, birds, crickets, anything. She pulled the gas mask out, hurriedly slipping it over her head just as they had practiced, and tugged the strap at the back, making sure it was secure. If they'd put something in the air, like everyone said they would...If they'd let something loose from a plane flying high above them, something invisible...

Inside the mask, her gasps for breath were louder than ever, the air hissing through the filter of the nozzle, the blood rushing to her head. The black rubber sucked against her skin, and the cellophane eyepiece started to mist up. She couldn't see to either side because of the rubber rim blocking her vision. On an impulse she turned her head sharply, expecting to see someone, but the road behind her was still empty.

Breathe normally, Miss Mountford had instructed them during their drills. Breathe too hard and you'll hyperventilate and then pass out or go mad. You might even give yourself a brain hemorrhage, they'd been told. *You just need to breathe normally.* But she never had been able to breathe normally in a mask. From the very first time she had put one on she had nightmares that one day she wouldn't be able to take it off.

She tried to walk on, taking in gasps of air that never felt deep enough. Sweat and condensation began to collect inside the visor. It formed on her skin and ran down the sides, dripping around the rim of the eyepiece and into her eyes, making them water. Despite everything Miss Mountford had told them, she was breathing so hard and fast now that she would almost certainly pass out. There were little tiny specks floating in the air around her. Tiny white specks. *Just seeds,* she told herself. Tiny seeds of something, she didn't know what, touching the visor and her neck and her hands and prickling, tingling all over. She scratched at her skin; tiny pinpricks, perhaps every one an infection. She furiously flapped her arms about her, whirling them out and above her head, swiping at the air and its contagion until she began to cry—and after all this time and all those promises to herself. Keep walking, she told herself. Keep walking. Don't stop. Everything will be all right.

The road through the village was deserted. There was no one chatting or cycling along the street. No children running along the pavements. No soldiers from the Liverpool Scottish leaning against the wall in their kilts and smoking; no Archie Chittock or Tommy Sparrow or any of the other Local Defence Volunteers messing about outside The Cricketers, their bikes piled beside them. Just dried leaves and dust blowing across the street.

As she reached the school, she saw the drawings that had been stuck to windows peeling away from the glass in the heat. Inside, the two classrooms were abandoned, the chairs upside down on the tables so that Mrs. Sturgeon could clean the floor underneath. She pressed her hands against a window to look in and felt a sudden pang to see Rosie or Cath, or any one of the others, even Joe Pitcher, dashing in and sliding on his socks.

When she reached Pringle's, the little village store was locked. In the doorway was a small printed card that read, in block capitals, WE ARE NOT INTERESTED IN THE POSSIBILITIES OF DEFEAT— THEY DO NOT EXIST. Despite this, the shop was closed and empty, gummed brown tape crisscrossing the windows in case a bomb blast blew them in.

She crossed to the other side of the street, then undid the latch on Mr. Morton's gate and walked nervously up the steppingstone path to the front door. The sandbags stashed against it were green with mildew and sprouting grass, and on either side a gnome stood sentry with a rifle held against his red painted shoulder. Above her a tatty British flag hung limp from a pole. She pulled at the bell cord and stepped back as the two-tone chime announced her in the distant recesses of the house. She hitched up her socks as she waited and shined her sandals against the back of her legs as she always did, but all she could hear was her own voice, trapped in the mask with her, *Please be in. Please be in.*

She opened the letter box and, bending down, peered through. She could just about see down the hallway into the kitchen where Mr. Morton always sat, his shirt stretching across his enormous back as he bent over his crosswords. He wasn't there.

"Mr. Morton! Mr. Morton? It's me—it's Lydia. Are you there?"

There was no reply. Not even from Mr. Biggles, Mr. Morton's ill-tempered parakeet, who was known for throwing abuse at every visitor that called.

She shut the letter box and scrambled over the flower bed to the sitting-room window. Like the windows at Pringle's, it had sticky tape crisscrossing the glass, and the curtains were drawn, a blackout cloth pulled across. She couldn't see in. She stepped back and tried the letter box again, pressing the nose of her mask against it.

"Mr. Morton! It's me!"

She bent a little lower, staring through the murky visor down the empty hallway, then called again. She could hear the crack in her voice, the tears coming once more.

"Please! *Please!* Are you there?"

But the house remained silent, and her hand slowly let the letter box squeak back into place. She walked back down the path, shutting the gate behind her, and looked up and down the empty street. Everybody, it seemed, was gone.

*   *   *

The lane led her out of the village, over the bridge, and across the flatlands. She hauled the heavy suitcase with her, her gas mask still pulled tight across her face. No matter how hard she tried to calm herself, her stomach churned. The road rolled out endlessly, the heat washing over her in waves. She could feel the sweat sticking her dress to her back, the air in the mask now so hot that even her breath seemed to burn her skin.

The car, when it came, met her halfway down the lane. It wasn't a German patrol car, or the British infantry, or even a member of the Local Defence Volunteers. It was an old black Hillman Minx, like Bea's, but caked in mud and with its exhaust pipe dragging and scraping along the road, making a racket. She watched it from a distance, rattling towards her, then stumbled up onto the bank as it drew near. But there wasn't anywhere to run, and somehow she knew before it had even started slowing down that the driver was going to stop. He pulled up ahead of her at an angle as if he was trying to cut her off. Inside, the man was large and bulky like the car itself, with thick-set shoulders and barely any neck, his arm hanging out of the window. His tweed jacket sleeve had a muddy elbow, and he was chewing on something, tobacco perhaps, his waxed hair slipping down across his eyes. The pockmarks on his cheeks scared her.

She stood on the verge, suddenly feeling ridiculous in her gas mask on such a sweltering day, with the visor steamed up so she could hardly see through it. She wiped the front of the goggles with her fingers but all the condensation was on the inside. She wouldn't talk to him. She would carry on walking, stumbling over the uneven verge if she had to, mindful of the rabbit holes and the sudden dips into the ditch.

He leaned further out of the car.

"Young lady!"

She took no notice.

"Hey! Excuse me! I'm talking to you!"

She stopped and looked.

"You shouldn't be here," he said.

"I know," she said.

"What?"

She struggled but managed to peel the gas mask off and felt the relief of dry air against her sodden cheeks.

"I know," she said.

"So?"

"Where is everyone?"

He laughed, slapping his hand against the door of the car. "Gone. And you should be too. Where have you been for the last month?"

She stared at him. His eyebrows were thick and met in the middle.

"Where are you off to anyway?" he said. "I'll give you a ride. Come on—hop in."

She shook her head.

"I won't bite."

"It's all right," she said. "You're going a different way."

"Don't matter."

"No, I'm all right."

He pulled his head back in and did a cumbersome five-point turn, hitting his bumpers against each verge, until he had turned the car around in the middle of the road and stopped.

He leaned across and ratcheted down the passenger window so they could talk again.

"There, see," he called over the spluttering engine. "Now we're going the same way, so come on. Get in. You shouldn't be out and about here anyway. No one should."

"I'm going to my aunt's," she told him. "She's just up here. She's waiting. We're going to Wales. My brother's there already and—"

"Really."

She bit on her lip to stop herself from saying any more.

"Come on," he said. "For heaven's sake, hop in! You'll only get into trouble wandering these lanes on your own. Come on—in you get!"

He leaned farther across the passenger seat and pushed the door so that it swung open on its hinges, but she took a step back.

He watched her for what seemed like ages and then, maybe realizing that she wasn't going to get in, said, "Suit yourself," pulling the door shut again with a slam.

"You're being rather stupid, you know," he said through the window. "You'll get yourself shot."

He put the car into gear with a grinding wrench, and she watched as the car's bumpers hit each verge again as he struggled to swing it back around; then he drove off, the exhaust still clattering. She waited on the verge until the car was safely out of sight and just a distant mumbling; then she stepped down into the lane and, pushing the gas mask back into its box, carried on walking.

A little while later, she saw the fork in the road and the red post-box at the end of the drive up ahead. The box wobbled on its stand as the heat shimmered off the camber and everything rippled, the view down the lane turning to liquid in the sun. When she reached the old crossbar gate, she stopped and looked down the drive. She'd expected all the windows and doors to be wide open, the breeze blowing through the large house, but everything was shuttered up. The gate squeaked when she opened it and she crunched across the gravel up the drive, then dropped her case on the doorstep, pulled up her sagging socks, and tried to open the door—but it was locked. She stepped back and looked up at the house. The bottom half was neat red brick, the top half painted a crisp white between the dark beams. Ivy crept up one wall, edging its way around the windows. There were patches of moss on the roof tiles and grass sprouted between the two chimney pots. She walked around the outside but everything was closed. The shuttered windows on the ground floor even had planks of wood nailed across them. She tried the back door but she couldn't get the handle to turn no matter which way she twisted it; instead, she stood on tiptoes to look through a glass pane, but something was covering the window inside and she couldn't see in.

She went back to the front and tried the door again.

"Hello!" she called as she peered up at the windows. "Hello!"

She tried to force the handle one more time, shaking it, then looked around. The house and its garden were surrounded on three sides by woods, the trees standing silent in the heat, and beyond them it was a good mile back to the village, or half a mile in the opposite direction to the shore if you knew your way across the salt marsh and mudflats. She slung her gas mask box down by her suitcase and walked across the scorched lawn. The splintered door of the chicken run was hooked open, the chickens gone. She crouched down beside the rabbit run but that was empty as well. She scanned the undergrowth of the trees for the white bob of Jeremiah's tail, and she called out to him, but there was no sign of the rabbit. The flower beds had been turned over to vegetables but most of them were dead now, the soil sucked dry and the leaves crisp and withered. In the middle of a circular flower bed, now surrounded by rings of shrunken cauliflower heads, stood a stone cherub on a granite slab, his skin freckled with lichen. It took all of her strength to wiggle him far enough to one side so that she could pull the spare key, wrapped in paper, out from under him. She ran with it across the grass to the door, but the key wouldn't turn at first and she had to rattle it around in the lock for a while, until finally, reluctantly, it clicked. She pushed the door open and the sunlight glanced in ahead of her.

The house smelled unfamiliar. Her feet creaked over the floorboards and the oak paneling was cool to her touch. All the doors from the hallway were closed; she opened them one by one, finding the rooms dark and musty, the fixtures and furnishings indistinct. All the windows were filled with blackout frames.

She stood at the foot of the stairs and called out again.

"Hello?"

Holding on to the banisters as she went, she followed her voice up the staircase. At the top she looked both ways before nervously making her way down the corridor. The bathroom light didn't work; even the tiny window in there had its blackout frame in place. There were no towels hanging over the rail. No toothbrushes or toothpaste in the blue spotted mug.

She stepped back into the corridor and stopped outside the next door, her sweaty hand on the cool, brass knob.

"Hello?" she said quietly. She turned the knob and nudged the door open. The room was dark and hot. At first everything seemed to be in its place. The neatly made four-poster. The old oak dressing table. The slightly tarnished mirror. The little side table and tasseled lamp. But no bedside book. No half-drunk glass of water. She took a step back and found herself staring at the bulky oak wardrobe. Her breath quickened as she reached out for both handles, and then, after a silent count of *one, two, three,* she flung open the double doors. It was empty. Her mother's clothes were gone.

★　★　★

She sat there on the four-poster bed, her feet dangling, until her eyes slowly adjusted to the dark and shapes began to emerge from the wall: pictures hanging from the picture rail, her mother's treadle sewing machine, the corn dolly hanging on its hook. She began to feel cool again as the sun fingered its way around the side of the house, no longer pressing at the shutters. She tried to think, forcing her eyes shut in the hope that when she opened them again, the room would be full of light and everything as it should be. Twice she got up and shut the heavy wardrobe doors, hearing the careful click setting everything back into place, but when she opened them again the wardrobe remained empty.

Eventually she wandered downstairs. The front door was still open, the sun still streaming through now that it was lower in the sky, but the kitchen remained dark.

She sat up on the work surface—something her mother would never have allowed—and leaned over to fill a glass from the tap. The water drooled out, cloudy at first and then finally clear, and she drank it and then filled the glass again, drinking it more slowly this time.

Her mother had gone to the cinema at Felixstowe with Bea, or Joyce, or somebody else. There wouldn't be a bus back till late, and that was why she'd already prepared the house for the blackout. Her mother was like that—organized. That was why they'd wanted her in the Women's Voluntary Service, and on the parish council and the school's board of governors and heaven knows what else. And she'd moved out of their bedroom and into the spare one. That was it. It might have got damp in her parents' room, because, after all, her mother had always said that the house was damp, she said she could smell it, while her father contested it as he contested almost everything, arguing that it was her imagination. *It's barely thirty years old, Annie. How on earth can it be damp?*

Lydia sat for a moment, letting the heel of her sandal bang rhythmically against the cupboard. But that didn't explain the empty station, or the empty village either, or the empty road and fields. Other than the man in the black Hillman Minx, the only sign of life she had seen had been on the train: soldiers with their kit bags, air force officers eating sandwiches or playing cards or sleeping with their heads gently knocking against the window as the train rattled on its way. Two or three women had been sitting in other carriages. She'd seen them on the platform getting on when she'd changed at Reading—a plump lady with a suitcase and a couple of WVSs in their funny green uniforms and hats. She had hoped that one of them would sit by her, but they hadn't. Something about them had made her think of her mother.

Have you a ticket?

Her mother had it, she had told the ticket collector. *She's just powdering her nose.*

Right, he said, although he didn't seem sure. *Most lassies your age are going the other way, you know.*

She nodded.

Everyone but the army is going the other way.

He asked her how old she was, nibbling at his mustache as he did and leaning against the compartment door as if he was getting himself ready for a long wait.

She told him, almost twelve.

He frowned as if even that were questionable, scratching his head under his cap, and then stood there watching her, waiting. Finally he asked her if she was all right in there—*your ma?*

She stumbled for a moment, wondering what to say, and then blurted that her mother was feeling sick, that was all—sick. *She doesn't like trains.*

No? Well, nor do I much on a ruddy 'ot day like this, he said. *I'll be back later for the ticket, mind. I've another four carriages to do before Ipswich, so you make sure she has it ready.*

She nodded and forced a smile, but the man never did come back and the train clattered on.

She hauled her things up the stairs, along the landing, and into her darkened room. She dropped her gas mask on the floor at her feet, heaved her suitcase up onto the bed, and lit the oil lamp. The flame's light flickered across the walls, teasing shadows up to the ceiling and smearing them across the floor. She pulled the evacuee tag off the case's handle and, screwing it into a ball, netted it into the wicker waste bin beneath her dressing table, then clicked open the catches and lifted the lid. She took Mr. Tabernacle out and sat him plumply on the bed. At eleven years old she had thought herself too old for bears, but her mother had suggested that she might want a friendly face with her, even if it was just one-eyed Mr. Tabernacle wearing her father's school tie.

She emptied the rest of the suitcase on the bed and then felt too hungry and tired to put any of it away. What was the point? If her mother had been planning to leave the house, she was sure that she would have written to her. But then her mother still thought she was in Wales, safe and sound.

She slumped on the bed with the bear on her knee and reached over to pull out the six letters from the gas mask box along with a storybook she'd made, the pages threaded together with string. Now it was all crumpled, her writing half-washed away where one of the Welsh boys had thrown it into the brook. She tried one more time to smooth out the creases where it had dried all out of shape, but the story was ruined. She put it back into the box, then laid out the letters, folded tight, in a semicircle on the bed between her and Mr. Tabernacle.

"You choose," she told the bear. Then, taking his arm, she made him pick one.

She unfolded the letter.

She knew them off by heart, her mother lamenting at how quiet the house was now that she and Alfie and Lydia's father were all away. The petrol pump in the village was out of bounds, she wrote—needed by the infantry apparently—so she was feeling desperately cut off and she never had been good on a bicycle, as Lydia well knew. The Germans had given them a bit of a bashing the day before, one of the Jerries emptying a load on the harbor at Lowestoft and another hitting the airfield at Martlesham. Joyce had apparently felt the rumbles in the pub, and her mother wrote that half the tins in the kitchen larder had fallen out. It had put the frighteners up them all.

They're calling it "terror attacks" on the radio. It does make me laugh, the funny terms they come up with. I expect they'll have another shot at us tonight (they seem to be coming every day). I hate going down to the shelter with no one to talk to. I keep thinking that your father has overloaded that tin roof with all his veg. The slightest blast in the village and I swear the whole lot will come down on top of me. Can you imagine Archie Chittock and the rest of the boys trying to haul me out from under all that muck and your father's carrots and cabbages?

There was no news of Alfie or of Lydia's father. She wrote instead of WVS meetings and her disastrous fruitcakes, as if nothing else mattered, and of Mr. Morton.

I told him you wouldn't be back until all this nonsense blows over. I said you were having a ball in Wales. You are, aren't you, Darling? Do write and tell me that Mrs. Duggan is looking after you, and Button too.

And so Lydia had written one of the special postcards they'd given all the children. Everyone is being lovely, she said. What did another lie matter?

She slowly folded the letter again and put it back in the box with the rest. Then she picked up Mr. Tabernacle, gathered the blanket from the bed, and took up the oil lamp. She stepped out onto the landing and walked along to the junction outside the spare room. The door at the far end of the corridor was closed, the rim of darkness around its frame sealing everything in. At some stage, if no one came back, she thought, she would have to go in.

She stood for a moment, looking at it, then turned back as far as the narrow flight of stairs that led up to the attic. The steps were steep, and near the top she had to set Mr. Tabernacle and the oil lamp down, her blanket wrapped around her shoulders, so that she could heave the hatch open. After a struggle it tipped back on its hinge and clattered down, throwing up dust. She hauled herself and everything with her up through the hole and then dropped the hatch shut and pulled the bolt across, pushing it into its socket good and tight.

The attic had been many things: a submarine, or an airship flying out across the Channel, or a courtroom, or the offices of a spying agency, or a dragon's lair, or just the very best and most secret of hiding places. It was rather poky, being in the only part of the roof that was high enough to stand in, but it had a single square window that she could see out of if she stood on one of the crates. She looked out now. The sun was finally sinking beneath the horizon. Clouds rolled in from the coast, their underbellies orange and pink.

She stepped down off the crate. There wasn't much room. An old ottoman stood in the corner, containing some of her mother's coats from when she'd been courting and there must have been more money. A few cardboard boxes were stacked full of disused china plates, cracked saucers, and chipped teacups. And everything—even the things supposedly sealed up safe— was furred with dust.

She checked the bolt across the hatch and, emptying the coats to make her own nest of sorts in the corner, heaved the ottoman across the hatch as well—just to be doubly safe.

She tried to make herself comfortable but the coats smelled of wet fur, and she wondered how long they'd been abandoned there, slowly rotting. It was getting dark. She would keep the oil lamp going as long as she could; that way at least she might stop the night from completely swallowing her.

She squeezed her eyes shut. Alfie was in his cricket whites out on the lawn, bouncing the ball on the underside of his elbow and catching it as it flipped into the air. She could see him quite clearly—his blond hair, blue eyes, the golden tan to his face. She concentrated on making him real, on remembering something good. They were playing cricket—Alfie, Eddie, and her—and she was infield as usual, which meant she spent the whole time chasing the ball and never got to bat.

Alfie tossed the ball to Eddie and took position—*Bowl!*—and Eddie bowled, his ginger hair flapping. The ball arced through the air, and as it came down Alfie leaned forward on one leg and hit the ball with a *whack*. It whistled off to the left and struck a tree on the edge of the garden where by some magic it was stopped short, caught within the fork of two branches.

Out! yelled Eddie.

That's not out! said Alfie.

Tis!

It's not!

It is! Out!

I'm not!

You are!

Alfie looked up at the ball wedged in the tree. *Oh, bugger it!* he said, swearing with his usual gusto. *Look at that! In the damn ruddy tree!*

She remembered watching from the terrace as the two boys stood around, hands scrunched in pockets, staring up at the branches and trying to work out how to get the ball down— an image of Alfie in her head pushing his hair out of his eyes, Eddie next to him, always the less impressive with his pale skin and gangly limbs, and yet, as her mother said, such a dear. Alfie was training to be a carpenter and always had dusty arms and splinters in his hands, and looked rather fine, Lydia thought, in his overalls. *People are always going to need carpenters,* he said, *'specially in a war.* Eddie had his eye on the air force, but of course that never worked out because, with his epilepsy, Eddie wasn't going anywhere. He would end up spending his days sitting in a field in a damp pillbox stocked with iron rations and toilet paper, with nothing for company but a battered rifle and the chums his grandfather grew potatoes with, while Alfie gallivanted around Europe having all the fun.

Alfie kicked his shoes off and clung to Eddie as Eddie hoisted him up on his shoulders. From there, in his socks, Alfie climbed up into the tree. He pulled the cricket ball out of the branches and dropped it into Eddie's hand.

She could see Alfie now, standing in the branches, the sun washing through him in his cricket whites. She would always remember it: a tall, lean figure with a shock of blond hair standing among the illuminated leaves, almost illuminated himself in the sunlight, like something heavenly. But only ever for a moment, because he was soon scrambling down and onto Eddie's shoulders, Eddie setting off with him, running across the lawn, both of them laughing and yelling until they fell sprawled across the grass in a terrible tangle of limbs and set to wrestling like they always did, rolling around on top of each other and trying to pin each other down, grunting and laughing and shouting, *Submit, submit!*

That had been the end of May, less than two months ago; it was the day before Alfie had left, sent out on a draft to France by his own choice, and two days before she was packed off herself to Wales. Within a week they were all scattered, a whole family blown across Europe—Alfie, her, and their father too, who'd been sent off with the navy. Only their mother had been left behind. Now even she was gone.

She pulled the blanket tighter around herself.

In the morning she would walk to the railway station and somehow get herself back to Wales and Mrs. Duggan. She'd shut her eyes and her ears to everything there and not let it eat at her. She'd leave a note for her mother and tell her to come and rescue her. Perhaps that was where her mother had gone. Perhaps they had passed each other on different trains, meeting for that split second as their carriages swept by each other on the tracks. Perhaps her mother was on her way to the little Welsh village now to look for Lydia when Lydia was here instead, in the dark and too scared to sleep, scared of the man in the Hillman Minx coming back for her, scared he might have followed her and knew where she was living, scared of the gas.

In their drills they had been taken to green gas vans parked by the school and told to put their masks on and step into the van, which had been filled with foul-smelling smoke. That way, they'd been told, they'd know if the masks were working.

But what if the gas isn't like smoke? someone said.

Of course it's not like smoke! said the woman from the WVS, and she laughed.

But no one said what it *would* be like. What if it was like tiny seeds in the air, or the sparkling particles she'd seen in the hall-way as she sat on the kitchen worktop? What if it looked like the dust in the attic, or like nothing at all, just bad colorless air, un-wittingly breathed in and out?

She sat upright and fumbled under the coats for the box. She took the mask out, then took a deep breath and pulled it over her head.

She tried to breathe normally. She took long, deep breaths and heard the rasping back and forth of all the air and tiny particles being drawn in through the filter, into her mouth and down her throat, deep, deep into her stomach, where the poison would lie twinkling in her lungs.

She tugged the mask off again and laid it on her chest, trying to catch her breath, and shut her teary eyes. She couldn't wear it; she wouldn't. She didn't want to die here, but if everyone else was dead and gone, what did it matter? She sat for a moment, then she slowly opened her mouth, opening her throat as wide as she could, and took in as much air as she could manage, breath-ing in every mote of dust and every poison particle.

She woke with a lurch, and it was a moment before she realized that she was no longer in Wales, sharing a bed with Button. She had heard the wailing of a beast in her dreams, had seen the eyes from her own stories watching her in the dark. The room felt clammy, and she could just about make out Mr. Tabernacle and the sheen of his single black eye.

There was a soft creak of wood downstairs, and she listened. Footsteps. She got onto her knees and pressed her ear to the floorboards, listening for her mother, waiting for her voice. She tried to trace the movement, holding her breath as one stair creaked, and then another, before it went quiet again. Then more footsteps, going in and out of each room, but too cautious perhaps, too careful. She pressed her ear harder to the floor. She heard the throb of blood in her ear, like the soft pulse of the house, and then the squeaking tap in the bathroom slowly being turned, something scrambling up through the pipes, and then a sudden retch of water and a voice, a profanity, almost like a bark, that didn't sound like her mother at all.

She sidled nervously across the floor and hunched beneath the window. For a while there was nothing but an uneasy quiet. Then the footsteps came again, quietly coming right up to the steps of the attic this time, and suddenly, from inches away, a rattling. The hatch in the floor bucked and jolted, and she almost shrieked but the bolt held firm, and, under the weight of the ottoman, there was no way in. She clamped her hand across her mouth, the other pressing at her heart. *Don't breathe. Don't cry out. Don't make a sound.* After a moment the attic steps creaked and whatever was there moved away until it was gone, and for a long time she could hear nothing but the slight quivering of her breath.

She was used to sleepless nights. They all were. She was used to lying in bed, hearing the sound of bombers droning overhead, followed sometimes by the snarl of pursuing fighters. Even in Wales there had been disturbed nights as a lone plane tore up the sky, and for a moment you could imagine a single package of death whistling down through the clouds to you, *From Mr. Hitler, with Love.* The silence was worse. The silence made room for other things to creep in, from her dreams and from the stories she wrote, her imagination turning real.

She sat there now, listening. It must have been an hour or two, maybe more, since she had heard the noises downstairs. She stood and pushed the ottoman back as quietly as she could, squatting down to listen again before she pulled back the bolt and slowly lifted the hatch just enough to peep through. The attic stairs were shadowy, the hallway a somber gray. She hauled the hatch open and laid it gently on the floor. With her toes fumbling in the darkness for each step, she eased her way down, pressing herself against the wall at the bottom of the attic staircase before she found the courage to look around the corner.

Along the landing, a single slip of moonlight fell across the carpet from her mother's room. She used it as a guide, allowing it to take her footsteps to the top of the stairs, where she peered down over the banisters and waited. After a minute she sidled her way down, one careful step at a time until she was at the bottom, her feet curling on the cold floor.

She crept sideways down the hall, her hand feeling along the walls, edging up to the corners and door frames. At the end, the kitchen waited dark and empty. The sitting-room door was open, and she took a few small steps in, her hands held to her mouth to smother the sound of her breath. The room seemed somehow darker than the others, just the heavy silhouettes of furniture: the lumpy backs of leather chairs, the blackout sheets pinned, the bony legs of a side table with the Bakelite telephone crouching on it, and her mother's piano and stool, both ghostly beneath old sheets.

She took another step in and, as her eyes readjusted, the darkness shrinking back a little, she saw the silvery glass of water on the floor at the far end of the room and then a figure huddled beside it in the shadows beneath the window. She must have made a sound, because the figure moved slightly, and something clicked. It was a man, holding a pistol, the barrel pointed towards her. The sudden sense that she was the subject of his gaze lit the room up around her as though he were shining a torch. She wanted to move, to run, but her feet were rooted to the floor, and panic had snatched away all her breath.

She could barely see his uniform in the dark, but it reminded her of the Essex Regiment when they'd come up this part of the coast the previous year. When he finally spoke his voice was quiet but firm, and she glimpsed his teeth. For a moment she thought he was grinning—then she realized they were gritted in pain.

"Why are you here?" he said.

She tried to answer, but couldn't find any words. Her throat was clamped tight.

"I said—why are you here?"

She couldn't even swallow. Her fingers found the button of her cardigan and twisted it on its threads.

"I live here," she finally ventured.

His eyes remained fixed on her.

"Where is your family then?"

"Out," she told him, the lie slipping from her before she could catch it.

He watched her from beneath his scowl. "Out?"

She nodded. "They'll be back soon though. Any minute..."

The man laughed.

Without taking his eyes off her or lowering his gun, he rose to his feet and she stumbled backwards.

"Where are they then?" he said.

He held her in his stare. The pistol wavered in his hand and she saw then that it was wet, bloody perhaps, and that there was blood on his shoulder and down his arm too, a smear of it across his face. He took a step closer, and she clamped herself rigid; rubbing at his forehead, he took a couple of steps back—and then, as if changing his mind, came towards her again, straightening his firing arm now and pointing the pistol with some certainty. She waited for the shot, for the hot impact, but his arm dropped again and, with a sudden bellow, almost simultaneous with her own shriek, he kicked at the glass of water and it exploded into shards against the wall.

He leaned his hand against the window frame, catching his breath and watching her from beneath his scowl. His breath came like snarls through his gritted teeth and his gun hung loose in his hands; then he straightened up and pointed it at her.

"Go back to bed," he said. "Go on! Now! And don't leave your room. Do you hear me?"

She backed towards the door, still saying nothing.

He jabbed the gun at her. "Do you understand?"

She nodded. Then, scrambling out through the doorway, she ran down the hall, up the stairs, and into her room, slamming the door behind her and pushing everything from her bed to the floor. She jumped in and pulled the covers to her nose. She lay there, holding herself as still as possible and listening as hard as she could, but all she could hear in the darkness was the sound of her breath blasting against the bedsheets and the throbbing of her heart.

He gathered up as many bits of glass as he could find in the dark and emptied them into a teacup on the dresser, rubbing the dusty shards from his hand. The pain in his shoulder was excruciating, burning right through to the bone and sending piercing stabs down his arm and across his chest. The blood was soaking through the dressing and his shirt. He covered his eyes with his hand and listened. He had to focus. Stay calm. He couldn't let the girl being here trip him—not now.

He moved to the window and tried to look through the slit in the blackout cloth that he had cut with his knife. It was almost impossible to see anything through the rip and the dusty glass and shutters, but he'd see a torchlight if someone was coming, and that was enough. He leaned back against the wall and allowed himself to breathe, tipping his head and glancing at the ceiling.

He checked his pockets. Everything was still there: identity card, letters, the photograph, the dog tags, the ten pounds in English notes, the Browning back in its holster, the spare magazine. He had to keep checking these things; had to know everything was in its place.

He looked up at the ceiling again. The child. The bloody child! His hands were clammy and tacky with blood, and his heart hammered. He could feel the grit and sweat in his hair, the taste of salt still on his lips. Stay calm, he told himself again. He couldn't afford a mistake.

After a couple of minutes he pulled his kit from the corner. His pack was sopping wet, but when he unfastened the buckles and opened the drawstring the contents were still dry, carefully wrapped in their oilskin bags. He emptied a box of cartridges out from one of them and took out a handful. Taking the spare magazine from its carrier hanging on his belt, he fed the bullets in and exchanged the magazine for the one already loaded into the butt of the pistol. Four bullets used already; he would have to be more careful.

He pushed his pack back into the corner, stepped lightly to the foot of the stairs, and listened. The girl would not be asleep. She'd have buried herself in the bed or would be crouching behind the door, listening to him listening to her, and neither would make a sound. He could sense her, just as she no doubt had sensed him: the pulse of another heartbeat, the soft breeze of another's breath.

He edged his way around the house, counting off the rooms as he passed through them: hallway, dining room, kitchen, study, sitting room, back to the hall. He pulled a small torch from one of his pockets that gave off a light so fine and sharp that it could make the smallest incision in the dark, and with it he checked in cupboards, cabinets, and corners, behind the three leather chairs, cautious all the time that something might jump out. He had learned over the last few months that if you find one child in an abandoned house, there were usually more, hiding away somewhere. He saw the flash of torches, frightened white faces, heard a rattle of gunfire, shouts, and screams, then sudden desolate silence. He tried to blink the images away. You shouldn't think back. Ohlendorf was right. Don't ever think back.

As he moved about the house, he could feel his shoulder seizing up, as if inch by inch, minute by minute, the pain was closing him down. He opened drawers, rummaging around, putting his whole hand in and feeling awkwardly along the top for things stuck there or secret catches; listening all the time for her, for any movement. In the study he flicked through the leather-bound books along the bookcase, his torch held between his teeth while he thumbed hurriedly through the pages or opened the books by their spines and shook them out. He pulled up the sitting-room rug, upturned ornaments, and poked around the soil of dead pot plants with his blade, foraging about in the corners of this other family's life. He tried the cupboards of the Welsh dresser, feeling for false backs, looking for even just a slip of paper—a document, a letter, a photograph, anything useful—pushed so far into a crack that only the tip of a corner might be visible.

In the sitting room, he stood at the side table and picked up the telephone receiver and listened to the buzzing crackle; then he quietly replaced it, pulling out the cord from the back and curling it into a loop, and with a sharp yank he severed the line. He switched the torch off and pocketed it, then paused again, scanning the darkness. He was already beginning to feel acquainted with the house. He had a sense of the space settling around him. *Greyfriars*. It was not at all what he had expected.

He went back to the window where he had cut a slit in the

blackout material and perched on the ledge. He had already hauled the sash window open, and, stooping a little, he pushed the knife through the slit and levered up one of the wooden slats of the shutter with the blade. He looked through the narrow gap and almost instantly felt the hot smog of the night slipping in, the slight drift of air from the coast blowing across his hands.

Beneath the blanket of clouds, everything was gray. The mound of the air-raid shelter. The meshed structures of the chicken coop and rabbit run. The stone angel statue in the middle of a vegetable patch where the ghostly circles of vegetables looked as if they were made of ash and the slightest puff of wind would blow them into dust.

Over the treetops the sky flared silver, then died again. He felt the tremble. An explosion out at sea. He wondered if the girl had noticed.

He scanned the trees, waiting for movement, a sense of something watching.

Their forms remained still and thick and heavy against the night: great English sycamores, oaks, and firs. And beyond them the marshes, the mudflats, the beaches, the coiling wires, and concrete blocks, pillboxes, and buried mines.

He left the window, going light-footed into the hall and up the stairs, moving from room to room and along the corridor, past family photographs on the wall.

When he was a boy growing up this had all been played out as a game. He and the other boys running around among half-built, abandoned buildings, shooting at each other with their stick guns and scrambling over the brick piles and timbers. They imagined that a new war was raging, greater and wider than the World War had ever been; that the abandoned building sites were not abandoned for lack of money but were bombed-out streets, that they were clambering up and down broken stairs, that the half-built walls had been blown away, allowing them to sit on bedroom floors, swinging their legs out into infinity. *I claim this half house in the name of the Republic!* And if a boy they didn't know strayed onto their street—perhaps a Communist—they would capture him and beat him and shoot him until he was dead.

Those were just games though. Taunts wouldn't kill a boy. The guns weren't real. You could point at another child's head and say "bang" and nothing much would happen, except maybe a fake slumping to the ground, followed by a giggle or, better still, a groan. Now there was a real pistol in his hand. He was standing over a bed with a child asleep in it. He held the gun to her temple, feeling the softness of the skin there through the metal, as though the weapon were an extension of his hand. There was no choice with this one; there had been no choice before.

FRIDAY

EARLY THE NEXT morning he went from room to room taking down the blackout frames and hauling up the sash windows in the hope of admitting the thinnest lines of sunlight from between the shutter slats. Even with the windows open the rooms remained hot and airless. He felt along every floorboard, shining the torchlight between the gaps and testing each board with the blade of his knife to see if it was loose. The wound in his shoulder was still painful, searing like a burn, and every time he lifted his arm it felt as if he were being cut anew.

In one of the bedrooms he found a wardrobe of men's clothing. There were shoeboxes in the bottom with brogues and boots but little else, and nothing in the pockets of the trousers, jackets, or coats but a penny coin, a few seeds, and some fluff and sand. He pulled one of the jackets out and held it up against him. It was well stitched and of a fine thread, and when he lifted the arm to his cheek he could smell the warm fug of its wool, as if the heat of the man who had last worn it were still trapped there.

A model boat stood on the windowsill, and he picked it up carefully in both hands, the torch clasped between his teeth. It was skillfully made with canvas sails and cotton thread for ropes, now slightly grubby. Every detail was delicately crafted: the varnished rim around the deck, the fine wire rails, the intricate etching around the wheel. He would commit it to memory like every other detail in the house, every knickknack, trinket, treasure, and vase. Nothing would go unnoticed. Nothing would be left to chance.

He lifted one of the wooden rungs of the shutters and looked down across the garden at the birdbath, hollyhocks, and buddleia below, the trees casting early morning shadows across the lawn. He couldn't let the girl go. Why hadn't he shot her when she was just a dimly lit face, a figure and no more than that, standing there in the sitting-room doorway?

In the master bedroom, pictures of flowers dabbed in watercolors hung from the picture rail: clutches of foxgloves, lilies, and bluebells, tiny thunderflies like pinpricks caught behind the glass. He ran his hand over the bedspread, searched under the pillows and mattress, but there was nothing. The wardrobe in the bedroom was empty too, as were the drawers of the dressing table, bar a few bits of makeup and a jewelry box pushed to the back. He took it out and opened the lid with a click. The gears coughed rustily inside, and three figurines stood frozen mid-dance on the circular mechanism. The device chimed once, then was silent, and he shut the lid and returned it to its drawer.

He picked up a wedding photograph from the dressing table: a bride and groom beneath the crumbling arches of a church door. The man looked mildly surprised, as if the camera had flashed before he'd had a chance to compose himself, while his bride smiled demurely, head cocked to one side like a bird. He studied them closely: the bride with her curls and coils of hair pinned elegantly; the groom's own hair slick and shining, his face sharp and youthful, with prominent cheekbones. He put the photograph down and looked in the mirror at his own face, the contours of his own skin. Sometimes he barely recognized himself.

In the bathroom, he took off his jacket and shirt and removed the dressing from around his shoulder. The blood was now clogged and black around the wound, which seeped a clear sticky liquid; every time he moved his shoulder the pain forced air through his clenched teeth. He gently bathed the wound in cold water, wincing as he went. The hole was deep, and he was worried that the knife had not been as clean as it had looked and that infection might be setting in. He could feel the throb of it, the pain of its pulsing, tiny spasms like fissures splintering down his arm and through his chest. He dabbed it dry with the corner of a towel and applied a fresh dressing from his kit bag, wrapping it around and tying it tight; then he tested his fingers, bending and straightening them.

She woke with a start. He was sitting in the chair beside her, his pistol in his hand. One finger tapped rhythmically on the arm of the chair, and a collection of wooden splinters were piled like a tiny bonfire on the other arm. Outside, the morning was silent. Behind him, a sharp rectangle of sunlight burned its outline around the blackout fabric at the window. He looked right through her.

She clamped her eyes shut, but when she opened them again he was still there.

"Get up."

He hauled the bedclothes off her and she sat up blearily.

"Come on!" he shouted. "Up, up!" He bent down for her suitcase and threw it on the bed beside her. "You can't stay here." He pocketed the gun and flung open the case; then he gathered the clothes up off the floor and threw them onto the bed.

"You have to leave."

Barely thinking, she scrabbled things into her arms and scrunched them into the case.

"Do not tell anyone that you have been here," he said. "Or that I am here or that you have seen me." He grabbed her by the arm and pulled her so close to him she smelled his dirty breath. "If you tell anyone about me I will hunt you down and kill you. Do you understand?"

She nodded and he released his grip, then gathered more clothes up, squashed them into the case, shut it, and threw it to the floor.

"Go on," he said. "Go!"

She stood looking at him, suddenly unsure.

He picked up the case again and grabbed at her wrist.

"Come on. Get out! Go!"

He hauled her out of the room and down the stairs, her feet barely touching them and the case dragging and scraping down the wall. At the bottom he pulled the front door open, and she expected him to push her out but he stopped short. She tried desperately to yank herself free, but he held her tight as he looked down the drive and across the road and fields. And then he muttered something—a curse, a word she didn't recognize—and suddenly pulled her back in and slammed the door shut.

"No!" she shouted. "Let me—"

But one hand was already clamped against her mouth and, with the other holding her around her stomach, he hauled her off her feet so that she hadn't the air or time to scream before she was being pulled—half-carried, half-dragged—down the hall-way, her feet scuffing and kicking at the floor, and him puffing and struggling as if in some pain. He shoved her into the kitchen and kicked out a chair from beneath the table. Throwing her down on it, he took his gun out and pointed it at her. Then, withdrawing it again, he paced up and down. His breath was ragged. Finally he turned to her.

"You are making my life very difficult," he said, catching his breath. "And I can still kill you. It doesn't take much. If you make me angry or nervous, anything but perfectly happy, the bullet will shoot into your stomach"—he gestured with the gun barrel—"or your face or your skull. You understand?" She stared at him, and he kicked the leg of the table. She flinched. "Do you understand?"

She nodded. Hot tears were running down her face.

He sat down opposite her then, nostrils flaring, face black with anger. His hands were dirty, nails black. His eyes were dark in the dim light and his hair hung damp over his lashes.

"I can't let you out," he said. "It's too dangerous. If you step outside this house, I will have no choice but to kill you. Do you understand that?"

She nodded.

"I don't trust you out there," he said. "And, you will get yourself killed."

She stared at the corner of the table where the varnish was worn away and tried to stifle her sobs, then raised her eyes to him. She could hear his breath slowly calming; she could smell his skin, his sweat.

"Where is everyone?" she said.

He held her firmly in his stare, the gun still pointing across the table.

"What have you done with them?"

He sat back in his chair.

"You're not English," she said. He sounded almost English—but something about his accent wasn't right, the care with which he worked his way around certain words. She wiped at her eyes. "Did Mr. Hitler send you?"

He laughed.

"You're coming, aren't you—the Germans? Everyone is saying it."

"Yes," he said. "England is shut, but, as you see, we are already here."

"I need to find my mother."

"You can't," he said. "I told you...if you try to leave the house, I will shoot you. And if I don't, someone else will." He laughed again. "I'm rather surprised you are not dead already."

She could taste tears in her mouth, breaths coming huge and ragged. "But..."

His eyes widened, questioning her.

"You don't understand," she said. "I don't know where she is."

"You will not leave this house," he said. "You will stay right here. You will not be seen by anyone. These are the rules. Do not stand at the windows. The shutters stay closed. If you disobey me in anything at all, if you try to leave, if you do anything to anger me, I will shoot you. Is that understood?"

He waited for her to respond.

"I said, is that understood?"

She slowly nodded again. She could hear it in his voice now. That slight accent, like the faint lingering of a smell, not noticeable unless you already suspected or knew it to be there.

His face showed a slight twist in his mouth, as if perhaps he was in pain. His hands kept the gun on her. Had he already shot her mother? Mr. Morton? Joyce? Bea? Had he shot the Local Defence boys from their bikes?

He poked the gun at her. "So," he said. "We have an agreement. These are the rules. Yes?"

She nodded.

"Good." He placed the gun down on the table and slowly leaned back. "So," he said, with a faint smile. "Here we both are..."

In the sitting room he pulled the sheet off the piano and opened the lid. He ran his fingers lightly along the chords, making the strings strum faintly. There was nothing hidden inside. He opened up the gramophone and emptied all the shellac discs, abandoning them on the floor, then went to the dining room and broke open locked drawers and cupboards with such force that the silverware fell out, clattering over the floorboards.

The drawers of the writing desk in the study were sticky and jammed, and he loosened them with his knife as he maneuvered each one free. Inside, he found letters, postcards, bank receipts, and mundane correspondence about village fetes and cookery recipes and an evacuee with an Eastern European name that he could barely read let alone pronounce. Between the edge of the drawer and a tin of ribbons and pins was a small leather address book, probably forgotten in the rush to leave. He slipped it into his pocket.

Back in the sitting room he tidied up the shellac discs, carefully inserting them into their respective sleeves. When he tried to slip them back into the cabinet beneath the gramophone, something was in the way. He got down on his hands and knees and shone his torch in. At the back, tipped on its side, was a small brass metronome. He took it out and stood it on the window ledge. He wound it up and turned the dial, setting the arm in motion so that it ticked steadily back and forth. The arm of the metronome swung this way and that. *Tick, tick, tick.*

If he shut his eyes he could hear it, the concerto swelling to fill the template of the metronome's beat, the auditorium rever-berating to its ornate rafters in that glorious wash of sound. He could feel the cello vibrating as if it were alive, trembling through his arms, his chest, his knees, the sound of the strings rising up high into the empty space above.

In the block-booked party seats at the front, rows of uni-formed men sat, their caps resting in their laps or hanging from the arms of the seats, one or two of them actually enjoying it, patting their knee with their hand or gently nodding their head. Further back in the stalls were families, a further scattering of uniforms, husbands with wives, fathers with sons, the buttons of their jackets sparkling beneath the chandeliers. The concert house had an opulence so fitting of Bach—the plush red of the seats, the golden columns and carved ceiling.

As her bow pulled across the strings of her violin, her eyes caught his beyond the swing of the conductor's baton, just as they had the first time he'd noticed her, two—maybe three—years ago now. She smiled at him, then tipped her head back a little as the adagio swept her up; her blonde hair pulled into a bun and tied with a black ribbon, her neck angled and taut so he could see the tendons as tense as strings, her black dress with its ribbed bodice tight around her breast and ribs, opening up into swathes of silken material that fanned out around her feet. *Eva.*

Her arm furiously worked the bow. His own arm ached, the tip of his elbow writing out the notes, his fingers pressing and squeezing the strings. And then the final note and the explosion of silence that followed, hanging delicately in the air for a moment like a held breath—before it was swept away by the applause and he could feel his arm relax.

The tram back to his apartment had rumbled through the dark streets of Berlin, the rain typing on the roof. Eva rested her head against his, keeping her hand warm under his coat. They passed lines of barricaded apartments, most of them empty and abandoned.

They made love that night. And when they were finished they slept soundly, waking to the sun streaming through the garret window. He got up. He dressed in his uniform. He left her in bed. But he took her scent with him, between his legs, on his breath, and just there, where he could still smell it now, in the warm curl of his hands.

★　　★　　★

Alfie was obsessed with German spies. He said that those who weren't already hiding in our communities would land by parachute under the shroud of night so that you would hardly be able to tell them from the darkness; and those who landed by day would be disguised as policemen, or nurses, or bus conductors, or teachers, complete with satchels and truncheons and ticket boxes, so that as they hit the ground and disposed of their parachutes they could walk out into the street and no one would think anything different of them. Before long, they would be everywhere, he said, and then, when the time was right, they would open up their satchels and truncheons and ticket boxes and inside would be guns.

That was why the Spielmans had left. She remembered cycling past their house and seeing it boarded up. That was almost a year ago now. Before that there had been firecrackers through their door, smashed-up plant pots in their front garden, kicked-in fences. Someone even painted the word *Traitor* across the side wall. Her mother and father wouldn't talk about it—you didn't always know what went on behind closed doors—and, a week or so later, the Spielmans were gone anyway.

Taken, Mr. Morton told her. *Best thing for 'em.*

Taken where? she'd asked.

The Isle of Man. That's where they take 'em. To the prison.

He said they were traitors. Fifth columnists. *And they had pigeons. You know what pigeons mean?*

She didn't.

Communication, he said, nodding knowingly. *Sending messages, I shouldn't wonder. You can't trust anyone.*

She huddled in the dark of the wardrobe, holding the torch she'd taken from beneath her bed close between her knees so she could read the pamphlet. She stumbled over some of the longer words, but she understood most of it. She'd read the leaflets with an exhilarating mix of fear and excitement maybe three or four times before, but that had been when she'd wanted the invader to come and had thought of it as a game; now that it had really happened, she couldn't stop her hands from shaking.

DO NOT BELIEVE RUMORS AND DO NOT SPREAD THEM. WHEN YOU RECEIVE AN ORDER, MAKE QUITE SURE IT IS A TRUE ORDER AND NOT A FAKED ORDER. MOST OF YOU KNOW YOUR POLICEMEN AND YOUR ARP WARDEN BY SIGHT; YOU CAN TRUST THEM. IF YOU KEEP YOUR HEADS, YOU CAN ALSO TELL WHETHER A MILITARY OFFICER IS REALLY BRITISH OR ONLY PRETENDING TO BE SO. IF IN DOUBT, ASK THE POLICEMAN OR THE ARP WARDEN.

She read on, reviewing some of the sentences several times until the words sank in and she was sure they would stay in her head when it came time to burn the leaflets, or bury them.

SEE THAT THE ENEMY GETS NO PETROL. REMEMBER THAT TRANSPORT AND PETROL WILL BE THE INVADER'S MAIN DIFFICULTIES. MAKE SURE THAT NO INVADER WILL BE ABLE TO GET HOLD OF YOUR CARS, PETROL, MAPS, OR BICYCLES.

The pamphlet seemed to assume that if invaders came there would be some time to prepare, and perhaps there had been. Perhaps her mother had already put some of the advice into practice, although the Crossley was still in the garage and her mother had made no attempt to hide any food. If anything, there were more tins and packets stockpiled in the larder than before, despite all the government warnings against panic buying.

She remembered reading to her mother from the first pamphlet that had arrived, following her about the house as she had done chores: up the stairs and along the corridor, a pile of sheets in her mother's arms, then into her parents' room, where her mother had set to changing the bed.

It says, Do not give a German anything, she told her mother. *Do not tell him anything. Hide your food and your bicycles. Hide your maps.*

Yes, all right, all right, her mother said. *Now, come on, you're getting under my feet. I've a WVS meeting at eleven, and at this rate I shall never make it.*

You can't take the car, she told her mother. *You have to dis . . . able all vehicles,* she read, stumbling over the word.

That's only if the Germans come, Lydia. And they're not going to, are they, not this morning anyway; I'm only popping out for a couple of hours.

And then Bea had arrived, always in her tweeds and hat, the front door opening, her voice yodeling up the stairs—*Yoo-hoo! Annie!*—sending her mother into a flap.

Oh Lord! Is that the time? Look at me—hair in a mess and still in my petticoat. She turned to Lydia. *Darling, be a poppet and hang the washing out, will you? And where is that boy hiding himself?* She stood and looked about her, as if expecting Button to suddenly materialize from beneath the floorboards.

And then she was gone, clattering down the stairs, Bea saying things like, *Annie, darling! Am I early?* And Lydia's mother saying, *No, I'm late as usual. Heavens, what a morning! It's all hands to the pump here. Any news from the boys?*

Lydia had walked over to the wardrobe and flung open the doors. There was Button, just as she knew he would be, staring up at her from between the racks of clothes with his big, watery eyes.

With her father and brother gone, and her and Button evacuated, she had huddled under the covers in Wales worrying about her mother alone in the house. And what now? What had happened here? Were the fields and marshes and woods and villages awash with German soldiers?

She flicked the torch off and sat in the darkness, listening to her own breathing. She pressed down on her heart to try to quiet it, but it only seemed to bump harder against the inside of the wardrobe, the sound reverberating through the floorboards and down the walls and along the floor and, no doubt, up through the soles of his boots, so he would know exactly where she was. She sat with her back to the side of the wardrobe and her legs outstretched so that, if she pointed her toes, she could touch the other side. After a while she brought her knees back up and squeezed herself into the corner. She had pins and needles, her throat was parched, and she was frightfully hungry. She had no idea how long she had been hiding in there. The wardrobe smelled of damp wood and dusty clothes, even though it had nothing in it anymore. She pretended that Button was huddled at the other end. After a while she heard his breathing in the pitch black, but when she reached out her hand to him there was nothing there.

No one knew why Button always hid in the wardrobe.

Perhaps that's how they live over there, Joyce from The Cricketers had said. *Perhaps he always hides in boxes. You know what these boys are like.*

Lydia's mother worried about his parents. You heard such terrible things.

Yes, and you wouldn't want to be stuck with him, said Bea. *I mean, it's all very well doing the right thing for a few weeks while this nonsense blows over, but you wouldn't want to be stuck with him.*

No, her mother agreed. *I suppose not.*

The truth was that no one had quite known what to make of

Button. He didn't speak a word of English, barely a word of any language, it seemed.

In Wales Mrs. Duggan took an instant dislike to him: his pale face, his scrawny limbs, that dark hair of his, and the slightly pointed eyebrows that gave him a look of constant surprise.

Looks a bit too primitive for my liking, she said to Lydia. *How come you've been lumbered with him?*

But Lydia didn't know. Button had just come, having been billeted with the McGowans at first, but that didn't go down well, not with them being Catholics and him being a Jew. *You have to look after him,* her mother had said. *He's a long way from home.*

The boy was definitely odd. A week into his time with them, he found Lamb and, from that point on, took to dragging him around the house. Lamb was a life-sized stuffed toy mounted on a narrow red trolley with wheels and a handle. She and Alfie had both used Lamb as toddlers, waddling behind him as they'd learned to walk. As she got older, she had attached a strip of cloth to him as if it were a dog lead, and it was with this that Button dragged the lamb about, his gas mask fixed over the animal's moth-eaten head.

Sometimes in the night, when she couldn't sleep, she thought she could hear him pulling the lamb with its mask along the hallway, the wheels of the trolley quietly squeaking and rattling over the floorboards. She imagined the silhouette of them in the corridor: Button's face and the lamb's rubber snout.

The wardrobe was stifling. She switched the torch on, changed her mind, and turned it off again. Better not waste the battery. If she strained very hard she could hear the wireless in the kitchen. There had been a soft hammering earlier but it had stopped now, replaced by the sound of swing music swelling up through the floorboards. Her mother couldn't bear silence so the wireless was always on, providing a constant bubbling of chatter and songs. She could hear her mother's voice now just behind the music, half singing, half humming.

Taking the torch and the pamphlets with her, she opened the wardrobe door and stepped out into the semidarkness of the room, placing her feet softly on the floorboards so as not to make a sound. It was only when she had shut the wardrobe behind her that she realized there was no singing, no sound of swing from the wireless at all. She held still and listened and, for a moment, thought that perhaps the man had gone.

On any other day like this, the doors and windows would have all been open, music playing from the wireless or from her mother's quick fingers as she sat at the piano. Her father would be in a deck chair with his newspaper, reading bits aloud to anyone he caught wandering past. Or listening to the news as he polished his brogues or filed down a bit of wood for some project or another: reports of German submarines and E-boats in the North Sea, or Luftwaffe planes flying inland. Or perhaps he would've just been catnapping. For months their nights had been restless, and everyone was tired and irritable; it was an unspoken rule that you slept whenever and wherever you could.

Once, before the war, a giant zeppelin floated over Bawdsey, down at the end of Hollesley Bay, like an involuntary thought. And for some time her mother had thought there were funny things going on at Bawdsey Manor. Rumors spread that it had been bought by the military, and they'd seen metal towers above the trees, lines of steel posts, and extra fencing. All very suspicious, her mother had said.

Her father turned the page of his newspaper and drew on his cigarette.

If something secret was going on at the manor, it was secret for a reason, her father felt. *I wouldn't ask too many questions, Annie, if I were you.*

Her mother thought they should be told. *But George, what if it's dangerous?*

I'm sure it's not, darling. I'm sure it's perfectly safe.

It was bringing too much attention to the area, her mother said. *We've enough eyes and ears about the place as it is.*

She sat on her parents' four-poster bed—a remnant of the times when her mother's family had been wealthy and they'd owned a paper mill at Bramford, now long gone. The man had been quiet for some time but now she could hear him prowling again. She heard kitchen cupboards being opened and shut. His footsteps were the slightest squeak of wood and nothing more, as if he was already getting to know the house, its loose boards and creaking giveaways.

She looked down into the garden, thinking for a moment that she might see Jeremiah's white tail bobbing up and down some-where among the undergrowth. If she had managed to get out, if the man had let her go, Lydia would have run away through the woods, to the village or the railway line, or just out across the marshes. But then where, she wondered. Who would she go to? What would she do?

As she padded back to the wardrobe, she had an idea. She hurriedly folded the pamphlets around her calves and pulled her socks up over them. She went to her mother's dressing table and checked the drawers, but nothing there needed to be hidden from him.

In her own bedroom she took her identity card from her suit-case and went to search through her books. Her *A History of England* had a number of maps of the country and of the local area, and she carefully folded the relevant pages, making the crease good and sharp, then tore the pages out and returned the book to its shelf. She gathered her own stories from the shoebox beneath her bed—she didn't want him reading them—and pushed them all up inside her dress, along with the pages of maps. When she was done she stepped out onto the landing. Looking down the corridor at the closed door at the end, she took a deep breath and slowly walked towards it. She stood outside for a moment and leaned in so that her ear was almost against the door. She thought she could feel the wood breathing. Something inside. She took a step back. Not now. Not today. But if no one else came back to Greyfriars, she would have to go in.

She could hear him in the hallway, then the front door opened and shut, followed by the sound of footsteps crunching across the drive. She went to the top of the stairs and leaned over the banisters, listening. More footsteps, stones crackling under boots, then a dull *twack;* something fell to the ground. She would have to be quick. She clung to the edges of the steps where they were less likely to squeak as she carefully made her way down. Creeping to the front door, she squinted through the keyhole. She couldn't see much, but the garage doors were open; her father's rusty lock and chain were lying broken in the gravel. She turned the handle and pulled but the door wouldn't budge. She tugged furiously at it, then felt in her pocket for the key, but it wasn't there. Had she left it on the little side table when she'd first come in? She must have done, but now it was gone.

She ran into the kitchen and tried the back door, pulling at the handle, and then twisting it and pushing at it. The bolt was pushed across at the top and she reached up on her tiptoes to pull it back. She tried the handle again, but the door still wouldn't open. Studying it more closely, she felt her stomach suddenly turn. The door was nailed into its frame.

She ran out of the kitchen and hurried from room to room, desperately now, trying to push open the shutters at the windows one by one—but the planks were still in place, nailed across them on the outside, so that no matter how hard she tried she couldn't push them open. She stumbled back into the middle of the sitting room and saw the telephone on the side table. She'd call someone. Anyone. Get somebody to come. But when she lifted the receiver and listened, the line was dead. She heard nothing but the sound of her own breathlessness and then her sudden, sobbing tears.

The motorcar was a Crossley Torquay Saloon with a sliding roof. He remembered them from when he'd been in London; his music tutor, Professor Aritz, had owned one too, although this was older, a '33 model. Still, it looked in good condition, and while the wheels' spokes were grubby, it had only a few dents and hardly any sign of rust. He walked around the garage admiring the vehicle and occasionally giving one of the wheels a nudge with his boot. Even in the dimness of the garage the front lights gave him a bug-eyed stare. He had never had a motorcar of his own, and this was a particularly fine one; the bottom half a milky cream, while the top half and the sliding roof were a smart jet black. Inside were brown leather seats, and the woodwork was so beautifully finished that even through the murky windows he could see the polished grain.

He opened the door and sat in the driver's seat, resting the pistol in his lap, then looked in the mirror at the garage doors behind him, slightly ajar, and the hot afternoon sun burning through the gap. He ran his hands around the steering wheel and across the polished dashboard. The seat was surprisingly comfortable, and he inhaled the slight tang of leather and polish. He studied the dials and pedals, familiarizing himself with them. There was no radio. He had tried tuning in the wireless in the sitting room to find German broadcasts, but all he could pick up with any clarity was the BBC Home Service.

On the back seat was a neatly folded picnic blanket of green and blue tartan. He imagined driving to picnics in this car, along the twisting, turning English roads. Out of London into the heart of the country. Henley, Oxford, and then, perhaps, on into the Cotswolds...

Eva had enjoyed picnics. Their first afternoon on their own together had been a picnic in the Tiergarten during the May Day celebration and parade. The day had been unseasonably warm, full of people enjoying the sunshine, kicking balls about and playing games, drinking and laughing. He could see them now, past the duck pond, more and more people joining the line along the parade route, shuffling about as they tried to find the best spot to take up their positions. Fathers carrying sons or daughters on their shoulders, wives and mothers with woolen blankets, children with paper windmills and footballs, bunting swinging from the trees and lampposts. And all the flags, hundreds of flags; everybody holding one. They had found a quiet spot beneath a couple of trees and laid out a picnic blanket along with the food they'd picked up from Hertie's department store on Dönhoffplatz. He had surprised her with a bottle of wine, pulling a couple of glasses from his pockets. She had looked so pretty in her summer dress with the sun dappled on her skin through the leaves. The light fluttered like butterfly wings across her face.

He pulled the starting control out to its fullest extent and turned it, then switched on the ignition and operated the starter. The car choked and spluttered, the whole vehicle juddering under him with the effort and then puttering out. He tried the starter again and the engine coughed and died. He sat for a moment, waiting. He didn't want to flood it.

He remembered the conversations. Even back then there had been the vague talk of war. Eva had a brother, Bernhard, who worked in the new Air Ministry building on Wilhelmstraße. He said the rumors were all unfounded. There weren't any plans to expand Germany beyond what it had already reclaimed in the Rhineland and Austria, and those had both been rightly theirs. Eva said she didn't believe a word of it. *What does silly old Bernhard know anyway? He's just a pen pusher.*

They were late joining the throng of people lining the parade route through the park. Although they ran along the line with their picnic hamper and flags, they had caught only the briefest sight of the official cars through the mass of excitable bodies. The noise—claxons, cheers, and music—had been almost deafening. And as the crowds dispersed again, he thought for a moment that he had lost her, among all the hundreds of faces.

They took a walk around the park in search of ice cream and stopped on what he now considered to be "their bridge," asking a passing couple to take a photograph of them. It was an act that he would soon learn Eva would insist upon, on every afternoon stroll they took there, on every future picnic and parade, as if this bridge was a reminder of that first delicate and quivering flush of romance, and each photograph taken in their usual spot and pose—half-turned towards each other with an elbow on the rail—fastened them just a little tighter together.

In the garage he tried to start the car again, but the engine wouldn't take and the air filled with fumes. He cranked down the window and sat, thinking. Then he tapped on the fuel gauge. Empty, of course. Not even the English would be stupid enough to abandon a car full of petrol.

If there is a war, Eva had said, *I mean another one, what will we do?*
The comment had come quite out of nowhere.
Do? What do you mean?
Well, we'll all get dragged into it somehow, I suppose. I can't just play in an orchestra. What good will that do? I'll have to turn my hand to something useful, something good.

Her mother, she had said, thought getting married and having children was useful.

And then she had stopped herself and laughed, thinking maybe that talk of marriage and children on their first turn together around the park was perhaps a little presumptuous.

But he hadn't minded at all. And, in time, that had been their plan, he thought as he sat in the Crossley, staring at the empty petrol gauge. After the war.

In the study she pulled out a road map of England, and another of East Anglia, a walking map of Suffolk, and another, barely used, of the nearby Fens. She took down her father's leather-bound atlas from its shelf and, with barely a thought, hurriedly ripped out several of the pages. She opened up the desk drawers. They were all in a mess as if someone had already been rummaging, the identity cards, ration cards, and her father's bank statements gone.

She could hear the car's engine coughing several times and stopping, then coughing again as he tried to start it. She gathered the maps and torn pages up inside her dress and hurried across the hallway into the sitting room. DO NOT GIVE ANY GERMAN ANYTHING. DO NOT TELL HIM ANYTHING. HIDE YOUR FOOD AND YOUR BICYCLES. HIDE YOUR MAPS. She pushed the piano stool aside and scrambled under the piano; then, taking a hair clip and bending it open, she got down on her hands and knees and slid it along the edge of one of the floorboards until she felt some resistance. She could hear him still in the garage, the car coughing and choking. She fumbled with the clip but it kept flicking out of the crack. She straightened it and tried again. Her mother had twenty pounds in cash hidden. *I know it's daft,* she had said, *but it makes me feel better, if anything should happen . . .*

Outside now, it had gone quiet. He'd give up with the car before long and come back in. She fiddled desperately with the hair clip, but her palms were sweaty and the clip kept slipping from her hand. Then, with a delicate *click,* the tiny catch her father had fastened unhooked, and with the tips of her fingers she managed to prize the broken floorboard up. She lifted a few folded bits of paper out of the hole and checked, but her mother's money was gone.

Before marriage and a family, there was Eva's father to contend with. His daughter being a musician was something to be proud of. But a future son-in-law? *Pah!* He had made it quite clear that music was a profession delicate enough for women, but any man participating in it must surely be of questionable character. Germany hadn't been made in the music halls after all, but in the trenches, in the thunder of battle. With the exception of Wagner and a few traditional folk songs, he pronounced, music had done nothing to cajole the German people and was, at best, a passable distraction on a Sunday afternoon— and only then when there was nothing better with which to occupy the soul. It would certainly not make Germany great. Or a son-in-law worthy.

He had only recently signed up again, feeling like so many others that it was his duty and privilege. In those first few weeks of the training he had felt a camaraderie with other men that he had never experienced before—the sense that together they were on the cusp of something great, something worth fighting for. And in the months preceding the war he proved himself to be an elite soldier. He had a level of awareness matched by few and could tune his ears to the slightest sound, while his ability to remain undetected out in the field had brought him to the attention of the NCOs. None of this mattered to Eva's father though, who still branded him a "musician"—and no amount of hobnail boots or cross-fire action, or even his later Brandenburg training, was likely to change that.

He climbed out of the car and looked around the garage for a petrol can. In the corner, piles of black sheeting lolled about on a workbench, cloth sacks sagged against the wall, pot-bellied with potatoes, and tatty spiderwebs drooped and dripped from the overhanging beams. He dragged aside cans of paint, a tool-box, a scuffed water bucket, and the sleeping coils of a hose, but there was no petrol.

That first afternoon, they had walked about the Tiergarten and eventually found themselves back at the same picnic spot. She had lain on her back, her hand drifting across the grass and picking the heads off daisies, casually flicking them at him. He had lain beside her, propped on an elbow and swigging the last remnants of wine, and had told her about his childhood in Bavaria. How his grandfather had taken him hunting almost every day and poaching most evenings, so that he had learned not only the skills of stalking, he said, but also of survival; and then how, as an older boy, he had joined an Outward Bound group, refining his skills on weekend treks in the Rhön Mountains and the Black Forest and even Austria, where they'd spent a week walking the Eastern Alps and catching marmots and mountain hares.

She had laughed. *Do boys never grow out of hunting? That, and playing at wars.*

What do you girls like to do then? he asked.

We like to lie on our backs in the warm sun and pick daisies and look up at the clouds and find things in them.

And she had shown him: a bear with a frown, a plump bunch of grapes, the underside of a fluffy sailing ship as it passed slowly over them.

At some stage that afternoon they had watched a couple of

Brownshirts grasping each other in a drunken headlock and staggering around in circles, trying to pull each other to the ground.
Later the same pair would drag a young Jewish man out onto the
lawn and, forcing him onto his hands and knees, make him eat
the grass.

God, look at us, Eva had said. *We're turning into animals.* The
sudden change in her had quite surprised him. *People everywhere,
sitting around having their picnics, and no one does a thing. We all just
turn our heads and carry on as if nothing is happening.*

He hadn't known how to respond at first, and then had said
that there wasn't much they could do—not unless she wanted
the Brownshirts to turn on them instead.

That's just an excuse, she said to him.

Is it?

Yes, she said, *and that is why things won't ever change. No one takes
a stand.*

He walked around the car to the driver's seat and clambered
back in, pulling the door shut behind him with a click. He
needed petrol, damn it—it was the first thing that they had been
told to do: attain a reliable mode of transport.

If he shut his eyes he could still see Eva, feel the weight of her
head in his lap. A smile flickering across her face. Two dimples
no larger than pinpricks appearing in her cheeks and then just
as quickly disappearing. *We should spend all summer sunbathing and
having picnics. You're too pale.* Then she reached up and wrapped
her arm around his neck and pulled him gently down to her, rising from his lap so that their lips touched for the first time. He
felt her through the thin wrap of her skin, her flesh, her delicate
warmth.

He got out of the car, leaned against the bonnet and rubbed at
his eyes, then wearily turned his attention to the shelves, pushing
aside jars of nails, screws, and bits of wire, tins of varnish, and

offcuts of wood. Beside his feet a sack of potatoes fell and scattered across the floor. He picked one up and rubbed his fingers across its nubbed surface, then lifted it to his face and smelled its dry and earthy skin.

After sitting for a few moments beneath the piano, pressing her hand over her mouth to stifle any tears, she took some deep breaths and tried to pull herself together. From under her dress and within her socks, she emptied the maps, the torn pages, her identity card, her stories, all the bits and pieces she'd gathered, hurriedly stuffing them into the hole. She pushed the board back, hearing the click of the catch snapping into place. Outside, the garage door grated over the gravel as the soldier pulled it shut. She crawled out from under the piano and slid the stool back into position, then ran into the kitchen and jumped up onto the work surface as if she had been there all the time.

The front door opened and shut again, and he came down the hallway towards the kitchen, clumping in his boots. He stopped in the doorway and caught her for a moment in his stare.

"You've been running," he said.

She shook her head.

"I can hear it on your breath. Don't lie. What were you doing?"

"Nothing."

"Nothing?"

"I wasn't doing anything," she said.

"Listen to me. I can hear every sound, every breath, every single beat of your heart," he said. "So, some advice. Do not creep about. You will only make me nervous." He took hold of her by the chin, his fingers pressing gently. "Do you understand?"

She nodded.

He turned and walked back along the hall and up the stairs.

She heard his footsteps passing over her head, just the gentle give of wood.

She let out a held breath.

On the windowsill was her mother's mint plant in a cracked terra-cotta pot. She poked her finger into the soil. She wondered how long her mother had been gone. Long enough for the soil to become as dry as dust, but the plant was still alive, the leaves limp but not yet dead. She lifted it and held it under the tap, letting the water drizzle slowly into the earth. Then she returned it to the sill, turning it so that when the light was finally allowed back into the house again, a new set of leaves would feel the sun upon them.

He was intent on making a first aid kit, supplementing the field dressing, needles and thread, and iodine he had already with what he could find in the bathroom cabinet and a small drawer in the kitchen. He found plasters, more dressing, arnica, and a tin of pink cream called Germolene, which he took to be some kind of antiseptic.

He was aware of the girl creeping down the stairs after he had gone up to the bathroom and then of her going back up once he had come back down. It was as if they had the same magnetic charge, keeping to opposing corners and pushing each other around the edges of the house. All the while, he sensed her listening to him as he listened to her. Feet padding over floorboards, groaning giveaways, and telltale squeaks, her eyes watching him from behind a door or a chair.

"Why don't you come out," he said, "and stop creeping about like a little mouse?"

But she stayed silent; he could hear her holding her breath.

In her bedroom he picked up the discarded clothes from the floor and folded them—a pretty little blue dress that was soft to his touch; a white cotton vest with a fraying hemline; a pair of white cotton panties with three mauve flowers stitched onto one side. He put them neatly back in the drawer. Dried leaves shed from a dead plant on one of the shelves crinkled under his feet, and further down the shelves, parked between books of fairy tales and poetry, was a wooden Noah's Ark, a menagerie of carved animals boxed up inside. When he pulled down the blackout frame at the window, he uncovered a dusty line of seashells set out in order of size along the windowsill. He held the largest to his ear for a moment and listened to it whisper.

What was it she had run from? It intrigued him that she seemed to have no idea where her mother was, where anybody was. An adult would have been so much simpler to deal with, he knew from experience. There would have been no delay, no hesitation, no mistakes. But then the house—this house—was supposed to be empty.

Greyfriars, he thought. The word had been an abstraction, as, of course, had Lydia herself, but now he was here and everything was real. It felt odd, but satisfying, to have honed in across Europe to this one place, this house, this moment; the surprise of actually finding the girl exactly where he had imagined her to be.

Back downstairs in the porch he found plant pots and wooden trays, sacks of compost, gardening gloves, propagators, and canes tied in bundles with fraying string. His grandfather had taught him gardening, among other things, but there had been no space for it in Berlin. He thumbed through the seed packets, all opened but folded down and held together with a single wooden clothespin. He carefully read the names, feeling the shape of each one in his mouth: delphinium, lupins, fuchsia, geraniums. He tipped a few seeds into the palm of his hand and moved them around with his fingertip. Each seed in itself was a little packet of hope, a tiny new beginning.

When he shone his torch around the kitchen larder he was relieved to see that they were set for a siege. Ceramic containers and
earthenware jars and columns of tins and packets were piled precariously, and it took some time to divide the tins and packets into
two tottering heaps. The smaller of these he would not touch: it
was just about as much as he could carry when the time came.
The rest they could eat as and when, for as long as they were
here. Skipper sardines. "Woppa" processed peas. Baxters chicken
and mushroom soup. One or two tins he had trouble deciphering,
even from the pictures on the labels. Those words, once he'd understood them, he repeated to himself as he went about the house.

"Tap-ee-o-ca," he said as he sat on the bottom step of the stairs
picking gravel stones out of the tread of his boots. "Tap-i-o-ca.
Tapioca. I will have tapioca pudding, please. And cauliflower
cheese."

He put his boot back down and turned, looking up the stairs.
The girl had materialized at the top, coming out of nowhere as
she had been doing all morning. She looked down at him, embarrassed perhaps and indecisive, then slowly she made her way down
the steps, her sweaty hand squeaking against the handrail as she
inched her way towards him. He didn't move as she reached the
bottom, and she squeezed past him into the hall without catching his eye, walking swiftly into the kitchen. He heard a cupboard
door being opened, a packet being torn, more rummaging. The
girl must be hungry. He had no idea what time it was.

Through the crack in the door she watched him draw the blade
down his neck, gathering up the grubby soapsuds and the dark
flecks of hair along its shine. He sloshed it around in the sink and
slowly dragged the blade down the other side of his cheek.

Beside him the bath continued to fill, the pressure in the pipes
so low that the water was a trickle. He was slender but more

muscular than her father or Alfie, and he was covered in cuts, bruises, and grazes, some of which still looked red raw. Worst was the hole in his shoulder, as if a bullet had gone right in and was still embedded there. It was inflamed and caked in clods of black, dried blood, and the skin around it looked pink and tender. Every time he raised his arm a twinge shot across his face, pulling at his cheek and his eye.

He bent over and washed the soap from him, droplets running down his face and along his arms. His hair was dark and damp in the steam, trails of it drooping down over his eyes that, in the mirror's reflection and sharp sunlight, were the deepest blue she'd ever seen.

He reached over the bath to turn the taps off, but the water still churned up the pipes, and deep in the belly of the house there came a juddering groan. The floor beneath her trembled. The beast in the pipes.

He unbuttoned his trousers and slipped them off, then tugged off his socks, hopping about as he did. Everything was neatly draped over the chair. He tested the water and flicked the droplets from his hand, before drying it on the towel. Then he slipped his grubby white underpants down and stepped out of them. She watched him drop them on the chair and step cautiously into the bath. She covered her face with her hand but couldn't stop her fingers from opening or her eyes from looking between them at his neat, pale bottom and the sore-looking cuts on the back of his thighs. He lifted the other foot into the bath and made a quiet gasp, followed by a short sharp hiss; he murmured something as he slipped into the water, and, for the slightest moment, she thought she heard him sobbing.

He had laid his uniform blouse and collarless shirt out on her parents' bed. His black leather boots were under the dressing table, laces neatly tucked inside; his pack on the floor. She recognized the uniform; it had the same shoulder flash the Essex boys had worn before they'd been sent up to Northumbria and replaced. When was that? April or May. Definitely before the summer and before she'd been sent away. She let her fingers touch the khaki woolen fabric, the fly-flap to conceal the buttons down the middle, the small belt tab, the patch pockets on each breast. The wool was rougher than she had imagined, and tacky, as if something had been spilled on it.

By January all the local regiments were serving abroad. They were replaced by the Territorials or recent recruits that in time would include Alfie. Several army infantry divisions that were not fully equipped or hadn't been trained enough to be dispatched to France had been sent this way to protect the East Anglia coast. The Essex Regiment had been in the area since the previous November. She'd seen them patrolling Shingle Street before they'd started cutting off the beaches, putting up all the barbed wire and blockades. By the time Lydia was evacuated, there were soldiers and defenses up and down the beaches, and now she wondered what good they had been and what had happened to them all.

She opened up the shirt, laying it out flat. A name was written on the label inside. Red capitals, the ink of each letter seeping into the fabric like jagged little teeth.

JACK HENRY BAYLISS

She stared at the name for a while and folded the collar in on itself so she wouldn't have to think about how a German soldier might have acquired an Englishman's uniform. She wondered why he hadn't killed her, why he was keeping her in the house. Perhaps he was playing a game.

She lifted the arm of the uniform and smelled it. It had a familiar odor, like the louse dust Mrs. Duggan had brushed into Button's jacket that had made him sneeze.

Poor Button. The first thing her mother had done with him when he had arrived at Greyfriars was take him out into the garden and wash his hair over a bowl with kerosene mixed with sassafras oil, and then rinse it in vinegar. Lydia had laughed at him. But then the first morning in Wales Mrs. Duggan had done the same to them both. Out came the washing bowl and the Jeyes Fluid, and they were ordered into the yard.

This is a clean, ship-shape house, she said as she tugged Lydia's dress off over her head and then pushed her head down over the bowl. *I don't work at it all day long only to have scallywags like you coming in full of creepy-crawlies. Filthy little vackies.*

For the first two weeks either she or Button had cried in the night, until Mrs. Duggan came in and said, *If you don't pipe down, I'll put you out in the baily and give you both a clout.*

She looked out of the bedroom now, across the landing to the shut bathroom door, her heart suddenly bumping harder. Wisps of steam drifted out from under it. No sound though, not even the slop of bathwater; she wondered if he had drowned.

She fumbled in his shirt pockets. The two outside ones were empty, but there were two more inside. The first had lots of shiny tacks in it, and when she pulled out a handful a golden St. Christopher medallion was caught up among the pins as well. She untangled it and lifted it up so that the cross twirled around on itself, catching the dim light. She let the chain trail through her fingers, then she put it and the tacks back and carefully felt inside the second pocket. She found small, flat bits of metal, and when she pulled them out she saw that they were half-moon-shaped tags made of steel or tin. Six of them, and all broken, it seemed, in half. She spread them out across her hand.

"What are you doing?"

He grabbed her arm and snatched the tags away, scattering them to the floor, then pushed her hard against the dressing table, causing her to gasp. He scrambled around gathering the tags up, wearing nothing but one of their towels tied tight around his waist.

"Do not touch or look at anything. Do you understand?"

"What are they?" she said.

"They are nothing."

She pressed herself back against the dressing table and watched him feed the tags back into the pocket and fasten the button. He took the shirt from the bed and shook it out and draped it over the chair. He still had water dripping from his hair, dripping onto his shoulders and down his stomach. It trickled down the side of his chest and seeped into the towel about his waist. She thought she ought to look away, but she didn't.

"I didn't mean it," she said. "I'm sorry. I didn't mean to be nosy."

"I have given you many chances," he said. "So many. That was your last. Do you understand?"

She nodded.

His chest lifted as he breathed. How was it that she hadn't seen him, hadn't even heard him enter the room? The bathroom door was wide open now. All the steam was gone.

"Now," he said. "I am wet. I want to get dressed."

She stepped away from the dressing table. She wouldn't let him see that she was scared. "You can't keep wearing the same clothes," she said.

"What is it to you?"

"They smell."

He glanced at her but said nothing, so she walked slowly to the door, then stopped again. He lifted his shirt off the back of the chair. "I know how to make egg omelets," she added, "if you're hungry."

He nodded but that was all.

She felt stronger now. She stood in the doorway, waiting.

He turned his head to look at her. "I want to get dressed," he said again, and then he flitted her away with the flick of his shirt and she quickly left the room.

They ate in silence, the small lamp casting a vague light across the blackout cloth at the dining-room window. Their shadows played across the walls. They did not speak. She kept her head down but strained her eyes to watch him without looking up. He had opened one of her father's bottles of wine, but he barely had more than a few sips. He sat in her father's seat in his collarless shirt, his jacket hung over the back. Perhaps it wasn't *his* shirt, but that of Jack Henry Bayliss or some other English hero. His dark, damp hair kept falling into his eyes, and occasionally he would push it away with his finger; and then she would see the blue of his eyes again. When he laid his hand flat on the table she wanted to reach across and touch it, just with the very tips of her fingers, to see if he was warm.

When he was finished eating he folded his napkin. He watched her as she pushed the dried-egg omelet around her plate. She had been famished but now she couldn't eat—not with him watching her—and anyway, the omelet had tasted powdery, the egg so tough she could have soled her sandals with it. If her mother hadn't let the chickens go they could have had real omelets, real chicken. The man probably wouldn't have thought twice about killing one with his bare hands.

She gave up and put her fork down. He was tapping the table with the nails of two fingers, tapping out a rhythm, a marching drumbeat, the wineglass tilted in his other hand. *Tup-tup-tuppity-*

tup. He looked right through her, as if a film or a dream was playing out against the wall behind her. *Tup-tup-tuppity-tup.* His lips were red with wine. His skin almost dark in the candlelight.

His fingers fell still and he glanced at her.

"Have you finished?"

She nodded.

He pushed his plate aside and stood up and, taking his jacket from the chair, he walked out of the room.

"Thank you," she whispered to herself.

"Oh, that's quite all right," he said.

In the sitting room she watched him put the blackout frame back up at the window, pressing it into place, a tiny torch gripped between his teeth. She held Mr. Tabernacle to her chest and watched him as the room grew darker and smaller, frame by frame. Soon he was not much more than a dark figure up against the wall, only his hands occasionally seen in the torchlight as he worked. She felt as if she were being packed away into a box.

"Do you have blackouts in Germany?" she asked him, because she was becoming afraid of the silence between them.

He looked at her but didn't answer and she fidgeted awkwardly in the doorway. She held on to Mr. Tabernacle so tight that she thought he might burst in her arms.

They'd had blackouts in England since just before the war had started, so that now the only nighttime lights seen with any regularity were the beams of searchlights crisscrossing the skies on the coast. Hardly anyone left the house after dusk for fear of falling over something or not being able to find the way back home again. Even before Lydia had left, there had been several incidents in the village with people stumbling off pavements or into the ditches along the sides of the road. No one dared drive anywhere on a cloudy night, and with no street lighting in the village even her father had given up risking the walk to The Cricketers; he'd have his own brew at home.

Lydia's mother had wanted everyone safely indoors by the time it got dark, but Alfie had proven to be a law unto himself.

What time do you call this? her father would say when Alfie finally tramped in. *And where in God's name have you been?*

Don't worry. No Jerries are coming tonight, said Alfie.

Oh, is that right? And how do you know?

With the blackout fabric in place, the soldier set candles in jam jars out on the floor and then opened up his pack and pulled out a canvas case, each narrow pocket snugly holding a pencil. He unbuckled the main flap and took from it a large map, torn and crumpled and stained in places. He opened it up and laid it out on the floor, then repositioned the lights around it. He looked up at her standing in the doorway, her eyes suddenly welling.

"What is it?"

She stared at the map, brought of course by him, then shook her head and said, "Nothing." Her endeavors to hide anything useful from him had, it seemed, been pointless.

He turned back, bending over the telltale lines of roads and rivers and the target dots of towns. The map was of England, but it was only the southeast coast that he seemed interested in, and, taking a pencil from one of the bag pockets, he placed a small X where she supposed Greyfriars must be. She nervously walked across the room to one of her father's leatherback chairs and sat with her feet up on it and her knees huddled up. He followed the roads inland with his finger, occasionally writing something down on a scrap of paper and mumbling to himself, then took a coil of thread from his pocket and measured out one of the roads.

"Are you a spy?" she said. He probably was. "I know that's not your uniform. Where did you get it?"

"It doesn't matter."

"Did you kill him?"

"No."

"Then how did you get it?"

He said nothing but turned back to the map, following the different roads with his finger and occasionally looking up, not at her but just to think, his lips moving ever so slightly as if the thoughts were words that he was trying to shape but he didn't quite know how. He scribbled things down, finding another road, maybe measuring it with his thread.

After a while she lowered herself out of the chair and onto the floor beside him, taking Mr. Tabernacle with her, and he edged a candle away to make room for them. She leaned in close so she could read some of the towns: Ipswich, Colchester, Felixstowe...

He had drawn little circular symbols at Yarmouth, Lowestoft, Brightlingsea, and Harwich, and she wondered if they were naval bases. When she asked him he didn't answer.

"Did you fight in France?" she said.

He raised his eyes to look at her.

"Yes."

"Where else? Did you fight in Poland?"

He made no response and turned his attention back to what he was doing, and then he changed his mind. He ushered her to move out of the way as he lifted the map, getting up onto his knees to do so. He turned it over and laid it back down. The flip side covered the whole of Europe and was scribbled all over in washed-out pen and pencil so that almost every inch of sea was covered in such a scrawled tangle of words and figures and numbers and symbols that she couldn't pick out anything that made sense.

"Here," he said, showing her a point on the French coast where there was a similar penciled X. "And here," he said. "Poland. And here too."

She bent closer to look. "Norway?" she said. "Isn't it cold there?"

He nodded. "Very."

She looked at the map, Europe obliterated under his notes, and wondered where her father was among all of it. She missed his hugs, and the tang of his Woodbines, and the way he'd call her *missy* even though she used to hate it. *I'll be home before you know it.*

"How did you get here?" she said.

"To England?"

She nodded.

"On a boat," he said. "This is to be our first post. We have to prepare. More men will come soon, and then more, and then more."

"Here?" she said.

He nodded.

"And then what?"

"Your country will fall—just like the rest," he said. "You will be overrun."

She looked at the map again, at the tiny island that was Britain and all the bits around it that she knew Germany now had; it seemed the only way they might escape was to push themselves further out into the Atlantic and not let the rest of Europe gobble them up.

"Where are the rest of your soldiers then?"

"Coming."

She had meant the others in the boat that he had arrived with, but perhaps he hadn't understood. She looked at the windows, all boarded up and blacked out.

In the autumn, just after the war had started, Alfie and Eddie had found a rowboat washed up on the beach. They had thought then that the Germans had landed—Alfie had been quite convinced—and made such a terrible fuss of the matter that the police had set to combing the nearby fields for more signs. But in the end it turned out to be a fisherman's boat from Boulogne, with its black hull and yellow and white bands, set adrift in a storm perhaps and blown across the Channel until it was washed up on Shingle Street Beach for Alfie and Eddie to find.

For months they'd watched bombers flying overhead, and over the last few weeks the ports and harbors all along the east coast had been targeted by German aircraft. She'd heard it on the wireless at Mrs. Duggan's. The aerodromes and military installations had been targeted too. There had been a raid on Garrett's munitions factory in Leiston, less than ten miles away, her mother had written. A stray bomb had even blown out the greenhouses at Wetherby's fruit farm. Lydia had imagined the shards of glass taking to the sky like a swarm of glittering insects.

He folded the map away, returning it to its canvas case. She sat back up in her chair. In the weeks before they'd been evacuated, the boys from school had spent most of their time lying along the hedgerows, wooden sticks ready to fire, waiting for someone like this man to arrive. She wondered how brave they'd be if they were here now, and thought of how silly they'd look with their sticks.

"You've run away, haven't you?" he said. "That's why you're here, on your own. You're not supposed to be here."

"I am," she said. "This is our home. Not yours. What happened to your shoulder anyway?"

"Nothing," he said. "It is just a wound." He switched on his torch and then went around the room blowing all the candles out. As the torchlight flickered she saw the pits and shadows in his face.

He went to the window and used the tip of his blade to hook open a tear in the material just enough for him to look through.

He switched off the torchlight and the sitting room fell into darkness. Lydia did not move.

She remembered that first night of the blackout, when her mother couldn't bear being trapped in the house. They'd taken their tea outside and sat in the moonlight on a blanket, having a picnic. *We can make this fun. Look, Mr. Hitler!* her mother had yelled out into the dark. *Look what fun we're having!*

"Does your bear have a name?"

The sudden question surprised her. "Mr. Tabernacle," she said.

He laughed. "That is not a name. That is a word. A Jewish word as well. Is he a Jewish bear?" He laughed again. Then he turned his back on her once more and stooped down to look through the slit in the blackout frame. For a while longer, he did not move.

Her hair was fanned across the pillow, a thin clump of it lying across her face and gummed with moisture as if she had been sucking on it. Pale cheeks, a button nose, freckles spattered across its bridge by the summer, nostrils barely moving as she drew air in and out. He moved closer, the mouth of the gun against her jaw. He tightened his grip and felt the tension in his hand, tendons straining wire tight in his arm. He heard the soft sound of her breathing and saw her flickering eyelids, dreams or nightmares chasing through her sleep.

After watching her for a while, he lowered the gun's barrel towards the floor, and left the room as silently as he had entered.

Midway down the stairs he sat and rested his elbows on his knees, his heartbeat thundering. He watched the hallway and the front door, the gun still held in his hand. He let the darkness close in around him until, like the girl—whose name he knew but wouldn't say—he was swallowed and lost within it.

★　★　★

They had trudged slowly through the trees, pushing up the Norwegian mountainside and away from the town. The snow was thick and dry, their feet sinking into it over their boots, each man weighed down by his rucksack, rifle in one hand, the other grasping at branches and tree trunks for support. Groups of four dragged sledges carrying heavy machine guns and mortars strapped on with ropes. He had never known such tiredness.

War was a long and arduous slog. It dug at the back of your heels, and pinched and rubbed and cut and gnawed, and hung heavy from your shoulders, and dragged you to the ground. It was better not to think of yourself as human or alive. You were an organic machine, nothing more, with wheels and pistons and bellows and cranks that somehow kept you walking.

As they climbed higher he remembered seeing the mountains circling them through the treetops; at their most vertical points the grazed rock faces were bare. The air was thin. Gusts of wind blew between the trees and slapped at their faces until they were red and chapped.

The ground eventually leveled, and when they reached the summit they found nothing growing but tufts of gorse and small clumps of birch bent over by the wind. They cautiously picked their way up to the highest point, where they stood around clapping out the cold and squeezing their hands deep into their armpits as they looked down into the gorges beneath them, and out across to where higher peaks lost their tops to the clouds.

Many of them were inexperienced—too old to still be considered schoolboys and too young by far to be men. He had shared a cigarette with one of them, who had round-rimmed mountain goggles hanging around his neck and a look of terror so frozen into his face that the boy could barely chip out a smile.

He told the boy to put his gloves back on and make sure that all his buttons were fastened. *If the wind gets in you'll have frostbite and then, by God, you'll be sorry.*

They had arrived on ghost ships through fog, coming up through the black waters of the fjord. In the harbor they made short work of two Norwegian defense ships, blasting the keel out of one, striking the battery of the second. The detonation rolled around the cliffs behind the harbor like thunder. The water was clogged with civilian ships, merchant ships, smaller vessels, all torpedoed; the harbor water burned around the wreckage. The landing boats nosed their way through floating bodies.

Within twenty-four hours the British navy had arrived, appearing through the mist and snow just as the German flotilla had done. Cannons and mortars thumped. From behind their defenses in the town, he had watched his destroyer, the *Wilhelm Heidkamp,* break up in flames. Around him guns rattled, zips of light flickering out in lines across the darkness. Mortar shells exploded. People ran. Even their supply ship, the *Rauenfels,* had gone down, taking all their artillery with it.

Now though, up on the mountainside, everything was quiet and subdued. Cigarettes were lit and smoke dispersed in the air. Men talked in muffled whispers and coughed at the cold.

We should go back. This is madness, one of them murmured. *We're going to die up here. We're never going to find our way.*

Weber, warned another. *For God's sake, shut up.*

I'm telling you, these fucking mountains are going to swallow us—

I said, fucking shut up! The man took Weber firmly by the collar and for a moment it seemed that a brawl would start.

Hey! shouted Ohlendorf. *You two!* And, just as quickly, the moment passed. A flurry of wind blew snow up into their faces, and the men all turned their heads or covered their eyes as the flakes chased around them.

Ohlendorf gave a signal, tossing his cigarette butt into the ravine, and they slowly made their way down from the mountaintop. Their faces were solemn and nobody spoke. Later one of the sledges would be lost down a channel between the rocks, and it would take thirty men almost an hour to haul it and the equipment back up onto the path, their hands frozen and boots struggling to find grip in the snow.

Walking became almost mechanical. In the days and weeks and months that followed he would do it in his sleep, tramping ever on towards the railway line, seeing it sometimes in the distance, but never any nearer, the wooden scaffolding underpinning the tracks as it wormed its way around the mountainside, occasionally disappearing into a crudely cut tunnel and then reappearing further on: the Ofoten Railway.

SATURDAY

HE WENT FROM room to room, opening the sash windows to let some morning air in and awaken the house. Though the shutters remained in place, he pushed up a slat or two in each so that thin slices of sun could stream in.

He had slept badly, cramped into one of the chairs in the sitting room, head thick with dreams. He remembered running down endless dimly lit corridors, dark and narrow, the smell of damp and cordite pervading, and his feet echoing. There were hundreds of doors: doors opening onto more corridors and more doors and more corridors. He had been trying to call out, to shout, *Where are you?* But he had no voice, and when he put his hand to his mouth the contour of his face had been wrong; he had no teeth, no tongue, just a bloody hole. Panic had settled on his chest and he had shouted a single word up at the ceiling as he woke.

She pushed up one of the slats at her window and could see early morning mist drifting in off the salt marshes. She wondered, not for the first time, why nobody had come.

She found him in the kitchen digging around in the drawers and set to spying on him from a safe distance as he busied himself about the house. She watched his every move through the gaps in doorways or from behind sofas and chairs. He moved things about, spread maps out on the dining-room table, emptied his kit bag, and raided things from cupboards and drawers (screwdrivers, she noted in the back of an old exercise book, sticking plasters, Germolene, pencils and a pencil sharpener, candles, and a new tube of toothpaste). All the while she heard him mumbling to himself in English. *A rabbit run, but with how many rabbits? Tapioca pudding,* he said to himself. *Cauliflower cheese.* The man was barking mad.

When she got bored, she lay on her bed, her ear trained to his movements about the house. She thought about writing a letter, some sort of SOS, but she didn't know how she would get it out of the house. Having an idea, she went to the window, but it was too high to jump and there was nothing on the wall outside that she could have climbed down. She leaned back against the windowsill. She should do something, but what? She held still, listening, her heart suddenly quickening. Her ears strained to hear him somewhere in the house, the slightest footfall or disturbance or just the sense of his presence, but there was nothing.

Originally he had planned to set the sitting room up as an operation room, but once he'd started pushing back the furniture it didn't feel right. The sitting room, he realized, reminded him of his days in London and his professor's house in Pimlico, Baxter running circles around him whenever he arrived and yapping at his heels. So he moved instead to the dining room, spread his maps over the large walnut table, and cleared the tops of the dressers and sideboards to make room for candles and oil lamps, aware as he did it of the girl sidling out of the sitting room and slinking along the hallway, carrying her Jewish bear with her, then padding soft footed up the stairs. Somewhere above him a door clicked shut.

Here at Greyfriars, he could imagine days gone by, the sun streaming through the open windows, voices in the garden, the tinkling of the piano, the shelves of the study filled with books. His mother would have liked it. The pretty furnishings. The flowers and frills. Water-colored farming scenes hanging from the picture rail. A scent of lavender in the air.

The year *1909* was inscribed in a keystone embedded in the brickwork above the front door, which he rather liked; it was as if the date in the stone somehow marked the birth of the house, which in turn signified that the house was alive. He thought he felt its warmth when he ran his fingers lightly down the banisters or pressed his palm against the door—not a warmth burned into the wood from the summer's heat outside, but something that seemed to be emanating from deep within. Now that he had recognized it, it made him feel at ease, as if somehow the house was welcoming him.

He sat on the floor of the sitting room and took the record sleeves out from the cabinet. Most of them were jazz and swing, including a collection by Fred Astaire that he considered playing but changed his mind.

You couldn't buy anything like that in Germany now, not even on the black market or in the secret backstreet record shops. For a while Eva had taken a fancy to Negerjazz, particularly an American trumpeter called Erskine Hawkins. The Reich Music Chamber had put a stop to all of that. Even Mendelssohn was banned, labeled a mere "imitator" of genuine German music, while Mahler was the composer of degeneracy and decay, and Irving Berlin a Jew.

You'll have to toss your copy of A Midsummer Night's Dream *out of the window if anyone comes around asking awkward questions,* Eva said.

And you'll have to be at the bottom to catch it, he told her with a smile.

The recording had cost him almost a week's wages.

During the economic depression many musicians had left the country or had been purged or simply quit; so many in fact that there had been a shortage of quality musicians commensurate to the shortage of quality compositions that they were able to perform. The situation had been exacerbated by the expansion of organizations like the army, the SS, and the Labour Front, all of which wanted their own military bands and orchestras and demanded the very finest performers to provide them with the necessary pomp. In 1933, just as he had been leaving for London, there had been an assault on Jewish and left-wing musicians organized by the Fighting League for German Culture. Even the Jewish players of the Berlin Philharmonic had been fired, many of them Eva's friends. With the expanding number of orchestras required by the Reich and the vacant positions left by the expunged Jews, he had often wondered whether—if he had remained focused on his music, if he had shown enough dedication—he might have managed to eke out a living from it. Instead—and with perhaps some sense of pride, which only now could he concede—he had ended up consumed within the wheels and cogs and chomping teeth of Field Marshal Keitel's Wehrmacht.

She lay on the floor beside the banisters at the top of the stairs, slowly and carefully lowering a small square mirror tile that she'd managed to tape to a ruler. This was something that Alfie had once taught her—a way of looking into rooms without being caught—and was what all the best spies did. She wouldn't let herself be beaten by a Jerry, even if she was only a girl. She would play him at his own game. She would be a spy too.

But as she tried to maneuver the mirror around, all she saw were reflected glimpses of the ceiling and the top of the walls, and very occasionally the passing glint of a light fitting as it swooped by. She leaned a little farther over, her whole arm pushed through the gap in the banisters and the side of her head pressed awkwardly against one of them. It was just as she was beginning to feel that she was in position and was trying to steady her dangling arm that he came out of the dining room. She hurriedly pulled the mirror back up, but it got caught between the banisters and the tape gave way. With a silent gasp, she saw it fall and smash at his feet. He bent down and picked it up, the mirror now cracked in his hand. He studied it for a moment and glanced up at her. He held it up as if offering it back.

"Is this yours?" he said.

The girl had left him some biscuits for lunch and a tin of Fray Bentos Corned Beef, together with a jar of rhubarb and ginger preserve. He found them on a plate in the kitchen with a note on a scrap of paper written in wobbly green pencil. *For you,* it said.

In Norway they had always been famished—cold and tired and empty. He remembered the platoon stopping midway up a mountainside where the ground leveled and the trees gave some protection from the wind. A flock of rooks reeled above them.

The boy who had been suffering from the cold had sat next to him. He had a bread bag with him but the bread inside was frozen solid, and he had turned and smashed it against a tree until it broke.

You can't eat that. Here.

He offered the boy some of his own black bread that he'd wrapped in paper and insulated inside a sock, and the young private had taken some and nodded his thanks.

Unlike the boy, he had trained with the 3rd Mountain Division under General Dietl, and he was used to this terrain—they had been put to the test in the Austrian Alps only the previous year—but this kid was like so many in the company: new and ordinary infantrymen scrambled together from other regiments and completely ill equipped.

They sat and smoked awhile as he examined the state of his feet and changed his socks. He had blisters on both heels and on the anklebone that were the size of fifty-pfennig pieces, two of which were burst and sore, leaking sticky liquid. The boy pulled his rifle through as he sucked on his cigarette and said nothing. They listened to the boom of artillery shells in the distance, sitting together for half an hour or more before they set off again. Only now, thinking back, did he realize that he had never asked the boy's name.

Later that afternoon, he saw her walking down the long corridor with her arms full of folded pillowcases and bedsheets trailing around her ankles. When he later walked past the spare room he saw that the bed had been made up—the sheets tucked in and folded but ending somewhat short of the bottom so that they stuck out at the edge like a flap.

He imagined Eva living here, walking down the same landing, her own arms full of sheets, making their bed up perhaps, tucking in the sides, patting out the pillows, a sprig of lavender tucked beneath the covers. She'd sit in the sitting room reading the newspaper. She'd worry about the world, the things that were happening that she could do nothing about. She would catch him watching her over her half-rim glasses—*What's so funny?* she would say—and then she would laugh at him and it would make him smile.

In Berlin he had rented a small garret room in the corner of a large tenement block. The building had been constructed in the 1920s—part of a new architectural movement designed to bring functional living space to the masses—but already it was looking worn out and tired, as if functionality was a hard grind. There was a kitchen area in the corner with a surfeit of cupboards, most of which remained empty. In the living area they'd hung paintings over the walls to hide the patches where the plaster was pulling away. Eva would sometimes bring him flowers, holly, grasses, even clutches of twigs if that was all she could find. She'd tie a red ribbon around them and put them in a chipped glass vase—and there they'd sit, bold and defiant in their color, until they turned gray and dry.

He had chosen the room solely for its window and view. They would sit opposite each other, legs thatched together, feeling the snug of each other's toes beneath their buttocks, or Eva leaning back against him between his open thighs.

From up high Berlin looked peaceful, all the sound drained away, all the disturbances, smells, and struggles. They would watch the sunsets—the reds and pinks and oranges unfurling themselves from behind the buildings. *We're halfway up to heaven,* Eva told him.

Yes, he said. *Or halfway down to hell.*

They had no table and would eat cross-legged on the floor, Eva laying out a red checked cloth with tassels around the edges so that every day was a picnic day. They would listen to the dripping tap, to the tick of the metronome swinging, to the wireless or the gramophone—Bruch's "Kol Nidrei," Kreisler's "Liebesleid," Ponce's "Estrellita"—all of which they themselves had played on some occasion or another. Sometimes they would push the furniture back and waltz about the room, bumping into things as they went, their feet drawing invisible patterns on the floor. The waltz was the only dance that he could do without tripping over his own feet. Eva would tease him, saying that he made the dance his own, and he would tip her back into his arms and pretend he was going to drop her so that she shrieked and laughed.

Now, in the sitting room, he lifted the sheet from the piano and opened it up, then sat on the stool and gently rested his fingers on the keys.

If you ever go to fight, she had said, *I want to fight too.*

He had laughed. *And what would you fight for?*

Freedom and justice. I don't know. The rights of all people . . .

German people?

Everyone.

You can't fight for everyone, he said. *You have to take a side.*

Why?

Why? He laughed again.

I don't want to be left here dangling, worthless. I'd have to do something, she said.

He let one finger play its droll note and hang for a moment in the air.

"I can play 'Clair de Lune.'" The girl was standing in the doorway, fingering the buttons of her cardigan. "I could play it. If you want me to."

"No," he said. "No, thank you."

He closed the lid and she stood there a while longer, perhaps thinking he might change his mind or do something, but he didn't; in the end, she backed out into the hall and disappeared. He draped the sheet back over the piano; it was better not to touch.

She slowly retraced her steps back upstairs and found herself drifting into the bathroom. She perched on the edge of the bath, its numbing coolness under her thighs making her feel suddenly helpless. She wondered what to do. Earlier she had made them a lunch of sorts but had left his on the sideboard along with a note so that she didn't have to speak to him. Then she'd made herself busy, getting a room ready for him, because if she were more like her mother perhaps her mother would come back. Soon, surely sometime soon, someone would come to look for her. She had taken clean, ironed sheets and pillowcases from the cupboard. Her mother always put clean sheets on the bed when a guest arrived, even if the sheets on the bed hadn't been used. It was better to have fresh sheets, she said, and, besides, the spare room often smelled musty. Fresh clean sheets and an open window, her mother said, soon fixed that.

She'd tugged the old sheets from the bed and set to making it up again with the new. As she worked, she had pretended that she had a little girl of her own who today was insistent on reading something to her, a pamphlet she had found.

"Yes, yes," she said to the girl. "Now come on, you're getting under my feet, and I've a WVS meeting at eleven and washing to hang out and cakes to bake and dinner to cook for your father. Go and read that thing in the sitting room if you want to read it, but not under my feet."

She shooed the girl away, then turned back and looked at the bed appraisingly. The sheets' corners could have been tucked in better but she had at least made an effort. She supposed it only right that she treated him like a guest.

Alfie said that spies were the people that you least suspected, and in Wales the boys had always been talking about codes, symbols carved into the trunks of trees, shapes cut into the sides of stiles to give the Germans directions; even an ordinary pile of stones might mean the invasion was coming. She had spent hours in Wales hiding under the bed, trying to find secret messages in her mother's letters. They were so dull and ordinary that they must have been hiding something. She wrote of nothing but shopping trips and days out. She'd gone up to Southwold, she wrote once, and half the shops were boarded up. *It really was a waste of a day. The place was like a ghost town. The galloping horses were still there though, and that funny little man. Do you remember?* And when Lydia wrote back and said that she did, she put a tiny dot next to the letters that spelled out I LOVE YOU. When her mother's reply arrived, several days later, she studied it for hours to see if she'd used the same code and then had been disappointed and quite surprised that she hadn't.

She looked at her face in the bathroom mirror. She was definitely looking older, and rather pale despite the summer. She bit at her lips to make them red, then refastened the clips that kept her hair out of her eyes. *You can't let yourself go,* she said to herself, just as her mother did, and then she sighed as her mother did too. *You've got to be strong.* She took the cloth from the cabinet and wiped it around the sink bowl, clearing it of the dried specks of white foam and tiny bits of hair spattered from his shaving. Just like her father, she thought—leaving bits of himself in the sink.

If she went down to the kitchen now, she might suddenly find him there, or her mother. *Oh there you are,* her mother would say, as if nothing much had happened. *We wondered where you'd got to. Didn't you hear me call?*

Voices. Always voices. It had never been a quiet house. The sound of the wireless or the gramophone or the piano coming from the sitting room. Alfie and Eddie's shouts and cheers coming from the dining room where they shot the bagatelle ball around the board that their father had made and it clattered about among the pins. *Cheer up, darling,* her mother would have said to her. Her father would say, *Don't cry.*

They all had something they tried to think about to take their minds off the march. Some counted in foreign languages or wrote poems or letters to loved ones in their heads. He made up rhythms to walk to that fell in line with the long, hard slog. A slow base beat: left, right, left, right, one-two-three-four. He would lay tunes over the top. A mournful song for his cello or, if the march was flat and easy, a fanfare of trumpets, bringing in a lone violin sometimes or a clarinet or a soprano, turning it operatic. The starting point was always the rhythm though. He could write concertos, adagios, or waltzes to it. It didn't matter, as long as the rhythm kept his feet moving, kept him somehow alive.

Occasionally, low over their heads, came the deep-throated grumble of a plane circling—paratroopers perhaps, but beneath the tree cover and thick cloud it was impossible to tell.

The weather worsened and they became sluggish and despondent, staggering through the snow and battling against the wind. As they moved downslope to lower ground, the mist thickened and he began to feel nauseous. The packs on their backs had grown heavier with every passing hour, and they could barely see more than ten feet ahead of them.

They pushed on, but as the dimly lit afternoon seeped away the gale winds drove the snow hard into their faces. They struggled to make headway, lurching and staggering through the blizzard like drunkards. Eventually they dug in for the night and fastened their tent quarters together in groups. Some, himself included, lit small stoves, but they offered little warmth. Where they could they dug shallow trenches in the snow between the trees as a feeble line of defense and took turns watching long into the frozen night.

They hadn't had much equipment when they'd landed; the majority of it had been washed overboard on the journey over, and the supply ships destined for Narvik had failed to arrive. Most of the weapons and provisions they had they'd seized from the Norwegian arms depot at Elvegårdsmoen, but it wasn't enough. A few winter bivouacs, but no skis and no camouflage equipment. Against the French Alpine troops they would be easy pickings. Their clothes were insufficient. The snow clung heavy to their greatcoats, slowly soaking through the material and freezing them from the inside out.

He shared a tent with three others, one of whom spent most of the night coughing. The night was long and bitter, and full of strange forest noises. In the early hours of the morning there was shooting, bullets puttering into the snow. Norwegians, they supposed, but none had seen a thing. The platoon took their positions and fired back, but the night was too dark and they were too exhausted to do much but shoot blindly into the trees. When the gunfire ceased some tried to sleep. They crawled out of their tents at first light to find the men on watch blanketed in snow, seven of them dead—not shot but frozen inside their clothes, their lips sealed shut with ice and eyelids stitched closed with frost.

In the spare bedroom he remade the bed, laying the sheets and folding them tight around the corners of the mattress, so it now looked as if made for a welcomed guest. He smoothed down the blanket and plumped the pillows. The bedroom was small but adequate.

He opened the wardrobe and, checking the girl was not watching, he flicked through her father's clothes, picking out a tweed suit that was frayed around the cuffs but looked smart enough, a crisp white shirt, and a pair of black boots not too dissimilar to his own. He turned down the framed photograph on the dressing table, then undressed and put on the man's shirt, his trousers, some brown socks, and button-down braces. He sat on the four-poster bed as he heaved on the boots. Eva had always liked him looking smart.

There was a job, she had told him. She was going to apply

for it. A hospital. Out in the country. Not even in Berlin. It was paying thirty marks a week, she said. Think what she could do with that.

He had looked out of the garret window and slowly let out a sigh. The sky over the city was turning mauve. Dvořák's Cello Concerto was playing on the gramophone. It wasn't that he didn't want her to be happy or to feel that she was doing something good, it was just...

But now he couldn't remember.

It's a psychiatric institution, she added. *So you don't need a state certificate. They train you on the job.*

But what about the orchestra?

All this talk of war, she told him. Everyone was getting involved somehow. *All the most experienced nurses will probably end up being transferred to the general hospitals, and institutions like this...they'll be left with no one. I need to be doing something more useful.* Always it came down to that, he thought. *And anyway, no one has the time or even cares about going to music recitals anymore. Music won't save anyone; it won't win us a war.*

She was being ridiculous of course. All this talk of war would blow over by Christmas. *You'll see,* he said. *And then you won't need to worry about saving people. We'll all die old and gracefully, and incurably bored.*

But Eva was adamant.

He closed his eyes for a moment, then opened them again. He had almost forgotten where he was: standing in a strange room in front of a mirror and looking at himself or someone very much like him. The boots were a little big but everything else fit perfectly. He adjusted the braces and straightened his collar, leaving the top two buttons undone. Too hot for the jacket but he'd perhaps wear it in the evening. He would invest in this house, he decided; give himself to it until every detail of it was embedded within him—boots, books, bricks, and all.

He ran a comb through his hair and gently patted it into place, then studied himself once more in the mirror, with the faintest flicker of a smile.

Her mother had probably spent hours sewing the shillings into the cuffs of her cardigan, *Just in case,* and now, sitting on the floor of her bedroom, Lydia had unpicked them all and taken them out and she didn't know why. The broken threads still hung from the ends of the woolen sleeves, and she pulled them out like needle-thin worms. *I want to make sure you've always got some money with you, whatever happens,* her mother said. *Just in case.* She looked at the pile of coins on the floor, all her mother's work undone, and felt rather sick. *You're always meddling,* her mother would say, but Lydia couldn't help it.

Now her mother wouldn't come back. Lydia didn't deserve it. And what had she been thinking, talking to the man? She shouldn't have made the bed for him. She shouldn't be helping him at all.

She got up and brushed the bits of thread from her grubby dress. Her legs were covered in scratches and bruises. *You're not a girl's girl, are you, dear?* Joyce had once said. Lydia had never been one for dolls; she had always preferred to be with the boys, charging through the house barefoot, fighting with sticks, kicking at balls, making camps and going on adventures. The boys in Wales had been a different breed though—they were savages, and she had no mind to play with them. They seemed to think that evacuees like her and Button had been sent for them to torment. *Get the vackies!* they'd yell as they came bursting out of the woods and down the hill, waving sticks and throwing stones. It was almost always Button they got, and when they did, they gave him a pounding so that he came back to the house bruised and bloodied.

She climbed into the wardrobe and carefully shut the door. She felt oddly safe in there, in the dark. She understood now why Button had hidden in wardrobes—here, and in Wales, and maybe back in his homeland too. You could pretend that you didn't exist, that nobody could find you, that outside the wardrobe everything was ordinary and exactly as it should be.

I was about your age when the last war started, her father had said. *It will be all right, you'll see.*

Through the darkness, she heard the sound of Alfie running up the stairs, bounding up them two at a time as he always did. She pushed the doors open and tipped herself out onto the floor, scrambling quickly to her feet, and ran out into the corridor. She looked both ways.

"Alfie!" she called, feeling an inexplicable tremor of hope. "Alfie! Are you there?"

He sat on the floor of the study, taking each drawer out of the desk in turn and painstakingly sorting through its contents. He kept a notebook beside him, and every now and again, as he pored over letters and photographs, newspaper clippings and receipts, he jotted down items of interest: dates and names and past holidays, a week in Southwold last August, a wedding in the New Forest...The Torquay Saloon, he discovered, had been bought from a dealer in a town called Stowmarket for what he thought was an extortionate price.

He thumbed through photograph albums and a collection of postcards tied together with string, most of them from a woman called Em. He would take a small collection of letters and photographs, he had decided, and he picked out a few and put the rest carefully back in the drawer.

★ ★ ★

She sat cross-legged on the floor outside the door at the end of the corridor. He had slowly been searching the rooms of the house, for what she didn't know, but she had come to the firm decision that he wasn't to go into this room. She dug at cracks in the floorboards with a broken match she'd found on a windowsill and listened to the house slowly expanding in the heat. Every hour brought more dust in the air. It got inside her, filling her lungs. She imagined being dead, her body like an empty shell containing nothing but dust. Or she imagined throwing open the wardrobe door and seeing her mother crouching in the corner, just like Button. *Ah, you've found me,* she would say, as if everything was a game. With her eyes squeezed tight and her concentration pulled taut and steady, Lydia could put them anywhere she wanted. Her mother at the piano. Her father in his work shed, or out on the terrace with his newspaper and carpet slippers, the smell of his Woodbines drifting in through the window. Alfie in the garden with Eddie bowling a few overs.

She could put them all in the garden, a whole throng of people. She could put them there on a Sunday, one of her mother's annual garden parties for the Red Cross, perhaps. Last year, she remembered, in the morning they had gathered around the wireless—Chamberlain had been speaking to the nation. But in the afternoon they held the party anyway, war or no war— her mother had insisted because everything was planned. Trestle tables on the lawn. Her mother put out cream teas, strawberries, cider, and their homemade elderflower wine. Some of her father's chums played a banjo, a guitar, a trumpet, and a slide trombone. There were flags in the trees, and streamers. People squatted on the edge of the chicken run or fed carrots through the grill to Jeremiah. Some of the ladies from the WVS danced barefoot in their summer dresses on the lawn, and one of them tried to do cartwheels, laughing, with cornflowers and celandine poking out of her hair. Alfie and Eddie served drinks on trays and threw each other wry expressions.

Lydia could hear the echo of everyone's voices, could imagine what they might have been saying to her: *Gosh! Look at you! Haven't you grown? You look the bee's knees in those sandals! Are they new?*

How did our Government ever think they could help? said Joyce, who every year lent Lydia's mother extra glasses from The Cricketers.

Joyce, do you actually know where Poland is? her father asked.

Good Lord, George, of course I know where Poland is, she said, laughing from under her enormous hat. *It's in Europe somewhere. Near all those funny little countries in the east. Hungary and whatnot. We'll all be getting evacuees, I expect. I hear they're going to be quite the rage. But where do you put them? I swear to God, they'll eat us out of house and home—these city children are like dustbins. You wait.*

Be over by Christmas, said Old Mr. Howe as he puffed on one of his homemade cigarettes and blew Lydia a smoke ring that smelled oddly of chrysanthemums. *Don't you go frettin' over this, little 'un. You young 'uns got nothin' to worry 'bout. Our boys will sort that Hitler out. I tell you, the fellow's crackers.*

The day before her father went up to join his ship, he took her mother out into the garden with his rifle.

He had paced across the lawn and drew chalk crosses on the trees. Lydia's mother had yelped every time she pulled the trigger, the end of the gun lurching up and the shot pelting over the treetops.

Steady on, girl—I want you to shoot an oak, not take down a bloomin' Messerschmitt!

They practiced for an hour and only once did she hit a tree.

Then, later, after her father had left, Lydia found a pigeon in the wood, a single bullet through its chest. She took it in to show her mother, its body cold and hard beneath the softness of its feathers. *Look, Mother. Look!* But her mother had just taken the bird in her hands and, sitting with it on the floor of the kitchen, she had sobbed.

She was aware of footsteps up the stairs and then the man appeared. He came down the dark corridor, his heavy boots clumping. She realized how silly she must look sitting there cross-legged on the floor, and she averted her eyes. She waited for him to turn off into one of the rooms but he didn't—he kept coming. She pulled her knees in tight.

"Excuse me," he said. He wanted to get past, get into the room.

She glanced up at him and quickly looked away, but she didn't move. All of a sudden, sitting guard at the end of the corridor didn't seem like such a good idea.

He pushed past her and she scrambled to her feet.

"You can't go in there," she said.

But he was already at the door, his hand on the knob.

"You're not to go in. It's private."

"And you're going to stop me?"

"There's nothing in there."

He turned the handle and started to open the door but, before she knew what she was doing, her hand was on his arm and she tried to pull it away.

He yanked her off him. "Let go!"

She grabbed at his arm again.

"I said, let go!" He pushed her hard against the wall with a thump, and for a moment he had her pinned to it, his hand pressing firmly against her chest.

"You're not in a position to tell me what I can or cannot do, or where I can go," he said, his face almost against hers so that she could smell his breath. "If you don't want me to put a bullet through your skull here and now, you'd be wise to remember that."

His hand released her and she felt herself sinking. He opened the door, walked through, and then shut it behind him. She sank to her knees, her mouth wide open and gasping. She could feel her whole body shaking. She held her hand to her chest and felt where his fingers had dug in like bent nails. She looked down the corridor and sensed the tears forming. All around the house was silent. She would not let herself cry.

The work shed, when he found it later, reminded him of his grandfather's outhouse. From the high horizontal window the light spilled onto the blades of the tools, lighting up the bradawls and pliers that were arranged along the shelf and walls. The shed was called "The Pottery," according to a piece of slate nailed to the outside, although that must have been the work of previous occupants—all evidence suggested that a different sort of craftsmanship was practiced there now. The workbench was thick legged and solid, with a number of wrenches and clamps attached at one end. He had been here once already, his torchlight sweeping across the tools, frantically searching. Now though, in the clear light of day, everything was calm and still but for the soft scrunch beneath his boots of the curled shavings from the lathe.

In Bavaria his grandfather had carved woodland scenes into slabs of oak and maple that he'd collected from the forest, and once finished these were hung about the house: animals foraging, birds taking flight, and scenes from German fairy tales, like the Erlking haunting the forests and luring travelers into the dark, or Bearskin, the soldier who made a pact with the Devil and became a bear. The carvings had scared him, for they were extraordinary—and if life could be so extraordinary, what control could he have over it? What protection could there be?

You hunt or you are hunted, his grandfather said. *You need to be invisible and silent and full of tricks if you don't want to be caught and eaten, or turned over to the Devil.*

Resting on several nails attached to the wall was a long handsaw. He smiled as he took it down, feeling how light it was, how thin. His finger traveled up and down the flat of the blade, and he bent the saw into an S-curve, flexing it this way and that, and then he put it back for now. He would need to find a bow.

On the workbench, beneath a box of matches, he found intricate pencil designs sketched out on graph paper. The next project: a yacht. There were fifteen sheets or more, each plotting out the boat from various angles, or elements of it, labeled and precisely drawn, complete with measurements, swatches of painted colors, and the type of wood or material to be used. He studied each diagram in turn, in awe of the detail, dedication, and precision. This was all there would ever be of the vessel now.

Sitting at the workbench on the high stool, he opened up the matchbox and laid one of the matches down on the bench. He chose the knife with the sharpest tip and, holding the match down by its head, he carefully made an incision halfway up the stick from its base, following the steps that he remembered seeing. The wood broke, a piece splintering off, the cut not straight enough. He tried with a fresh match, getting the length of the cut just right, but it broke again, as did the third and fourth. With annoyance he put the box of matches in his pocket for later; he was doing something wrong.

He was about to leave when he noticed a model rowboat high up in the window ledge called *Annie, Darling.* It had the same degree of detail as the sailing boat he had found on the windowsill of one of the bedrooms. He reached up for it.

There had been a boat like it at a hunting lodge their string quartet had played at just outside Berlin. He remembered the sun had pounded off the white flagstones of the terrace and into their eyes so that it was almost impossible to read the sheet music. They had been positioned by the open doors of the conservatory, and people kept pushing in and out past them. The party was to celebrate a birthday and the recipient, a man who was allegedly a close colleague of Ribbentrop's in the Foreign Office, had been drinking since breakfast. He seemed to spend most of the afternoon colliding with things, including the quartet, or hanging off people's shoulders and nuzzling into their necks. Around them were Party officials and one or two ministers who had nothing better to do on a Sunday. Waiters drifted about the terrace and the lawns serving glasses of Sekt and canapés. Everybody was smoking.

Midway through the afternoon the quartet took a break, and Eva suggested they take a rowboat out onto the small lake at the bottom of the lawn to escape from the rabble. On the other side, perching in the overgrown grass, was a stone folly shaped like a miniature Greek temple, and he had the idea that they would row across to it and back, but they got midway across when Eva said, *Let's just float awhile.*

She reclined back against the boat's rim and let her fingers trail in the water. Now, he thought, was as good a time as any to tell her that he had been called up.

She looked at him blankly.

He told her that they were being moved to the border. They were being sent in.

Sent in, she said. *Sent in where?*

Poland, of course.

She looked down at the water. *Oh.*

He rested the ends of the oars in his lap so that the paddles were lifted from the lake and water drizzled from them. As the boat slowly turned, he could see that someone on the slope leading down to the lake had fallen—a man in a sharp suit—and people were helping him back onto his feet.

Eva said something and turned her head away, and then, as he thought she would, she started to cry.

This, he explained in a faltering voice, was why he had come back from England—for Germany's great revival. The Führer had turned the country around, dragging it out of the desperate doldrums of its depression. There was pride and confidence, a new resurgence, and he wanted to be part of that. But saying it aloud then, he knew it to be only half the truth.

But you're no good at it. Look, she said, still teary eyed, taking his hands in hers. *These are cellist's hands, not . . . not . . .*

She stared out across the water to the party, the drunkenness and the larking about, all the noise and shouting and laughter.

I don't want you to go, she said. *I'm going to lose you.*

You won't lose me.

She wouldn't.

She straightened her hair, tucking a strand of it into the bun that she so hated and only wore when she was performing and was required to be neatly presented.

She looked at him. *I had something to tell you too, but I don't think I've the heart for it now. I got the job.*

At the institute? he said. *Oh, Eva, that's marvelous!*

Yes. But there wasn't any enthusiasm; he had somehow ruined her plans.

They sat gently bobbing, listening to the revelers on the bank and the soft lap of the water.

Perhaps we could take a trip out there, he said. *I'd like that. I'd like to see where you are going to be working.*

Yes. A trip. That would be nice. Then she turned to look back at the party and wiped at her eyes. *I suppose we had better get back then and entertain the monkeys.*

She lay on her parents' bed, trying to write her mother a letter. It didn't matter if it never got posted, or got out of the house, or was even read. What mattered was to write it—she needed to talk to someone. Balanced in the silky swells of the bedspread was the framed photograph of her parents taken at their wedding. Over the last few hours she had developed an unreasonable and terrifying panic that she might suddenly forget what they looked like.

Her father looked out at her from the arch of the church, so smart in his wedding suit and so young. He was always in a uniform: either his naval uniform or his cricket whites, just like Alfie. Even when he was in his workshop he'd wear all-in-one parachute gear, his motorcycle goggles pulled over his eyes. They helped him focus his mind, he said; blinkered him like a Shire horse. He'd spend hours in his work shed, working late into the night, the oil lamp burning and voices quietly singing to him through the stuttering wireless.

Her mother, in comparison, had been early to bed and early to rise, busying herself in the kitchen sometimes before the sun was even up. She'd waft through the house in a silk dressing gown or she'd be dressed already in a narrow tweed skirt and a smart pair of Oxfords, their heels clicking efficiently across the hall-way floor. Looking at her in the wedding photo, her mother had barely changed at all: that same slender waist and curling hair, the slightly prominent chin that both Lydia and Alfie had shared. And now they were all gone.

She didn't deserve to be rescued, Lydia thought. That was the truth of it. She had been mean to Button long before they had even got to Wales. *I don't see why we have to have him,* she said to her mother. *He's not English. I don't see why we can't just send him back to where he comes from.*

Her mother was not impressed.

Well! He doesn't talk. He doesn't do anything. He might as well not be here. He just gets in the way.

Excuse me, young lady, her mother said, *but where is your charity? What do you think God would make of you saying such things? You'll never go to heaven with an attitude like that.*

And so she had tried, but it wasn't easy. She told Rosie and Cath about how her mother had burned his clothes in the garden and bought him new ones; she had been worried about fleas. Fleas were the least of her troubles, they told her. Jews—especially Jewish boys—had all sorts of diseases, diseases that sometimes could not even be seen.

This troubled her, and she decided that it was in her best interests to pretend he wasn't there.

Sometimes though, in the night, she heard him in the spare room next to her, the sound of him climbing quietly into the wardrobe, the click of the door.

We don't know what he's been through and shouldn't ask, her mother said. *He's a long, long way from home though, and all on his own, and the very least a lucky girl like you can do is be nice to him.*

So, rather reluctantly, she had made an effort, and as the days passed and she grew more used to him skulking about the house and suddenly appearing from behind pieces of furniture or closed doors and making her shriek, she found herself warming to him.

And now, after all of that, here she was without him. She'd undone all her efforts. No one, she thought, would come and save a girl who only thought of herself.

Somewhere outside there was a boom, so loud and near that she felt it reverberate through the house. Windows rattled and downstairs something fell from a shelf and smashed. She scrambled off the bed and ran into the hallway. It had sounded like a shell blast.

"Hello?" she called. "Hello?"

She looked up and down the corridor. Bits of dust were falling in trails from the cracks in the ceiling.

"Are you there? Mister! Hello?"

Eventually his head appeared at the bottom of the staircase—"Are you all right?" he said—and she sighed with relief.

You hunt or you are hunted, his grandfather had said. *You need to be invisible and silent and full of tricks if you don't want to be caught and eaten or turned over to the Devil.*

And so he had taken the boy out hunting in the night, far into the dark Bavarian forests that surrounded the farmhouse.

You have to train your eyes to see through your blindness and train your ears to hear sounds in the silence. The forest is full of living things, he would say, *and if you are to be the hunter, you have to know that they are there.*

They would go deeper and deeper, and the boy would learn how to listen with new ears and see with new eyes, his grandfather teaching him how to walk so light footed that barely a leaf beneath him would crinkle and barely a twig would crack.

You see things that others think are invisible, and you hear things that others think are silent, but you yourself need to be silent and invisible, he said. *That is all that differentiates the eater from the eaten.*

Through the darkness of the forest his grandfather would cock his gun and fire into the pitch black, and although the boy saw nothing, somewhere he would catch the sound of a wood pigeon dropping through the trees. His grandfather would send him off to fetch it.

That will do for tomorrow's dinner.

But I didn't see where it fell, the boy would say.

His grandfather would shake his head with solemn despair. *You need to look with your ears as well as your eyes,* he would tell the boy. *If someone magicked you into a bat, what a mess you would be in.*

Then his grandfather would send him off rummaging in the darkness to find it. But one night, when he eventually found the pigeon in a soggy pile of forest debris, he turned around and the old man was gone.

He stood there for a moment and then called out. *Grandfather? Grandfather,* he called. *Grandfather, where are you?*

He stood there, quite still, holding the dead pigeon and feeling the darkness of the forest thickening around him, the trees growing taller out of the ground, the lofty tops closing in and thatching themselves over him, until the darkness was immense and complete.

Where are you? he said again, or whispered, or perhaps just thought. A panic surged through him. *Where are you?* He let the pigeon drop to the ground and for a moment he stood, listening hard, and trying even harder to see; and then, rather timidly, he stepped forward and began to fumble his way.

How long it had taken him to feel his way out of the forest, he did not know. Long enough for his hearing to grow acute and his sight to sharpen, so that, after a while, the darkness began to retreat and shapes started to emerge. His toes were stubbed and his fingers were pricked and grazed as he slowly made his way, half-blind, slithering over fallen tree trunks, his clothes occasionally catching on briars, his feet slipping in the sodden, uneven ground. When he finally broke out of the forest into the clearing, it was with a rush of relief. He found his grandfather sitting on the front steps of the farmhouse, casually lighting his pipe. A thread of smoke lifted from it. An oil lamp burned from inside one of the windows.

Where were you? the boy said—almost demanded—as he tried to hold back his tears.

There, his grandfather said.

No you weren't!

I was. I was right beside you, all the way. You just chose not to see me.

She slopped along the landing with the buckles of her sandals undone, now that her mother wasn't there to say, *For goodness' sake, Lydia—take them off or do them up!* The house was a furnace, every surface hot to touch. She paused at the top of the stairs and looked down the dark corridor to the closed door at the end and the room she had tried to stop him from going in. If no one came, she had told herself, she would have to go in as well; and now it was her third day here and nobody had come.

She walked nervously towards it—a door no different from any of the others and yet the wood seemed darker somehow. She reached out. The brass handle was warm in her hand, and the metal squeaked its resistance as she slowly turned it.

The room was just as they had left it, just as she remembered. FROG model planes lined up and waiting in their squadrons along the shelves, books on ships and tanks and wars, thickly packed between stone bookends carved as crouching monkeys. A man with a big mustache pointed his finger at her from a poster above the desk. YOUR COUNTRY NEEDS YOU, and Alfie had given himself to it, blagging himself into a war that, at his age, he had no right to take part in, her father had said.

She stepped inside and leaned against the door until it quietly clicked shut. There was the photo of Alfie and their father taken on a beach somewhere in Norfolk—Alfie in his swimming belt aged no more than fourteen, his dimples opening up in his cheeks as he grinned. On his bed sat his golliwog. A folded pair of pajamas was sticking out from under his pillow. Several cricket bats and tennis racquets were propped in the corner, with a pair of white sports shoes. One shoe had a balding tennis ball pushed inside, the other a cricket ball—the same ball perhaps that had once been wedged in the tree. Looking about her, she had the odd sensation that everything in the room had somehow been hollowed out, leaving just the skin of things.

On a shelf stood a wooden soldier carved by their father—a rectangular hunk of wood turned into a roughly shaped man: a little taken away from either side of the top to form a head, a slight rounding of the shoulders, the wood sliced away beneath the hands, and thick cuts to differentiate the arms from the body and the stocky soldier's legs from the base. It had been painted and varnished once, but the varnish was now cracked by many summers of heat and sun. She picked the soldier up and held it in both hands. It looked as if it had been broken into a thousand pieces, then delicately stuck back together, piece by tiny piece.

It angered her that the German soldier had been in there; nothing was safe now. She wondered if he had taken anything or moved anything. Whether he'd found her father's workshop too at the bottom of the garden, whether anything was left untampered with and still theirs. She didn't want him having it all, making the house his own. Some parts of it were meant to be private; some rooms were not supposed to be touched.

She returned the wooden soldier to his shelf and looked around the room again. She opened the drawers and saw the clothes all neatly laid there by her mother. Her fingers touched the white cotton T-shirts, the woolen winter socks, his navy Argyle jumper. She gently pushed her nose into its tickly warmth to take in the smell of him, but all that was left was the scent of camphor balls.

She sat on the floor beside the bed. Next to her were his

piles of magazines, *Flight* and *Aeroplane*. He had collected them for several years, but they had become especially important to him once the war had started and each issue began including full-length articles on the identification of various planes. They would lie on their backs in the garden and imagine what it might be like to watch dogfights over the marshes, two planes chasing and wheeling high above, the lines of vapor coiling out behind them like tangled laces.

At the end of April a Heinkel 111 was shot down over Clacton. It came down in the town, ploughing into a row of houses. It still had a belly full of mines that it had been laying off Harwich, and when it crashed the mines took out fifty houses and blew the windows out of every building for over half a mile. Alfie had read it in the paper and announced it over the dinner table, much to their mother's annoyance, who didn't like any talk of war over the craggy landscape of their toad-in-the-hole.

After months of nothing the skies had suddenly been full of planes. Her mother worried so much that she lost weight and had to keep taking her skirts in, and Lydia had seen it in her face too, the worry graying her skin and giving her bags and lines that shouldn't have been there. She kept a suitcase packed by the front door, next to a bucket of sand. *It's daft, I know,* she said to Bea, *but it makes me feel better.*

It's going to be all right, isn't it? Lydia had asked as they'd listened to the reports of the Germans marching into Denmark and Norway.

Of course, darling, she said. *Of course.*

But before long Lydia was being evacuated, and Button too.

Just a precaution, her mother had said.

She laid herself down on Alfie's bed and felt the warmth of the covers beneath her. The cotton sheets smelled musty. Just the slightest hint of him.

God will look after him, she had said the day that Alfie went.

Her mother had been staring blankly out the window at the driveway and the gate through which Alfie had gone, one hand held around her stomach, the other pressed against her cheek where he had kissed her. It would be all right because God would look after him, Lydia had repeated.

Yes, darling, her mother said. *Yes, of course he will.*

On the wall above the bed, rows of insects were pinned to the felt board. Alfie had spent hours out on Sutton Heath with his net in one hand and, in the other, a bag with a packed lunch. It was home to some rare species, *Some real gems,* he told her, including the silver-studded blue butterfly. He'd seen one on three different occasions, which, he said, was three more than most ordinary people ever saw. He killed one of everything he came across and skewered it with a dressing pin to his board, but there was an empty place still in the middle, saved for the studded blue. Three times he'd caught one but he'd never been able to kill it. *Too damn special,* he said. *Had to let the buggers go.*

She lifted one of the slats of the shutters and peered through. A small downy-white feather drifted against the glass, caught in the warm air, and she poked the window open wider in case it wanted to come in. As she watched it drifting there still, she saw her father walking past the side of the house towards the garage. She recognized the trousers, the shirt, the braces, the glossed sheen to his hair. He walked with casual purpose, his long strides taking him along the edge of the lawn, his arms loose at his sides. Her breath caught in her throat. He strode across the garden as if he'd just returned from a walk across the fields.

And then she saw that it wasn't him, not at all, but the soldier in her father's clothes. She wondered why she hadn't noticed the clothes earlier. How dare he, she thought. *How dare he?* She jumped off the bed and ran out onto the landing and all the way round to her parents' room and the window at the front. There she caught him as he disappeared into the garage, and she had to wait several minutes until he came back out again with a tool of some sort. He walked back around the house, and she ran from window to window to see where he was going until he paced out across the lawn. There were lines of sweat down the back of his shirt where the braces pressed against his spine and great wet circles under his armpits. He looked so much like her father. She shut her eyes and tried to make it true, but when she opened them again he'd disappeared completely, as if he had never been there at all.

The certificates were in a large paper wallet hidden among a dozen other paper wallets, packed within a box within a box that, on first glance, held nothing but torn-out knitting patterns. He sat in candlelight at the dining-room table and pored over each one in turn, carefully making notes in his pocket note-book. Certificates of the man's naval cadetship with records of efficiency, as well as the conduct reports completed at the end of each year and an ancient order of promotion from Midshipman to Sub-Lieutenant. There was even certification for a provisional swimming test, signed by a Commander and Gunner and dated September 1923, which made him smile. He sat back in the chair, stretching, and wondered how much more he needed. A marriage certificate would be good; a birth certificate, better.

Marriage. That had been their plan after the war.

He remembered the two of them sitting on a bench beside the Neue Wache memorial, and, not for the first time, he had thought about proposing—the words had been right there, shaping themselves in his mouth.

How many steeples can you see? she had then said, the question suddenly tipping him out of his thoughts.

After a while he had counted five.

I can see six.

Where?

There's one in the sky, as well. Can you see? There, in the clouds.

Was it this childish innocence, he wondered, that had so endeared her to him? The way it conflicted so completely with her political acuteness and philosophical viewpoints, as if—like a child—she was still questioning everything, and sat ever so precariously between two very different worlds?

Perhaps this was why she had struggled to understand so much. Why was it that they had fired the Jewish players from the Berlin Philharmonic, she said, when everyone with half an ear knew they were the best players the orchestra had?

Because they were Jews, he had told her.

Yes, yes, I know that. Of course I know that. But they play so beautifully. It doesn't make sense.

He closed his eyes for a moment, shutting her away, and then flicked through the pile of documents in front of him again, knowing already that they would offer him nothing more. He carefully returned them into the paper wallet, into the box within a box.

The new day was cold and still, the air thick with mist. Everything was bleached white and muffled silent so that all they heard was the crush of their own feet through the snow, the creak of the sledges behind them, and their panting breath. He had blisters within blisters that rubbed against the backs of his boots. He tried to focus on walking but ridiculous memories kept slipping into his head: a holiday in the Alps with his parents, having his photograph taken on a jetty with a bathing ring around his waist, playing Ping-Pong with his father, the back and forth and back and forth of the ball. He could play the memory eternal, just like the rhythm. Back and forth, back and forth. Step, step, step. He kept forgetting where he was going. Perhaps they were walking home.

The mist grew patchy and in parts they could see the mountainsides rising up over them, and occasionally rocks and rubble skittering down into the chasms, dislodged by the snow. In the distance a rusty bridge crossed the gorge. The Ofoten Railway line. They were to secure it east of Narvik, clearing out the Norwegians that were holding the railway between Norddal Bridge and the Swedish border. Often they would stop to scan the trees for sharpshooters. Ohlendorf said that the Norwegians would be almost impossible to see or hear, all dressed in white and moving silently through the trees on their skis.

Keep your wits about you, Ohlendorf had said.

They'll pick us off one by one, he remembered thinking.

Their path took them downhill again. The snow got deeper in the sunken ridges until it was almost waist high and it took every ounce of strength to haul their way through, following one behind the other through deeply channeled pathways and pulling each other out. Trying to drag the sledges through became impossible, and they stopped while Ohlendorf and his officers huddled in a circle with a compass and squares around their maps and decided what to do. The men waited, some lying flat out on their backs in the snow. Others leaned against trees, smoking. He opened his canteen but the water inside was frozen.

In the end they sabotaged the gear they'd dragged there on the sledges and abandoned it in pieces in the clearing. They set off again, slowly, traveling along the base of a gorge for some miles before heading uphill again. The mist would not lift, and as afternoon came it seemed to thicken around them.

As they walked through the trees a bough above them cracked

and snow thumped heavily to the ground. Someone's gun went off.

Jesus Christ!

No firing!

The men stopped and held still, nervously scanning the trees. He watched as up ahead Ohlendorf tried to radio the scouts. Then, after several minutes, he signaled them to move on slowly, and they did, straining to see through the mist, their fingers jittery at their triggers as the trees lumbered towards them out of the fog. *You hunt or you are hunted.* The mist swallowed everything until all but the men on either side of him had entirely vanished, just as his grandfather had done.

She held the glass of water to her cheek, her forehead, to her neck and to her arms, letting the cold condensation cool her before she finally drank it. She then upturned the empty glass on the windowsill over a fly, trapping it, and watched it bumping around inside for a while. She had never much liked flies. *Filthy little things,* her mother said, and Lydia was inclined to agree.

She tiptoed along the landing past all the portraits of her mother's family, the ones that she had never known. She wanted to go into the sitting room and search through her mother's *Good Housekeeping* magazines for survival tips, but he was in there and she didn't want to see him; she would pretend he didn't exist. She felt quite certain that today someone would come. She was getting agitated just waiting. She wondered if they'd be young like him, whether they would speak English too, whether she'd understand them. Every time she passed an upstairs window she looked out in case there were Germans in the garden or coming up the lane, maybe whole lines of men tramping through the fields towards the house. If only Alfie himself would walk out of the woods. If only he would come back.

They didn't know what had happened to him. The story had no final chapter.

Damn this bloody war, Aunt Em had said, and then she broke down, even though she had promised not to.

Sitting on a crumbling wall in Wales among the ruins of Cledwyn's Tower, Lydia felt sorry for her aunt, who had, perhaps against her better nature, driven halfway across the country for her with the news that Alfie was dead. Lydia hardly knew her. She was just a woman who lived miles away in London with a man called Ronald and an arthritic terrier called Mr. Chips, and whom she could only remember ever meeting twice before, once on a trip to the Tower of London and once at a wedding near St. Albans, or had it been a christening? Either way, Aunt Em had never ventured as far as Greyfriars. *She's allergic to us, missy,* her father joked. *Poor ol' girl can't travel more than a twenty-mile radius of London without coming out in a rash.*

Lydia couldn't quite think straight. Somewhere around her a fly was buzzing. Even the sound of the word was awful. That last *d* so abrupt and final. Dead.

But why didn't my mother come? she said.

We've had to put her in a special place, a type of hospital, her aunt said. *Not for long. Just for a short while, you know. It's for her own good.*

But is she all right?

Oh, she'll be fine. Grief's a funny old business. Some people don't take to it very well. You know what I mean.

But Lydia didn't.

She's had a terrible shock. We all have. So you must be brave, Lydia.

I will, she said, but she didn't want to be. She wanted to wrap her arms around her aunt and sob, but she didn't feel that she could.

★   ★   ★

Flaming timbers crashed down through the broken rib cages of buildings. Behind the men the hulks of ships, blasted and blazing in the harbor, lit up the darkness. Huge columns of black smoke poured up out of the wreckage. They moved up the street in short bounds, going from corner to corner and doorway to doorway through the blizzard, rifles at the ready. An explosion across the road blew the windows from a hotel, and they buried their heads as glass and chips of wood and masonry rained down over them, shrapnel rattling on car roofs or hissing in the snow.

It was quieter on Narvik's back streets as they headed away from the harbor where there had been no air, only smoke and flames and soot, the booms and blasts of warships slugging it out against one another. There was another blast and he woke with a lurch. He was hunched in the chair. His throat was parched dry and he rubbed at his eyes. It took him a while before he realized that he was in the sitting room at Greyfriars, before the chairs and cabinets, the gramophone and piano became familiar again.

He had stood on the pier watching as survivors from a coastal defense ship were brought ashore. Through the thick snow clouds the early morning sun sketched the tips of the mountaintops. Nearer, smoke still hung above the chaos of the harbor, wispy tails of it drifting around the debris. He remembered taking off his suede gloves; he had wanted to feel the cold biting his skin but everything was numb. Flakes of snow and flakes of ash fell from the sky, some melting when they landed in his hand, others lingering until he touched them and they turned to dust. Behind him he could hear the roar of motor vehicles moving through the streets. Below him bodies—young Norwegian sailors mainly—floated in shoals, caught against the stanchions of the jetty.

He suddenly had a weary sense of the distance he had traveled. What the hell had he been doing there, in France, in Poland, in Norway?

He had heard that the harbor of Narvik was the only Arctic port that did not freeze over and provided year-long access to anywhere in the west. The Ofoten Railway linked the port with the mining community of Kiruna one hundred miles eastwards over the border in Sweden. Thousands of tons of iron ore were mined there every year, and whoever controlled the Ofoten Railway line and Narvik controlled access to the iron ore. Ohlendorf had told them this during one of their brief stops on the mountainside, high up from the fjords. The platoon was supposed to trek eastwards towards the railway border station at Bjørnefjell, and from there they would secure the railway and the old navy trail that ran parallel to it—places that had seemed as distant and unreachable then as they seemed now.

He closed his eyes. He should try to forget. All that had happened there no longer mattered.

She found him in the sitting room, on the floor in front of the wireless. He leaned in close, his hand on one of the dials, turning it with precision. Among the crackles and buzz of the static she could just about hear a voice. He bent his head so his ear was almost against the speaker and raised his other hand to her—a *Hold still* and *Shush,* a *Don't make a sound.*

It was early evening, but while the world outside was still bright, the house with the blackout sheets at the windows was dark. He had set out candles as he had done the night before, and they glowed in jam jars around the floor, and on the nested tables and piano. Beside him was his folded map and a pencil, and her mother's metronome, gleaming golden in the candlelight. He made a slight adjustment to the radio dial and the static grew louder; then, as he adjusted it again, it fell away and a voice came, forcing its way through the crackling as if it were suddenly coming up for air.

It was male and spoke in German, issuing a steady stream of words with hardly a breath between them. If she concentrated hard she could hear beneath the voice and static the sounds of dance hall jazz playing, the ghostly whisperings of another radio channel bleeding in.

He twisted around and scrawled something in the corner of the map.

"What is it?" she said. "What are they saying?"

He put his finger to his lips to shush her, then leaned close to the speaker again and listened, his eyes still fixed on her.

It was then that she heard the word: *London*. It sounded strange—said in such an odd accent and trapped within all those other words that she hadn't understood—but she had heard it quite distinctly.

"What is it?" she said again. "What did he say?"

He motioned again for her to be quiet and lowered his head, straining to hear the announcer's voice. His eyes were locked on her so that she didn't dare move. The man's voice kept getting sucked under waves of static, and then came suddenly blustering out again as if he knew he was battling the noise.

He reached out and switched off the wireless with a sharp click of the dial. The room fell silent.

"What did he say?" she asked.

He sat up and looked at her. "The landings have started."

"Landings?" Her eyes filled. "Where? Where are they going to land?"

He repositioned himself and unfolded the map, spreading it out over the floorboards. Then he glanced up at her and motioned her to sit down.

He showed her the likely points at which they would arrive. He pointed out beaches from Ramsgate all the way around to the west of the Isle of Wight. He told her that it was all planned, down to the finest detail. They'd move up the Thames, taking London, Reading, Oxford, then they would sweep through the country, marching through the streets of Birmingham, Manchester, and Liverpool, across to Wales, to Cardiff and Swansea, and up north further and further, taking all the major towns, the ports, the aerodromes, the centers of academia, the cultural heritage sites, the museums, the churches, and the cathedrals. Every inch, brick, and step.

"Are they out there now?" she said.

"Yes," he said. "Everywhere."

"In London even?"

She tried not to imagine it but she couldn't help herself: the tanks in the streets, the grenades and the gunfire, houses burning and being looted, German soldiers, people running, people being shot . . . She could feel her stomach tighten as if a great hand had hold of her and was squeezing. She needed to get out, get some air, some light, some help, but he wouldn't let her, and where would she go? They'd be in the fields, on the roads, in the woods, everywhere. Alfie had said as much—they hunt like wolves in packs.

"You must not leave the house," he said quietly, "if that is what you are thinking. It is more important now than ever. If you leave the house I can't protect you."

She felt the heat of panic washing through her.

"But what are you going to do?"

"We have to prepare," he said. "We must get the rooms ready. We will need extra bedding for when they arrive."

"When who arrives?"

"The men, of course. My comrades."

"But, my mother...I don't know where she is." She finally started to cry.

He leaned forward and with his finger lifted her chin. "Look at me," he said. "Look." His voice was not harsh or cruel; it was almost a whisper. She looked up into his face, his round blue eyes, his hair falling over his eyebrows, the light stubble on his cheeks.

"If you help me," he said, "if you do exactly as I tell you, then, perhaps..."

His finger lifted her chin up higher so she could feel the crick in her neck.

"...perhaps, I might be able to help you...but," he continued, "only, only, if you help me. If you do exactly as I say."

"Have you killed anyone?"

The question had been smoldering inside of her all day, and only now had she found the courage to finally ask it.

He looked at her. They had eaten another silent dinner and were back in the sitting room, him with his maps, her in her father's chair with her knees pulled up, arms cradling Mr. Tabernacle. Around them candle flames fidgeted in their jars.

"This is a war," he said, "and I am a soldier. So, yes, I have killed people."

He carried on, marking up the map with his pencil. She leaned into the arm of the chair.

"What about children?" she said. "Have you killed any children?"

He stopped what he was doing and looked at her again.

"Why do you ask these questions?"

She shrugged.

"If you are wondering if I am going to kill you," he said, "I haven't made up my mind. Perhaps you ought to keep such questions to yourself. You might not like my answer."

She sat for a moment and watched the shadows cast by the candlelight across his face, his eyes almost disappearing into the darkness of their sockets.

"We could pray," she said. "It might help." Her mother always said it did.

"Who might it help?" he said. "Me or you?" He bent his head back down to his map. "There is no God anyway. God does not exist. So who are you going to pray to?"

Her face flushed. "You mustn't say that."

"Why not?" He put the pencil down and faced her. "It is the one thing I have learned in this war. If there is a God," he said, "if he is real, that is, he cannot be the good God that everyone says he is. If he does exist, he must want to strike us from this world he has created."

He rested his elbow on one knee and pointed his pencil at her.

"Let me tell you something. When I was in Norway," he said, "we broke into some offices, a railway administration office. A woman was there, shouting; she wanted us to leave and my men, they chased her into one of the rooms and they raped her. Six of them. One after the other. This is what war does to us. And do you know what I did?"

She shook her head. She could feel herself pushing deep into the chair. She didn't want to hear.

"I watched. I did nothing to stop them. Nothing. And God did nothing to stop them either. I have seen him do nothing good."

He poked the air with his pencil again, and Lydia's stomach tightened.

"And why? Because he does not exist. That is why. He is something made up to keep us under control, but it doesn't work anymore. We have become too clever. We know now. We have made him a joke. Worse than that, a swear word, a blasphemy." He laughed. "We say his name without thinking. He does not mean anything to anyone anymore. And without him, what is there to control us? What is there to stop us doing whatever the hell we like?"

"That's not true!" she said. "He's real. He is."

The man laughed again. "Do you believe in ghouls and goblins and the Erlking as well?"

She turned her head away. She would not let herself cry.

"It is a war," he said. "People get shot, hurt, killed. Not just soldiers, but women, children, babies... God has nothing to do with it. This is, this is..." He seemed to catch himself, his voice softening as if he had suddenly heard what he was saying. "It is our choice."

She pulled her knees into her, holding Mr. Tabernacle tight to her chest. The heat of the night was pressing at her, even her breath burned in her throat.

She looked at the pistol on the floor beside him, and she remembered how his hand had trembled when he had first pointed it at her, hands that had been so bloody. She had no idea where he had come from or what he had done, what terrible things he might have been part of.

"What's your name anyway?" she said. "I don't even know your name."

"It doesn't matter."

"I just want to know. I don't know what to call you."

"Heiden," he said. "My name is Heiden. That is my family name."

"But what do people call you?"

"Heiden."

"Don't you have another name, a Christian name?"

"Yes. But you can call me Heiden."

She rolled the name around in her mouth. It didn't feel right.

"I don't want you wearing my father's clothes," she told him.

"You said my clothes smell. You said it yourself."

"But they're not yours. They're his."

"Yes." He raised an eyebrow as if it were a question.

So, she thought, it wasn't right, but she couldn't find the courage to tell him that.

She pressed her hands in her lap and stared at them. She couldn't think of what else to say.

"My brother gave me wings once," she then said, suddenly remembering. "Like an angel. He took a photograph. Would you like to see? I could find it."

Alfie had made her stand on a stool against the sitting-room window so that the dark night outside formed a backdrop to the photo. *I'm going to make you immortal and give you wings,* he had said. The night had been cold and wintry, and he had drawn the outline of wings on either side of her in the window's condensation, lines of it dripping down the pane like threads. And then, when the flash of the camera went off, it lit a glow above her pale head that was still there in the photo, a burst of light like a halo in the glass.

"I could show you. I could take your photograph too and give you wings . . . then perhaps—"

"Do you think this is a game?" he said. "You talk about angels and God but you have no conception of what you are saying. Your head is full of stories. You have to grow up. Everyone has to grow up. Even you. Especially you. Do you understand?"

She stared at him, her eyes filling.

He got up and perched on the windowsill, pulling his fingers through his hair.

"I'm sorry," he said. "I should not have spoken like that. I am expecting too much from you. These times expect too much from us." He offered her a faint smile. "Let me see the photograph then. I would like to see it."

"No, I don't want to," she said. "I don't want to talk to you anymore. I wish you weren't here!"

He listened to her feet running up the stairs and along the corridor. A door slammed shut. In the sitting room the candles were burning out, the room folding in on its darkness and shrinking tighter around him. Was it any wonder that they could barely breathe? He could feel the heat sticking in his throat. All that nonsense about God. He had no idea where it had come from. Why had he said such ridiculous things? And to a child.

He pulled up a chair to the window and sat in it, twisting himself so that he could look through the slit in the blackout frame and prize up one of the slats.

He had killed three children in Poland. They had been hiding in a cupboard in an empty farmhouse outside a town called Olszanica. They had burst out as he had opened the door and ran at him and, in his surprise, he had shot them. Two girls and a boy. A reflex, not a decision. Not like this was. They had all three fallen face down, one in the hallway, the other two out in the yard. He had wanted desperately to turn them over to see their faces, to see what he had done, but Metzger had said, *Don't touch them. Just leave them,* and so they had. And when he dreamed about them now, they were still faceless. Even in that freeze-frame when the cupboard door opened, each face was erased, a pale, featureless blur.

Across the lawn in the vegetable patch the cherub statue glowed, bits of quartz in its stone sparkling. There was a bomber's moon tonight. Strange that these memories should come now. He had felt his mind drained of them in Norway, as they moved through the mountains. He would not become jittery like the other men had, a contagion of fear sweeping through the group, heads nervously twitching. They had been out there somewhere—Norwegian sharpshooters. They'd hear gunfire, shouting in the distance, but it had been almost impossible to tell how near.

He let the slit in the sheet close and paced silently about the room, into the hallway and back again, then sat back down and rested his elbows on his knees and listened.

He had spent some of the afternoon in the garage making fuses in preparation: breaking up cartridges and emptying the gunpowder into strips of material, and then rolling them up and binding them with tape, waterproofing them with tar. He had thought about asking the girl if she wanted to help or watch, if only for some company, but decided against it.

He crossed to the window and peered through the slit again, at the stone cherub watching him. In Norway, in the dynamite room, the windows iced up so much that you couldn't see out. Once he had held his hand against the cold glass until the heat of him had melted the frost and he could see through his watery finger marks, the cool, melted lines of water racing down the pane as he rested his head against it and felt the ice numbing him.

He leaned back against the wall. One by one the candles were guttering, the room darkening by increments. He tried not to think of Eva, to see her in the park, or on the lake that day.

I got the job, she said. *At the institute.*

And what was it he had said to her? He couldn't remember now. Something thoughtless. Careless. Or not. *That's marvelous, Eva! Well done!*

With a sharp tug he wrenched the blackout frame out of the window and put it down on the floor. He stared at himself in the glass reflection, then picked up the gun from the floor, released the safety lock, and pointed it at himself in the glass. Again, he tried to take himself by surprise, turning and pulling the gun quickly on his reflection, quicker and quicker, and wincing at the pain, his arms straight, elbows firm, his breath suddenly fast and furious. He wanted to shout out, to yell, to shoot. Then he stopped. He stared at the man staring back at him. His head was filled with the screams of others.

They were in a clearing where the ground leveled and the trees were thinly spaced. Flakes of snow drifted down through the thick mist. Even now he had no idea of what had happened or how the shooting had started. As they had made their way cautiously across the clearing, one of the soldiers in the middle of the platoon had stopped, his head suddenly twisting sharply, turning this way and that. *Jesus Christ! Oh, Jesus Christ!* Then the man had started shooting.

Closing his eyes he could still see and hear the men, gunfire rattling into the undergrowth. Someone near him was shouting *Fuck!* over and over again as he emptied his weapon; whilst slightly further away, another voice screamed at intervals. Bullets whipped out in all directions, pelting into trees and arms and legs and heads. He had thrown himself to the ground and buried his own head beneath his arms. Then he shuffled forward on his elbows and slid into a shallow ditch on top of two other men. He could hear their rapid breath, but, with their heads wrapped within their arms, he saw nothing of their faces.

She had her gas mask on and she couldn't get it off. It had suckered itself onto her face, clamping itself to her as if it were alive. She tried to breathe but the filter was blocked, and what little air was left inside the mask was hot and sweaty. She clawed and tugged and pulled but it wouldn't come free, and when her fingers fumbled for the edges she found that her skin and the mask were continuous.

Her body jerked and she woke, breathing hard. She stared at the wall in front of her, the blackout frame across the window. She wasn't alone. She felt the man in the room. She could sense him standing behind her, watching. Perhaps I'm not awake, she told herself. This is still the dream. She squeezed her eyes shut as she felt the springs of the bed straining, the mattress tilting from under her and sinking as he lay down next to her. His breath was hot against the side of her neck. She waited for his arm to reach around her over the covers, or for his leg to wrap itself over hers, but he lay perfectly still.

As he lay in the bed, staring, men struggled in the wall in front of him still. He remembered reading, a long time ago, that Leonardo da Vinci used to advise his pupils to stare at a mottled patch of wall until faces leaned out of it. He closed his eyes and listened to her breathing. How cold he had been that night. How much he had wanted to wrap himself in another's arms, to bury his face into the warmth of someone's neck. If he could just reach out to the girl, just pull her into him...But he didn't. He lay quite still.

When they had woken they were covered in a thin layer of snow and it was light. Inadvertently in the night they had pressed against each other for warmth, and he could feel the heavy weight of their bodies against him. Their faces were hidden and he had no idea who they were, and yet they had huddled into each other, burying themselves from the cold. Without speaking, they struggled out of the ditch, shivering and brushing the clods of ice from their uniforms. All tracks or footprints were buried beneath a blanket of white. Flakes still floated down through the trees. The three of them stumbled blindly about, weak-kneed and holding their guns at the ready, but there were no shots. No voices. No sound bar that of their breath and the soft crunch of their boots. Around them the bumpy outlines of bodies lay, half-buried in the fresh snow; as many as half the platoon, it seemed. The rest of them must have run. They turned the bodies over one by one with their boots. One was the young man who had been suffering from the cold, the one to whom he had given his bread. The boy's ice-blue eyes stared up at him, a bullet hole blown wide open through his cheek, a window into the architecture under his face.

They went from body to body, looking for men they knew, and softly mumbling the names as they were found or simply pushing the eyelids shut. He could barely see the shapes of his two companions as they drifted about through the mist on their own bewildered wanderings. One of them shouted. *Hey! Hey!* And then started calling out names—Röthke, Schröder, Studmann, Türke—his voice echoing through the trees—*Where are you?*—but there was no reply.

He staggered back: young and lanky and frightened. He was a Schütze, a marksman, and just a Private, not long out of school, whom Heiden would later know as Bürckel. The young soldier stared at him, questioning, and shook his head in disbelief.

When the third man came crunching back towards them through the snow, Heiden saw that he was tall and stocky, built like a bear. He'd lost his helmet in the cross fire, and he took another from one of the dead as he passed and smacked it against his hand to beat off the snow.

They're all ours.

Heiden nodded.

The man slapped the helmet on his head. *Jesus Christ,* he said.

They walked all day, exchanging names but little else. The older, bearlike soldier, Gruber, was a Lance Corporal and the same rank as Heiden, but he had served for twice as long and made a point of telling Heiden that. For most of the day Gruber lumbered on ahead through the snow, taking the lead without any consultation, while Heiden followed behind with the boy, feeling sick to his stomach. The more he thought about it, the more he felt sure that there never had been any Norwegians. Did the others understand? Should he tell them, he wondered? *I think we did this to ourselves.*

Bürckel bore the brunt of Gruber's anger. He was fresh out of training, and he had a way of blinking, slowly and thoughtfully, as though he was mildly but constantly surprised by everything. He would cry before the day was out; Heiden could see it in his face. He walked more slowly than the other two and froze every time Gruber coughed, as if he thought it might be gunfire. It wouldn't have surprised Heiden if it had been Bürckel who had started the firing. There was plenty of room for panic in his bewildered blue eyes.

The snow got deeper and their progress slower. The straps of his pack rubbed the skin raw under his clothes, and the cold bit at his nose and cheeks. Every limb felt dead and heavy. Not much further, he kept telling himself, although he had no idea where Gruber was leading them.

They stopped to change their socks and drink from their canteens, the freezing-cold water drizzling out from around the lozenges of ice that had frozen inside. He took out a compass and map, holding it to the trunk of a tree.

Ach! You're wasting your time, said Gruber. *We've no idea where we are.*

And so an argument followed. Heiden was adamant that the Ofoten line was up-country. That was where the others would head, and *that* was north, he said.

How the hell do you know? said Gruber. *You can't even tell me where we are!*

But by this point he had endured enough of the man. He hauled his rucksack onto his back, then folded the map and gathered up his rifle and slowly set off again through the snow.

So you're in charge now, are you? Gruber yelled after him.

Heiden did not reply.

She turned the handle as silently as she could and then opened the door just wide enough to slip through. She closed it behind her, keeping her hand on the handle until it had turned fully back again in case it made a sudden click. She leaned back against the door and breathed. Alfie's room was in darkness, all the shapes and silhouettes of his things losing their edges in the night as if they were slowly fading away.

She didn't know what time it was, but she knew it was late. Even after the soldier's breath had slowed and grown softer, she lay there staring out into the blackness for what must have been hours. Eventually she could bear it no longer and slid out from under the sheet, and now she was here with Alfie and already she felt safer.

She sat on the floor against his bed with Mr. Tabernacle held to her chest, his single black eye watching. She had never known where the other one had got to, falling out somewhere and forgotten, looking out now perhaps at a very different world: a dusty, fluff-filled corner beneath a floorboard or under a chest of drawers, or perhaps out there in the undergrowth of the garden or half-buried in the woods.

She lay on Alfie's bed and pulled a handful of blanket from beneath her and held it to her nose. A tiny white feather had caught itself within the wool and she picked it out and held it—so soft and downy in her hand it almost melted away. She concentrated all her thoughts on him, on squeezing him back into existence, until at last she could feel him in the room with her, sitting on the bed, the tips of his fingers gently pulling locks of her hair out from beneath the neck of her nightdress and stroking the back of her head.

Tears began to swell, trapped behind her closed eyelids. She saw Old Mr. Howe opening the gate and cycling awkwardly up the drive. She saw the tires of his bike slipping in the gravel. She had thought about it so often these last few days that she couldn't shake the images. Perhaps her mother had been there already, scrubbing at the doorstep or sitting on it shelling peas in a bowl and catching the morning sun on her face. Mr. Howe might have guessed what was in the telegram he was delivering. He wouldn't have cracked his usual quips, but her mother wouldn't have known. *Going to be another scorcher, Bill!* she might have said. Or *I'm doing peas. You can take some with you. I won't eat them all on my own.* And maybe he just handed her the telegram, or maybe he said, *Annie—I'm sorry.* And he would have walked with his bike back down the drive, his bag of letters in the basket at the front, the cycle clips around his ankles; and her mother would open the telegram but she would know it already. She would feel it in her stomach, in the dark space where he had grown inside her from such a tiny seed. She would know, and she would walk partway down the drive as if they were her own last steps before her legs finally buckled from under her.

For the rest of the afternoon no one spoke. Snow fell, growing heavier, until before long they were caught in a blizzard and he had lost all sense of direction; after two days of mist the mountainside, forests, rocky outcrops, and gorges were all starting to look the same.

He tried to remember the marching tune, because he was sure he had carried one with him all this way, and for some reason he was struggling to recall it. Without it he didn't feel that he could walk another step.

As it was though, it was the boy, Bürckel, who fell. He had been staggering for some time, weaving from side to side as if he was barely conscious, and then his legs crumbled and he fell into the snow, sobbing. Heiden struggled to haul him up but he was a slack weight in his arms.

Get up, he said. *Get up.*

The boy shook his head. He would not move. He sat half-collapsed, his gloved hands pressed into the snow, his lips blue and his breath short.

Heiden looked up at Gruber, who was standing some distance ahead watching.

Help me with him, he called.

But Gruber wouldn't.

Heiden struggled to pick the boy up.

Gruber, for God's sake, help me!

Ach, just leave him, the man called back. *If he wants to die, let him die. Look at the state of him anyway.*

But Heiden would not leave him.

You get up. You get up now. That's an order, he shouted. With both his arms around the boy and with every last bit of strength he had, he hauled Bürckel back to his feet. Over the howling blizzard, he spat the words into the boy's ear. *We are not going to die. Do you hear me? We are not going to die! So don't you say you can't go on! Don't you fucking dare!*

With their arms around each other, they slowly set off again, staggering to catch up with Gruber, but Gruber was already walking on ahead, disappearing into the storm.

From the chair she watched him as he slept. He didn't look "bad." She leaned in as close as she dared. His hair was straight and dark and fine, falling loosely over his forehead. He had long eyelashes for a man and his face was tanned and smooth. She wondered how old he was. When she looked closely at his face she could see the faintest of lines crisscrossing his skin. She wanted to gently lift his eyelids open to see his bright blue eyes.

The wound on his shoulder looked like a bullet hole, and yet the hole it had made seemed deeper, as if someone had stuck a finger into him or something had been dug out. Perhaps he had been chased like an animal, hunted down and captured and tortured. Perhaps inside he was all broken. She wanted to kiss the wound, like her mother used to do—to somehow magic it better. A German had probably killed her brother and yet, with his sleeping body there in front of her, she felt strangely safe.

She put the backs of her fingers as close as she dared to his nostrils so that the breeze of his breath blew warm against them and tingled, and then she lifted her hand to her own nose but smelled nothing but her own fingers. He did look a little like her father, such a strong chin, such sharp cheeks. They had the same slant to their noses, and there was something else, something deeper, a suggestion of her father that she couldn't quite name. She watched the flickering of dreams playing beneath his eyelids. She wanted to reach out and touch his cheek, just to feel if he was warm.

He dreamed of the men slipping over the side of a boat like oily droplets into black water. The boat was dark; lights off, engines silent, the swell slapping against its hull. A huddle of hooded silhouettes watched from the rail. Then a nod, a hand signal, and the swimmers peeled away, six men fanning out, their breaststrokes barely etching a ripple.

They made their way through a thin mist, the waves rippling almost silently against them; their rucksacks, strapped to their chests, clung like limpets; their ammunition boots, tied and hanging from their necks, dragging beneath them through the water.

They passed silently through debris—the remnants of a torpedoed tug: bits of wood, fragments of blasted crates, rags of paper and maps, the body of a seaman face down and bumping gently against a spar. A searchlight skated out across the sea from the coastal battery, and one by one the swimmers slipped beneath the water as it passed over them. Deep below them, moored contact mines hung like sticklebacked moons.

SUNDAY

THE CURVED CORRUGATED-IRON roof of the shelter had been buried, but now the earth was dust dry and the dead vegetables were lagging out of the soil, their roots bared to the sun. On one side of the shelter door were flowerpots shaped like amphorae and full of crisp dried lavender, bees busying themselves among the scented heads. On the other side was a pile of sandbags and a garden hand fork. High up in the cloudless sky he could hear the grumbling of a plane.

He looked up, waiting for the noise to fade, and pushed open the door. Ducking his head beneath the frame, he sidled in, his foot fumbling for the narrow steps inside. A sequestered coolness embraced him, and for some reason Keats jumped into his mind—"Cooled a long age in the deep delvèd earth." Professor Aritz, he thought, would be proud. A hurricane oil lamp hung from a hook in the highest point of the ceiling, and, taking a box of matches from his pocket, he struck one, lit the lamp, and dropped the spent match into his pocket for later. A warm orange light filled the tiny shelter. The floor was covered in duckboards. A slatted wooden seat ran along the entire length, and on the other side were two wooden bunks, each with a small pillow and blanket, chilled damp. At the end of the shelter a blackened metal box acted as a table and looked as if it had once been burned out. On it were two half candles, a few paperbacks and a Bible, a pack of playing cards, and a small photograph in a frame. The picture was of a boy of maybe eighteen or nineteen in a smart soldier's uniform. His hair looked newly cropped and he was trying not to smile. The photograph reminded him of Bürckel. Gruber had said, *That boy's a ticking bomb.*

He sat on the lower bunk and held the lamp up. The air was dank and earthy. Everything was dusty. As the oil lamp flickered he felt a little claustrophobic, as if, with his knees up and arms huddled to his sides, he was too big for the shelter or it was too small.

It was Gruber who had found the concrete store, tucked away from the edge of the mountainside beneath a canopy of trees. Its roof was covered to a depth of two feet, and great surfs of snow were blown up against its walls. A small square window at the front was shuttered up, and so was another at the side. They had stood outside as the storm howled around them, Heiden beside Gruber, rifle ready, while Bürckel hung back. Gruber pushed at the door and tried the handle but it wouldn't budge. Then he rammed his shoulder hard against it. There was a split and a crack as the door splintered and broke open; and inside there was sudden shuffling in the dark and hurried movement. Gruber fired once, then again. He shouted something and they crowded in to the smell of sweat and cordite, and the sight of three pale faces. A man in a naval uniform was standing in the far corner against the wall. A second was squatting in the opposite corner, wrapped in a coat. The third was slumped against the wall, Gruber's two blackened shots through the chest.

The two remaining men raised their hands.

Norwegian? Heiden shouted.

British. We're British, the man standing said. *Please. Please, don't shoot.*

★　　★　　★

Standing up and putting the lamp down on the floor he took the books, candles, and playing cards off of the tin box and prized the lid open. Inside were two cans of soup, some smelling salts and disinfectants, boric ointment, cotton and bandages, a torch, and some spare batteries. He considered taking them all with him but then changed his mind—he had enough to carry. He sat back down on the bunk, waiting like he had done as a child for his father to come home. Sometimes his father would come in bloodied. He and his Freikorps comrades were always getting drunk and into brawls. He'd spend his nights at a beer hall on Alexanderplatz looking for trouble. He wasn't like that when Heiden's mother first met him, she had said. Before the last war Heiden's father had never been an angry man.

It was at times like this that he missed his mother. She had been religious. His father had not. They had fallen on opposing sides of the fence on so many matters. His mother—being the family optimist—said it was good that she and his father had taken views on so many things. Every argument presented the boy with a choice. But it wasn't always that clear to him, between belief and nonbelief, black and white, right and wrong. Like many of his generation he had floundered with life's numerous options. The Third Reich had helped them on that. It had freed them of the worry of choice, giving his generation focus, something to believe in when God was no longer any good, or perhaps not even there.

The older he got, however, the more baffling he found it— caught between doing what was good and God's way, and what was right and the way of the Führer. As God fell out of favor, Heiden was happy for the National Socialists to take the upper hand. Many, it seemed, didn't care which way society was going so long as somebody was steering it somewhere. Eva had not been so sure.

He got onto his knees beside the bunks, taking the oil lamp down with him. In the narrow gap between the bunk and the floor a farmyard had been set out: herds of metal cows, ducks, horses, pigs, and sheep. At the far back, beyond the fields of tin animals, something was caught between the bunk and the corrugated wall, slipping down behind the makeshift bed. He moved the lamp closer and reached under until he could just about grasp the papers between his fingertips and pull them free. It wasn't a document, as he had hoped, but a homemade book of sheets of paper folded and threaded together in the middle. The cover was drawn in crayon and pencil—a large face with a wonky crown, and behind it a castle on a very rounded hill and what was perhaps a gray dragon or maybe just a large dog. Each letter of the title was written in a different colored pencil, and it ran all the way around the edge of the cover so that he had to keep turning the booklet to read it: *The Incredible Adventures of the Tiny Princess.*

He flicked through the story and smiled at the crudely drawn pictures. As he reached the end a photograph fell out. It was the photograph the girl had been talking about: She was standing in front of a window, a year or so younger, the flash of the camera shining in the dark glass behind her as if it were a halo. Someone had drawn lines in the condensation, two thin swoops arching up from behind her shoulders and then swooping back down like angel wings. He looked at it for a little while and then slipped the photograph into his pocket.

He pulled one of the spent matches from his pocket and put all but the head of it into his mouth until the wood had softened, and then took the small knife from his other pocket. He rested the Bible on his knees and, in the flickering glow of the oil lamp, he laid the match on it and made three incisions into the wood: one from the base to a point midway up the match, and one on either side just below the head. He carefully opened up these cuts until it was just right, then smiled to himself, for it had not broken. The secret, he remembered, was in the softening of the wood.

He stepped out of the air-raid shelter into the blazing sun. Midmorning but already hot. Another unendurable day. He tried to loosen the man's braces but they still dug into his shoulders, causing him some discomfort at the site of the wound, and he sweated beneath the straps. He unfastened another shirt button and looked up at the sky; the plane was long gone but it or others would be back.

From the corner of his eye he saw something moving in the vegetation beneath the trees nine or ten feet into the wood. Something small and white. It moved again and then stopped, half-hidden beneath the dock leaves and ferns. He took a few steps closer across the lawn, taking his pistol from his pocket. A creature of some sort, perhaps a cat. In the rush for people to leave their homes no doubt a great number of pets had been set loose into the woods and fields to fend for themselves. But this wasn't a cat or a dog; it was too small. He cocked his gun and waited for it to move again. The release of the safety lock startled it, and he watched as a pure white rabbit scampered deeper into the woods, its fluffy tail bobbing as it scurried beneath a fallen branch and vanished.

Now that he had taken the board down from the kitchen window, she could see him through the glass. He was at the back of the garden, past the water pump, disturbing the remains of her father's bonfire with the tip of his boot, the ash blowing around his feet. He had a half-eaten apple in his hand and he took another bite before tossing it into the hedge. He wiped his fingers against his trousers—Papa's trousers, she thought. He looked up at the sky and then over to his right where something had caught his eye. As his glance flashed across the window she stared down at the sink so that he'd think she wasn't watching him. She was aware of him walking away, down the side of the house across the terrace. She heard his boots on the gravel, and then the front door opened and he went up the stairs. She listened to his footsteps overhead. After a minute or so, he came back down, retracing his steps into the garden. He had the British uniform he'd worn that first night draped over his arm and what seemed to be a handful of papers. She watched as he dropped them all onto the fire pit and then stuffed the arms of the jacket and trouser legs with the paper. He lit a match and held the flame to the material. She saw the fabric slowly starting to smoke.

He watched the bonfire flames build and almost catch the hydrangea next to it. From the back she could imagine him as her father, standing over the bonfire as the garden rubbish burned: the same build, the same dark hair floppy at the front, the same blue eyes made brighter in the sun. She could just about see their glint when he turned his head as he nudged a jacket arm back into the flames.

She stood behind the sink just as her mother would have done, watching.

George! For goodness' sake, mind the hydrangea! It's only just started to bloom!

And bloomin' lovely it is too, he'd say, grinning at her. But he didn't. There was just a man dressed as him, burning a British uniform on a bonfire because, as he had said, the Germans were here now and he no longer needed disguises.

Perhaps her father would be the first to come back for her. He'd bring her back a memento—not something that he'd bought, but something that he'd found. Like the pebble with a face ingrained in it, all the way from Africa, or the shell that looked like a spider with eight bony legs. *You can hear mermaids singing in it,* he had told her, and it was true—the shell had indeed sung.

The soldier walked over to the water pump and pushed the handle several times, but the pump had long been out of use, the pipe's throat blocked with silt. He bent down to examine it, then tried the pump again. He leaned heavily against it, resting for a moment, and then he pulled something from his pocket— a letter. He didn't open it but just held it in his hand and ran his finger and thumb along the edge of the paper, sharpening the folded creases. She leaned in closer to the window. Would he protect her when the others came? Would he keep her safe from all the other soldiers when the house was full of them, when there were plans to be carried out and activities and exercises and noise and decisions and drunkenness and shouting, and all of it in a language that she didn't understand? People running up and down the stairs. Queues for the toilet or men just urinating in the flower beds. The thought made her want to spit. All their books being burned. All their letters. Everything that was to do with them. Every room being turned into something else. She would be in the way then. They would think she was under their feet, an inconvenience perhaps, an annoyance. She would have to make herself indispensable, tell them anything they wanted or needed to know; she would have to do whatever they wanted just to stay alive.

She lifted her hands from the washing-up suds and saw how withered they had become. She put them back into the sink and groped around beneath the bubbles and murky water. One last teaspoon was left, which she swilled around a few times and then wiped dry on the tea towel. If men came she didn't know how they would feed them. There were tins in the larder but not enough for an army. She should sneak a tin of sardines into her room, she thought, and hide it for herself.

She put the spoon in the open drawer beside her and then tackled the stack of drying plates and mugs and glass tumblers. Sunlight glanced off the steel knives and forks, dabbing a splash of rainbow on the windowsill. Now that she was a good six inches taller, she had no trouble leaning over the sink to put her finger into the shimmering pool of light and see how the colors reflected across her fingertip.

She repositioned the double lengths of string over both shoulders and then, gathering them up on either side of her legs as if they were puppet strings, she hauled them up and clumped over to the cupboard. She had turned the empty paint pots into stilts before the summer as part of an experiment to see what life might be like as an adult. Alfie had shown her how she could put a foot into the pots' handles as if they were riding stirrups, and then how to attach strings on either side of each pot and run them up over her shoulders and down the other side. The first attempt had been disastrous. Both strings had snapped as she had tried to haul herself over the doorstep, and she had fallen splayed across the gravel, grazing both knees. After some reconsideration, it was decided that they needed to use tough garden string instead and at double thickness so that the string could take the weight; and that she would have to pull them up with her hands as well as her feet if they weren't going to break. It made maneuvering awkward, but she eventually got the hang of it. After a couple of days she could clump all the way down the corridor and had once managed to haul herself all the way up the stairs when no one was around to tell her off.

The paint pot stilts had been abandoned in a cupboard after the third day, but they were proving rather useful again now; she could return any dried glasses or plates to the right shelf without having to get up onto the work surface or pull up a chair, or—worse still—ask him to put them away. She could even lean across the sink and turn the mint plant in its pot so it would grow evenly and a fresh set of leaves would feel the sun's warmth.

Outside, the man had disappeared, so she held still and listened. A wave of anxiety washed over her as it always did whenever she didn't know where he was. She half expected to be suddenly dragged away with a hand across her mouth.

She clumped closer to the sink and leaned into it, straining to see through the window as far as she could on either side, but there was no sign of him. She straightened up and turned around to look down the hall. The front door was open and beyond it the sun was burning bright. He had forbidden her to leave the house, and with the whole of England probably awash with German soldiers by now, it would be stupid to risk running. If there was any hope of finding her mother she knew that she needed his help.

When he finally reappeared he had taken her father's shirt off but still had the braces hooked over his bare shoulders. Even from here she could see the ragged-edged hole in his skin where maybe a bullet had gone in. He had their spade with him and was digging up the dead lettuces that her mother had so neatly planted out along string rows, a cigarette gently smoking between his lips. As he bent over the spade, his back was greasy with sweat and his shoulders had already started to burn. The muscles in his arms tensed as he unearthed the shriveled lettuces from the crumbling soil and one by one flicked them away into the undergrowth. All around him dust rose up into the air.

Once, last summer, Alfie and Eddie had taken her over Sutton Heath, nets and notebooks in their hands and jam jars hanging from string around their waists.

What are we doing?

Going hunting, Alfie said.

The heath was blanketed in purple heather that grew as high as Lydia's waist, and ferns that were even taller. The sun would have been relentless had it not been for the wind, butterflies battling against it and thistledown blowing everywhere.

You can use heather to make beer. Did you know that? said Alfie. *And tea.*

Eddie didn't believe him.

It's true, said Alfie. *Isn't it, Lyds?*

Yes, it is, said Lydia, but only because Alfie had said so.

They popped the seed pods of yellow gorse and scuffed at the rabbit droppings or struck down harebells with the rods of their nets. Above them the sky was endless. There didn't seem to be anyone else around.

Right ho. Let's start, said Alfie. *If you catch anything let me know,* he told her. *We'll pop it in a jar.*

Within an hour they'd captured a bumblebee, an earwig, a hawk moth, and a small tortoiseshell; and she then spent almost twenty minutes chasing another small butterfly, yellow and orange, that flew close to the ground as it fluttered between the gorse and was buffeted about on the wind.

Yes! Got it! she shouted as a sudden flurry of wind blew the creature into the gaping mouth of her net.

Or rather, it got you, said Alfie.

That's a small heath, that is, said Eddie. *That isn't anything special.*

What are you going to do with them all anyway? she said.

Fix them to a felt board, Alfie told her. *One of every kind. And I'm going to get myself a studded blue too.*

Not that day though. When they got home again, he and Eddie lined up the jam jars along his windowsill and for a while they watched the creatures inside, buzzing and bumping and scrambling around. The next day they were all dead. Creeping into Alfie's room she unfastened one of the lids and carefully lifted out the small heath that she'd caught. It felt so weightless in her palm, its legs like bent eyelashes. She gently pushed her finger against its body and thought she could feel the scrunch of its tiny bones breaking. She wished she hadn't caught it now. She wished it hadn't died. And when she tried to put it back in the jar its dust-dried wings disintegrated between her finger and thumb so that every bit of it was now broken and Alfie would not even want to pin it to his board.

As the British uniform burned on the bonfire he rested against the water pump, holding the folded letters in his dirty hands. He had received just two letters from Eva since the end of '39, although she said she had written many more and had put them in the nurses' "Post Out" tray in the secretary's office.

He held them to his nose and smelled them—her thoughts to him made real by the ink. The paper still held the faintest scent of her; her skin rubbing across its skin as her hand had moved across the page. *Sealed with a kiss.* And in the days and weeks and months that followed he wondered whether she had indeed placed her lips against the paper somewhere, there in the top-right corner, or at the bottom of the last page. He had tried to feel with his fingertips where a slight dampness had once occurred, where the paper was slightly puckered, and sometimes he thought he had found it and sometimes he wasn't so sure.

Her first letter was a predictable gush of enthusiasm. She had thrown herself into her new role with typical zeal and had, she wrote, already won the confidence of the senior sister, Nurse Hartmann—this seemed no mean feat when he considered the hour he had spent with her during their visit. The woman was so rigid and clamped tight that even when she smiled her teeth remained cemented together.

It was a Saturday in September, the day unseasonably hot but breezy. She led them in through the main hall and supplied them with lemonade, rattling out the history of the hospital as they drank.

Set among acres of ground the institute had all the grand delusions of a country estate, complete with Grecian pillars outside, disused stables, and even its own clock tower. The corridors were wide and echoing with tiled walls of pale green, and as they walked the sun shone through the large-paned windows and washed light across the floor.

People ask if we can cure them, Nurse Hartmann said, pointing out a step with her finger as they walked in case one of them missed it and fell. *It is not a question of curing, it is a question of making what life they have worthy of living. You'll find that our work here is highly regarded. We think of ourselves as progressive.*

He held Eva's hand and gave it the occasional squeeze of reassurance. She said little as they passed through the corridors, Nurse Hartmann showing them the offices, the dining rooms and kitchens, the nurses' quarters, the dispensary. There was a library, chapel, and what she called "the day area," although these were all empty. It was quieter than he had expected, he told her.

Dr. Kesselring insists that windows and doors must be closed softly, plates and utensils must not be clattered, Nurse Hartmann said. *No jangling of keys please,* she told Eva.

I was talking more about the noise of the inmates, he said.

We have our moments, Herr Heiden. However, we do not encourage them.

They crossed the paths of other quick-heeled nurses, each smiling politely as they passed. In her first letter to him Eva wrote warmly of the young nurse she was bunking with, Käthe, who had been particularly welcoming, showing her around and priming her on the unwritten rules and regulations of Nurse Hartmann's regime. There was, Eva wrote, great camaraderie.

There was no time to think though. They were required to be present around the clock: waking, bathing, and dressing patients, then supervising them at mealtimes, sluicing bedpans, changing bedsheets, and feeding them an array of pills. Dr. Kesselring, the physician, seemed terrified they would all be struck down with the plague, so everything was scrubbed and scrubbed and scrubbed again with carbolic soap: floors, bedposts, bedpans, clothes, and fingernails; she wondered that she had any skin left on her hands. Worse still was the endless counting; counting in patients, counting them out again, counting in forks and knives and spoons and anything that might cause some harm. Her biggest fear, Eva wrote, was that patients might accidentally hurt themselves or, worse, someone else while she was on duty.

Her violin was her one relief. She would play out the frustrations of the day in her room every night. She missed the window seat of the garret room, she wrote, and watching the sunsets over Berlin. She wondered where he was. *Are you still in the Hunsrück, or have they moved you on again? Please come back to me. I sometimes think you are the only reason I am living. I miss you. I love you. I think about you every night.*

He was in the Hunsrück mountain region on the Western border of Germany in reserve with the 16th Army. But by the time the second letter arrived he had been moved twice more and was at Cochem. This letter had been altogether shorter and more abrupt, as if her mind were elsewhere. She wrote nothing of the work she was doing, only that she was exhausted. There was nothing of the patients either, or Nurse Hartmann and Käthe. Instead she wrote of the gardens and how the autumn was turning the color of the leaves and starting to scatter them across the lawns.

On their visit, he remembered spending some time walking the gardens by himself while Eva was in one of the offices going through various forms and talking about the finer details of the job. The garden was functional, with just one or two small and unruly rose beds and benches set beneath bunches of trees: oaks and ashes and maples and conifers. They were only about a mile out of town, although from the front of the hospital where the gardens were there was little sign of civilization, just fields and forests and farms. He had been hot in his uniform and remembered crossing the lawn to sit on one of the benches in the shade. He watched two nurses in their own starched uniforms hurrying down a path. One of them gave a polite wave and he must have waved back. Then, feeling rather foolish, he looked back at the hospital, at the rows of tall windows blinking in the sun, the mock pillars lined up along the front, and the wide double doors that the two young nurses passed through. Eva would be happy here, he had thought.

How devastatingly wrong he had been. In the weeks and months that followed he had trawled back and forth through the memory of that visit, thinking that there must have been some clue, some way of knowing—a cracked paving slab or dead bird in the grass, some warning of what was to come—but, of course, there had been nothing. The afternoon had been so warm and bright.

He ran his fingers down the folded creases of the letters. He knew them word for word. *You are the only reason I am living. I miss you. I love you. I think about you every night.* He could forge her writing if he wanted to; he had studied every loop and curl. She always wrote on lined paper, each letter placed like a note, whole sentences plotted out like lines of music. He could sing the words—he could hear the song of them playing in his head.

Schizophrenia, epilepsy, senile disorders, therapy-resistant paralysis, syphilitic diseases, retardation, encephalitis, Huntington's chorea. Anything neurological . . .

Nurse Hartmann was leading them through one of the wards. It must have been earlier in their visit, not long after they had arrived.

I sometimes think it a wonder that we make it out of our mother's wombs at all without being struck down by something ghastly, she added. *They all have to be vetted and qualified before they're allowed in. The paperwork alone is quite disabling.* She laughed.

The beds were narrow and tightly packed, a dozen or more on either side with a small bedside table with a drawer between each. The men lay dozing or staring blankly up at the ceiling or some midpoint in between. They were quite comfortable and content there, Nurse Hartmann had stressed.

They stopped at one of the beds. The man beneath the sheets was withered, his face like a clay mask. His bony fingers curled around the top of the sheet that he'd pulled up to his chin. Beneath the covers there hardly seemed to be anything of him at all. The nurse lifted the clipboard at the end of the bed so she could read it. Heiden was about to ask what the man's prognosis was when she turned and asked her own question, as if there had been a reminder for her there in the man's notes.

You're not married?

We're to be married after the war, Eva said, smiling.

Ah, yes—the war, said Nurse Hartmann, as if it was something that in the confines of the hospital had somehow passed her by. Eva wouldn't be staying with them long then. Very few, she said, stayed after they were married. *Children, you know. Housewives' work.* She turned to Heiden. *Just so you know, visitors are not allowed after hours, and only on days off, not whenever it best suits you, Herr Heiden.* Men, of course, were not permitted in the women's staff quarters. *We have a lovely orangery though, which I am sure will be adequate for any conversation that you and Fräulein Winkler need to have.*

She looked again at the clipboard, lifting the various sheets of paper.

I'm very much looking forward to starting, said Eva.

Nurse Hartmann put the clipboard back and frowned at the man in his bed. *Your education is excellent. You are polite and professional, I can see that.* Most of the nurses at the institute, she told them, had done little more than domestic help before they were taken on. *People think "psychiatric nursing" isn't real nursing,* she said. *You will not be surprised to hear that I disagree. We are here to bring joy and life and relief to these patients. You will see for yourself when you start.*

They made their way further down the ward. He looked at every passing face. They were of all ages, some younger than he was. One of the patients, a middle-aged man with cropped dark hair, was fastened into his bed with leather straps.

You will have to keep your wits about you, Fräulein Winkler. If there is any possibility of disruption, our policy is to sedate them.

Like animals? Heiden said.

Nurse Hartmann gave him a stern look. *I appreciate your opinion—Lance Corporal,* she said, looking at the rank insignia on his uniform, *but you have no understanding of what we are dealing with here. God made us all animals. Some are wilder than others. These patients are not fully human. They need to be put right. It is, as I am sure you can imagine, a long and costly journey. We—all of us—are doing the best that we can.*

By this point they had passed through the door and were back out in the corridor. In the ward at the opposite end of the hallway a woman in a white hospital gown was shouting. Through the partially open door they could see two female nurses struggling to contain her and get her into bed. Nurse Hartmann, however, was keen to turn to the paperwork.

Fräulein Winkler, you are of course a member of the DAF?

Eva said that she was not and Nurse Hartmann tutted.

Well, that is the first thing we need to see to, then, get you joined to the Labour Front. She turned to Heiden. *And you, Lance Corporal, I'm sure would enjoy some air in the garden. I challenge you to find our strawberry patches. They are not where you might expect them.*

And indeed they were not, for he never did find them.

She was trying to sew the coins back into the cuff of her cardigan, but she was all fingers and thumbs. The end of the cuff wouldn't stay folded over and the coins kept falling out. Her mother had sewn them in with hundreds of tiny stitches and Lydia didn't have the patience for that. Even when she had managed to sew the hem down it was all puckered, but she kept at it anyway. Her mother would never come back if she unpicked everything.

For the third time the thread escaped out of the needle, and in her fury she threw it across the floor. She pushed the heels of her hands into her eyes so that she could block everything out. She would hide every bit of this away; the man downstairs, the German advance, the house like a buried box around her, the heat and the suffocation. She would push it all away into the darkness so that everything was gone.

Earlier she had stood out on the landing, shouting "Mother! Mother!" on the off chance that it was all a trick being played on her or just a silly dream, but it was the man who called up from the bottom of the stairs, "What are you doing?" And she didn't know. She told him she wasn't doing anything. She was just hoping. That was all.

If she could take her father's old watch from its drawer and wind it back and back, taking back one after the other the hours and days and weeks they had lost, she would. She would bring them all back one by one. Her mother first, and then Button, and then her father and Alfie. She would pop the bullet back out of Alfie's chest and bring him back to life.

She got up and left the room, walking along the corridor to the door at the end, Alfie's door. She had no urge to go in. She wanted to press the side of her face to the wood, to feel its warmth—a warmth that was his. She wanted to hear its creaking in her ear as if the wood, the door, the room itself were breathing his breath.

It was only when Eddie was there that Alfie wouldn't let her in.

She'd hear them laughing and fooling about, and knock on the door and open it, and then Alfie's face would be there, grinning.

Can I come in?

No, we're busy.

Come on, Alfie! Please!

No, you're too young, Lyds. Go away.

And she'd try to force the door, but with a slam he'd push it firmly shut.

She'd hear Eddie saying: *Shove a chair under the handle or something.*

And then Alfie would be doing just that and all the time she'd hear them both laughing.

I hate you! she would yell.

They were British naval officers; he recognized the uniform and the insignia on the cuffs of the man who was standing. The second man was huddled in the corner, wrapped in coats and a blanket; his skin was pale and his face craggy and pitted, with wisps of white in his hair. He looked at them with wild eyes, red raw in their sockets. Both men's faces were thick with stubble and their smart navy trousers were muddied and sodden. Against the wall lay the third man, slumped dead where Gruber had shot him—not much more than a boy, Heiden noted, and certainly no older than Bürckel. His eyes were open and glassy, the blood still trickling from the two holes in his chest. The air was still laced with smoke from the hurriedly stamped-out fire in the middle of the floor, some of the twigs still faintly glowing.

What are you doing here? Heiden said to them in English.

The standing man said nothing and Heiden repeated the question, poking the air between them with his gun. *I said, what are you doing here?*

We ran aground, answered the man.

What? said Gruber. *What's he saying?*

Heiden translated.

They had been on a British naval ship—the HMS *Hardy,* the man explained. It had been hit in the cross fire in the harbor at Narvik and had beached at a place called Vidrek, a small village to the west. The three men had been on the run ever since, the rest of the crew scattered by German soldiers, he told them. They had been trying to find another village where they could get help but the weather—

Heiden laughed.

You are lucky you found this place, he said. *You would be dead otherwise.*

Gruber dumped his kit bag down and peeled off his gloves, flexing his frozen fingers. *We should throw them out into the snow and settle in for the night, or just shoot them,* he said. *I'm not sharing with Tommies.*

Heiden bent down next to the older Englishman. He looked sick. He was crouched with his knees up and staring at them from behind the wrap of his arm, shivering and breathless. He already had a confused look in his eyes; lips almost translucent, eyelids pink and puffy. They'd been particularly diligent on the prevention of hypothermia in their training with Dietl's division, and Heiden had seen the symptoms before on exercises in the

Austrian Alps. As he leaned in closer, the man tried to push himself deeper into the corner.

I only want to see, Heiden told him. *Please.*

In the end, the man lifted his mittened hands out from his armpits and offered them to Heiden as if he wanted them taken from him. Heiden peeled one of the mittens off. The man's hand was blue and covered in white and yellow patches. The fingertips were black and waxy and hardened, and there were purplish blisters filled with blood. He put the mitten back on the man's hand and turned to Gruber and Bürckel. *We need to relight this fire,* he said. *This man mustn't get any colder.*

We shoot them, said Gruber. *He's going to die anyway.*

No. They are prisoners of war now. We're not shooting them, said Heiden.

Oh? And who put you in charge?

I said, we are not shooting them.

Gruber held his stare. *If you keep them alive you are putting our lives at risk, the campaign at risk, the whole fucked-up war. You hear?*

Heiden said nothing.

I won't be held responsible for them, Gruber said. *If either one of them so much as sniffs I'm putting a bullet through both of their heads, and if either you, or you,* he said, pointing at Bürckel, *have a problem with that I'll put a bullet through you as well.*

This was how the days would pan out: the operation reduced to school-yard bickering. The war in itself had become irrelevant. Trapped in the middle of nowhere, with the rages of a blizzard outside, all Heiden was concerned about was surviving the day and then the next one and perhaps, if he was lucky, the next. He could feel the odds stacking up against him.

He struggled out of his rucksack and motioned with his gun for the English officer to sit. He asked them what their names were.

Pendell, said the man. *British navy.*

Rank?

Lieutenant Commander. That's Harris, he said, pointing at the sick man huddled on the floor. *And that boy you've killed—*

We don't need to know, said Heiden.

His name was Lewis, the man said anyway.

Even in the dark of the shed Gruber had shot into the boy's chest with alarming accuracy. The blood soaking into his sweater and running down his front had stopped and would more than likely already be cold.

Heiden told Bürckel to let some light in, and the storm blew in as the young soldier hauled the door open, snowflakes blasting into the shed and across the floor in a flurry. Bürckel pulled the door shut behind him and began knocking the snow from the outside of the shutters and opening them up so that a pale gray light washed against the window and pushed through the grime.

They hauled the body of the dead English boy out into the cold and dumped it among the birch trees down the slope from the shed. Then they remade the fire, Bürckel and Heiden scraping up twigs and leaves from around the floor to act as fresh kindling while Gruber kept his eye and his pistol on the two Englishmen. Everything was damp and it took a dozen or so attempts and as many matches before the flames finally caught. He sat back against the wall away from the thick smoke drifting up from the twigs. Bürckel squatted next to him, shivering, while Gruber crouched beneath the window, occasionally tossing another stick onto the fire or stoking it with his flick knife. Heiden stuck his finger down the back of his boot and tried to relieve the pressure against his sore blisters. He could feel nothing in his toes.

I'm hungry, Gruber said. *Have they got food?*

Have you got food? Heiden said to the officers.

A little, said the man called Pendell.

Heiden took the man's pack from the corner and emptied it out onto the floor as the man watched. Gruber did the same with the bags belonging to the two others. Spare clothes and a few items of food fell out, tins tumbling and rolling through the dirt. There was a torn and dirty map too, which Heiden was quick to confiscate.

Gruber picked up one of the tins and showed it to him.

Peaches, Heiden said.

I'll take that, said Gruber, taking the tin back from him. *What have you got?*

A tin of chopped ham, a tin of dried egg, two tins of peaches, three or four small packets of biscuits, water purification tablets, and cigarettes, six whole packets. It wasn't much between them but it would keep them going for a day or two.

We share everything, said Heiden. *And them too.* He nodded at the Englishmen.

Gruber's eyes locked on him.

Them too, said Heiden.

They consumed a tin of cooked ham, then melted snow in an upturned steel helmet and poured it into Bürckel's canteen, which they passed around, sipping from the hot water and feeling the steam that lifted from it soaking into their faces. The three Germans drew lots as to who would take the first watch.

Ach, shit, said Gruber as he pulled the shortest twig.

The storm blew hard against the window, rattling the glass in its frame. With the fire now giving a tinge of warmth to the room, the man called Harris was already struggling to keep his eyes open. As the minutes and then the hours slowly passed Heiden felt his own exhaustion overcoming him. It seemed to disintegrate every muscle in him, turn every bone to lead. He jerked as his eyelids fell, and for a moment he seemed to lose consciousness—as if it were just a single connection in his head that was keeping him awake or even alive and it would only take a moment's lapse, a moment's disconnection, and then suddenly he would be gone.

She had been listening and waiting, and now that he had gone upstairs and closed the bathroom door, she crept into the sitting room. The wireless was still there on the floor where he had left it, and she knelt down beside it, huddling over her knees. She wiped her sweaty hands on her dress and slowly turned the dial until it clicked and the set buzzed and crackled. She flicked the volume as low as it would go and then edged the dial back round until it was just loud enough for her to hear if she held her ear close.

There were snatches of sound through the waves of static, and then eventually—yes!—a news broadcast in English, words rattling out through the static like short bursts of gunfire.

"French colonies...Africa have been...enemy territory." More crackling. "Ports...under naval blockade, following reports..." The broadcast slipped away through the fuzz, and then broke free again from the buzzing. "In London it was reported—"

A heavy palm slammed down on the set, and she was hauled backwards across the floor. His hand slapped across her face and then his boot kicked the wireless over. "No!" she cried, as his heel smashed down through its casing.

He wrenched his foot free of the wrecked shell and the burst of tubes and wires and pulled her up to her feet. "You mustn't. It's too dangerous."

"They were English. I could hear them!"

"German! A German broadcast delivered in English."

"No. It wasn't."

"It was. Now get to your room."

"No."

"I want peace and quiet."

"You're lying to me!"

The hand slapped her a second time, this time harder, knocking her into the table next to her, and he shouted something but she couldn't hear it through the ringing in her ears. The sting flared across her cheek and she stumbled out of the room.

He stood listening to her pounding up the stairs, followed by the slam of her bedroom door. It was going to hell; he saw that now in the mangled carcass of the wireless, felt it in the sting of his fingers where he'd struck her. He slumped heavily on the floor and stared at the mess, then pulled at the broken tubes, the crushed and bent amplifier. They had shown him how radios like this worked but the wires made no sense to him now. He was losing himself, everything draining away. He fiddled helplessly with the radio for a few moments and then gathered up all the parts into the shell and furiously shoved it away across the floor.

He shouldn't have reacted like that. He should have taken a component out of the radio, as he had been trained to do, so that she couldn't work it but he still could. Now he was without a radio. Idiot. Never trust anyone, they had said: women, Jews, gypsies, and children—especially children. And now that he had hurt her there was no knowing what she might do.

He rubbed at his eyes. His head ached. He was sick of feeling this hot. Even the floorboards he sat on were sweating. He almost wished for Norway. Here he felt so tired all the time, so heavy. And now he would need to find another house and another radio. He would have to summon up the energy to venture out, and all because of one stupid outburst, a moment's loss of control.

He glanced at the piles of books he'd taken from the study, books on English history, the English countryside, English poets . . . He shuffled across the floor and sat beneath the window.

He had no mind for reading now. He took his pistol and pulled out the magazine, counting the bullets lined up in it, and then he clicked it back into place. He turned his head and, with a sense of relief, felt the coolness of the wall seeping into his cheek, into his bones, and slowly numbing him.

After a while he could hear a dull *thumping* transmitting itself through the walls of the house; it sent a splintering through his skull. He lifted his head away but the noise remained. He wondered if he was imagining it. In the secret world of the house he had started to see and hear things that he knew weren't real. The previous night, he had sat up, sure that he could hear the sound of small wheels trundling across the floor above him; and when he had opened the door of the cupboard under the stairs he had been quite convinced that he would find children hiding there, just as he had done in Poland.

Thump. Thump. Thump, came the noise.

War tipped everything on its head: ethics, existence, common sense. That was surely why in a farmhouse in Poland he had shot three children dead; why in Narvik he had watched his men rape a woman and had thought nothing of it.

He needed to sleep now. God, he needed to sleep. But there were already too many images in his head, and it was in his dreams that they grew strongest, muscling their way in when he was trying so hard to forget. Gruber in the snow, stripping the clothes from a dead naval officer. Two nurses at the hospital doors. Children's faces in the dark. Or Eva in the park, her eyes bright as she leaned forward and kissed him. The touch of her lips. The struggle in the water. The thrash of limbs as they coiled and wrestled. The jerk of an arm, a slashing knife. Blood-red clouds in the water before waking and gasping with a sudden race for air.

He got up and walked out of the room, following the *thumping* into the hall and up the stairs. She was there in the corridor, frowning and throwing a ball against the wall as hard as she could and catching it, her face still wet from crying. He stood with his hands on his hips and patiently waited for her to stop, which she eventually did, but not until she'd thrown the ball extra hard one more time—*thump*—just to prove her point.

He watched the swing of the metronome's arc on the floor beside him, slow and steady. In his head he could hear music. Schubert's "Ave Maria!" He was lying on the bed in the Berlin garret room and Eva was playing to him in the dark. In his head he could hear the full orchestra accompanying her.

In early March the division had returned to Berlin and, for four weeks, he found himself stationed just west of the city, at Dallgow-Döberitz. He welcomed being so close to the institute and Eva, particularly as before long he'd be heading up to Wesermünde to board the destroyer *Wilhelm Heidkamp*. Word had already gotten out. *They're sending us to Norway.*

Eva had been granted some time off from the institute to see him, and they spent the day together. Lunch at Hertie's department store had been a disappointment—the menu rather more limited than he had remembered—and for the first hour together neither of them had quite known what to say. They whiled away the afternoon in the Tiergarten, navigating their way around the puddles and sharing a pretzel, and they had stopped at their special bridge to have their customary photograph taken, only for Heiden to realize that he had left his camera back in the barracks.

Oh, never mind. It doesn't matter, she had said, but he could tell that it did.

They watched a group from the League of German Girls being taught how to tend the allotments. The great park had been largely turned over to vegetables; the metal fencing and iron railings were gone too, and as they walked they could see a group of uniformed Brownshirts pulling down the iron lampposts from along the paths and replacing them with wooden ones.

Everything is being uprooted. Even the park lampposts, she said.

As she spoke, the iron post being dismantled in front of them fell heavily across their path with a thunderous clang, causing Eva, Heiden, and several others to leap back out of its way.

Careful, shouted one of the Brownshirts, and he laughed.

You could have killed someone, Eva shouted.

Well, we'll try harder next time then, he replied, laughing again.

To Heiden's utter surprise, Eva suddenly launched herself at the boy, seemingly intent on hitting him and shouting, *You pig, you're all ignorant pigs!* as they laughed and jeered at her.

It took all of Heiden's strength to pull her back and haul her down the path away from them, her arms still thrashing. *Calm down. For God's sake, Eva. What the hell are you doing?* Around them, people had stopped to watch.

It's all being torn down, she sobbed into his coat as he managed to walk her away. *I can't bear this any longer.*

I know, he said. *I know.*

Later they strolled alongside the lime trees between the two carriages on Unter den Linden and sat for a few minutes on the steps outside the Neue Wache memorial, counting steeples. In the evening, they visited their favorite little picture house just off Potsdamer Platz to watch *It Was A Gay Ballnight* with Zarah Leander and Marika Rökk, which Eva—seemingly forgetting the afternoon's drama—had immensely enjoyed, but which made Heiden inexplicably sad. Afterwards they rode the tram home along the darkened Berlin streets through the rain. She had snuggled into the wraps of his uniform. *Don't come back to me dead,* she said. *You are the only reason I am living.*

She had been out of sorts all day; and, of course, there had been the incident in the park. When he asked her what was on her mind, she finally said that it was the institute and the job. There were twice as many beds as there had been when they'd first looked around. He would hardly recognize the place. Getting from one end of a ward to another was an assault course, she told him. *We're not allowed to send any clothes to the laundry until we've at least tried to scrub the dirt from them, and if you attempt to smuggle in some that Nurse Hartmann thinks you could have cleaned yourself, she unleashes hellfire and fury. She flies at us over the slightest thing.* They'd had two resignations that month already—with no hope of them being replaced. *You wouldn't believe the deals I've had to make with that wretched woman just to get this time off.*

Dr. Kesselring had made a remark to one of the nurses that suggested that the institute might be turned into a public hospital as part of the war effort to look after wounded soldiers. He'd said nothing about where the current inmates would go. They barely had enough to feed the patients anything other than root vegetables, and there were numerous cost-cutting initiatives in place, although, despite that, the dispensary had been stocked up. Eva and Käthe had been told to put up new shelves to hold all the extra bottles of morphine and barbiturates.

And there had been the questionnaires from the Reich Ministry of the Interior. It had taken Nurse Hartmann the better part of three days to complete one for each of the patients, and that had put her in the most vile mood. When Eva had asked her what they were for, Nurse Hartmann had told her not to question. It was better not to know.

Just a few weeks back, Eva told him, four military trucks had pulled up at the institute. They were under the surveillance of the SS and all the windows were painted gray so you couldn't see in. They had come to deport some of the male patients elsewhere. No one at the hospital knew where they were going. Nurse Hartmann welcomed the transport nurses into her office and gave them tea and pastries, as if they had been expected; after that, she had gathered the nurses in the main hall and read out a list of patients—seventy-five in total. They had just twenty minutes to gather the men together and lead them out to the trucks. *And they just went,* Eva said.

Heiden wanted her to resign and not to get involved, but she refused. She had made too many attachments; she couldn't just leave.

Anyway, she said, *I don't suppose we will hear any more of it. And, for a while at least, we've a few less patients to worry about, and maybe we won't get any more. They're not curing them anyway. I don't think they're even trying.*

And so the tram rattled on through the darkness, shining its murky blue light along the steely tracks, and they spoke no more of the institute. They got off at their stop and ran across the street through the torrential rain and up the flights of steps to the garret room. Eva said the blackout frames made her feel like she'd been boxed up and put away somewhere, so they spent what was left of the night with no lights on.

From the bed he could barely see her as she played her violin. Just the thin threads of moonlight slipping up and down the strings of her bow; just the smoky shape of her swaying around the room. He tapped out the piano's accompaniment with his fingers against the metal frame of the bed. He could take that image now, that slow-moving silhouette, and transpose it onto the darkened wall of this sitting room. He could dream her into the house called Greyfriars and hear her playing for him.

He had woken to sudden laughter and the sound of sparks.

Look, said Gruber.

Yes, look, said Bürckel. *But you better stay well back.*

Heiden stretched his legs out and tried to shake the cold and cramp from them. His buttocks were completely numb.

He watched as Gruber plucked a match from the box he was holding and struck it, and then tossed it into the empty corner. As it hit the ground, there were instantly tiny sparks and crackles as if the dust around it was suddenly popping.

Fuck, said Heiden. *What is it?*

Neither Gruber nor Bürckel knew.

Gruber lit another match though and dropped it into the corner; and again there came the sparks and crackles, glittering on the floor.

It's debris from some sort of explosive, said the man called Harris, hauling himself up into a sitting position. He had barely said a word since they had arrived, and when he spoke his voice croaked, his breath heavy and labored. Heiden had been unaware that he and the man called Pendell were watching from the far side of the room; he had assumed they were still asleep. *It's in the air. Some sort of explosive dust. Highly sensitive by the look of it.*

What's he saying? said Gruber.

Heiden translated. *It must be there on the floor.*

It's a dynamite store, said the man called Harris.

Without dynamite? said Heiden.

All gone. Must belong to the railway line. Been empty some time, I'd say. They blast away landslides in the summer, I 'spect. Ice and snow in the thaw. They must have kept it in this room. There were a couple of empty crates when we arrived. They were something to sit on for a while, but in the end we had to break them up and burn them.

There must have been a spillage of whatever it is in that corner, where it's dry, said the man called Pendell.

Yes, said Harris. *I wouldn't light a fire near there if I were you.*

Heiden translated and said they should move the fire to the

opposite corner and sweep the floor as well as they could. *Otherwise the whole place might go up.*

Together with Bürckel he used a couple of scarves, brushing as much of the debris and dust away as possible, and then set to rebuilding the fire.

Occasionally, for fun, Gruber would toss another lit match into the corner and there would be fizzling and sparks. He and Bürckel laughed.

Enough now, said Heiden. *We don't want to waste the matches.*

You're heading for Norddal Bridge, aren't you? said Harris. *They've blasted it. The bridge, you know.*

The Norwegians, added Pendell.

Then we shall fix it, Heiden told them.

The mountains are littered with snow sheds and places like this, Pendell said. *Especially near the railway line.*

And how do you know?

That map you took from us. That's a Norwegian map, said Pendell. *Harris here stole it. It had symbols on it that we didn't understand but now we know.*

Show me, said Heiden.

He retrieved the map from his kit bag and handed it to Pendell, who unfolded it out on the floor. They gathered around it.

See? said the English officer.

He showed Heiden, pointing out various symbols.

Bürckel leaned in to get a closer look. *What is it? What's he saying?*

The little black squares are snow sheds, Pendell explained. *The green ones, like this . . . that's a dynamite store.*

Then we are here? Heiden put his fingertip next to Pendell's.

I don't know. Not for sure, said Pendell. *But, yes. Perhaps.*

Bürckel glanced at Heiden and Gruber and pulled a face. They scanned the map, hunting out signs of civilization.

Christ, mumbled Gruber after a while, *I hope none of you boys are in a hurry to get home.*

Shingle Street was only half a mile away. If she closed her eyes she could almost hear the soft lap of the waves, the water being hauled back over the shingle, the tiny stones being dragged back with it, the soft shushing sound of the tide foaming along its edges. The flat landscape was always windy, so that seagulls would struggle in the sky and voices were blown about, taken off and lost in the surf, words snatched away. The shoreline was constantly moving, the shingle shifting while the raised grassy ridge of the railway line marked the perimeter between the shore and the mudflat.

All along the beach now were coils of wire, pillboxes, dragon's teeth, and concrete blocks; all the clobber, Mr. Morton said, of England under siege. Before the beaches had become out of bounds, her memories were of brightly painted fishing boats lined up along the shore, while out to sea ships were on their way to Felixstowe. Yes, a war was going on then too, but it was being fought out on the horizon by people she didn't know. The weather that day—in her memory—had been mixed. A dark cloud smudged with rain seeping across the sky. She sat in the shingle, hiding among the tall tufts of grass that formed their own waves as the wind washed through them. And when she walked along the beach with Alfie he had pointed out the various plants, giving them names that she had now forgotten. Plants with little purple flowers nestled among the shingle. Plants that looked like cauliflowers with thick rubbery leaves and green buds like berries. Crinkly bits of seaweed that crackled as you stood on them. They'd seen a dried bit of bush blowing across the beach, down the slope to the shore, doing cartwheels all the way. Often boys prowled there, throwing handfuls of shingle over each other's heads, or hiding on the other side of the slope, lying in wait. Alfie stood on the top of the slope sometimes, in his shorts, long socks, and cloth cap, with his arms folded to the wind and his expression imperious.

There was a white-painted bungalow half-buried on the beach. Alfie and Eddie always wanted to break into it, as the house had been abandoned for years, but they never had the guts. One day the whole place would be consumed, Alfie said. Every room in the house filled to the ceiling with shingle, and, maybe in many, many years, when someone managed to open the door and all the shingle flooded out, they'd find the remains of a family, their mouths open and full, their bodies stuffed with stones.

Instead they looked for bullets, rusted tin mugs, tangled netting, or bits of amber or carnelian that were the color of toffee. And hiding among the grasses, she would run her hands through them, drawing them up the stems and hearing the wind, the soft whispers of the shore, or an occasional gunshot in the distance that set her heart a-jitter. Then off she'd go, scrunching through the shingle. You couldn't run. The shingle wouldn't let you. Uphill it pulled at the backs of her calves and, as she slid down the other side of the slopes, her heels would sink in, avalanches cascading down ahead of her and giving her a strange lurching feeling. She remembered Alfie waving and waiting, the silhouette of him against the sky.

He rapped on the shutters with the end of a garden cane: "Will you help?"

She lifted herself out of the depths of her father's chair. "I don't want to."

"Well, I need you," he said. "Come into the garden, please."

She wanted to say that she was busy but he'd already seen that she wasn't. It was probably his attempt at saying sorry for slapping her and breaking their wireless. He disappeared, and she sat there for a little while longer before she went out into the garden anyway.

The soil had become so dry that some of the cane wigwams had pulled free of the earth and fallen over, scattering the peas and beans. "If we're going to stay here much longer we need to do something with this," he said. "We have got to save as many of these plants as we can. When the other men come, they will all need feeding. We don't know how long we are going to be here."

She stood for a moment on the edge of the lawn, curling her toes around the warm, dry grass and holding her hand up to shield her eyes from the sun. It was such a relief to be outside, even if it was still hot. He bent down and pulled two canes out from the jumble of pea plants and glanced over his shoulder at her.

"Come on then. You need to get some shoes on. What are you waiting for?"

Together they managed to get the wooden canes back into the soil and pushed them in deep. The plants were already parched and withering, so dried out that some of the pods had cracked open and the peas inside were as hard as marbles.

"I don't think we'll get much from them," he told her.

He walked along the line of plants, checking that the other canes were pushed in deep. Then he looked out across the rest of the garden. "Now," he said, "what next?"

"You mustn't change anything," she said, suddenly worried that he might ruin it all. Her father had spent ages planning the garden. He had sketched it all out on boards and roughly colored the flowers with her old crayons.

"I am not going to change anything," he said. "I am just trying to save what is here. Or would you rather we starved?"

She frowned. She could feel the sun burning her skin, and sweat was forming in her hair and in the palms of her hands. He began hoeing around the drooping onions and bolting broccoli, and she walked behind with her mother's cane flower basket, picking out from the dirt the weeds that he pulled up. Clouds of earthy dust rose up around them and stuck to her damp skin and got into her eyes. The garden seemed to be choking. Even the soldier coughed.

"You have to be resourceful if you're going to survive," he told her. "It is important to get a good education, but learning about knights and kings and castles won't feed you or keep you warm." He pulled up a disheveled carrot plant and flung it onto the lawn. "Unless you become a teacher, of course," he added. "Do you want to be a teacher?"

She hadn't decided so she shook her head.

"Then we'd better teach you something useful," he said. He started to list things as he hoed up and down the row. His shoulder still seemed to be giving him trouble. "Firstly, you should never go anywhere without matches, and always keep them dry. If you're trying to catch fish with your bare hands don't make sudden movements; the vibrations will scare them. And put your hand just in front of them because water bends light, so objects and things like fish always appear further away than they are. Another thing is, you can eat dandelion leaves or sour grass, but never eat real grass—that will make you sick. And if you're lighting a fire make sure you only put dry stones around it."

"Why?" said Lydia.

"Why? Because wet stones can explode."

"How do you know all this?"

"My training," he said, stopping for a moment and resting on the hoe.

She had never heard of stones exploding.

"And from my grandfather. He taught me how to hunt when I used to visit him in Bavaria. We need to be prepared."

"Prepared?"

"This is a war. What if I wasn't here?" he said. "What would you do? What would you eat when there was nothing left in the kitchen? How would you survive?"

She looked back at the house. She hadn't thought about it before. What if he had never come? She couldn't imagine being here on her own now. How quickly she had got used to him.

"You need to be resourceful when you're on a mission," he said. "Know how to survive in the wilds, what you can eat from the land and what you can't, how to keep yourself alive, how to protect yourself."

He tossed the hoe onto the grass then bent down to study the giant fan leaves of a courgette plant. It was half-eaten and covered in a white dust. He broke off the leaf and then circled the plant, breaking off the other leaves that were plagued or turning yellow.

"What else?"

"I don't know . . . how to scale cliffs, how to make charges, defuse them, dismantle them, how to lay mines and traps. How to disguise ourselves."

Lydia giggled.

"Why do you laugh?" he said. "The training I had was brutal. There is nothing fun about learning how to kill someone, how to do it with your bare hands, silently, by surprise so they never have a chance. I could have killed you a hundred different ways before now if I wanted." He picked up the ball of twine that had fallen from his pocket. "I could kill you five different ways with this cord alone, maybe six. I could hang you from a tree with it, by the neck; stuff it into your mouth until you choke; tie it around your nose and mouth until you suffocate . . . I won't," he said, "but I could." He stuffed it back into his pocket and carried on tending to the plant. "War is not kind," he said. "Everything we were taught with the Brandenburgers goes against the Geneva

Convention, but tell me, has your Churchill got British soldiers being trained to do the same thing? Of course he has."

Lydia didn't believe that. Perhaps none of it was true.

He stood up and ran his hands through his damp hair, then pulled his shirt out from under his armpits. "Let's sit in the shade. I'm hot," he said, glancing over to the back door, ornamented by a selection of pots in which her mother grew herbs.

They sat on the back step in the shadow of the house, and she watched him trim the herbs with her mother's pruning shears. She could imagine her mother pottering about around the side of the house, rummaging around in the flower beds and slopping across the lawn in her wellies, her hair tied up scruffily in a scarf. "You need to trim them back and cut off the old leaves to encourage fresh ones to grow," he explained. "You need to take care of them."

He picked a leaf from one plant and rubbed it between his finger and thumb. He held it to her nose. "Tell me, what do you call this?" he said. The leaf was soft, grayish, and quite large. It smelled slightly peppery.

"That's sage," she told him.

He said the word quietly to himself. "We call it *Salbei*," he said. "And this?"

He picked a sprig from another plant and handed it to her. "That's easy," she said, smelling it. "That's thyme."

She gave it back to him.

"Thyme." He held it up. "It's almost the same. We say *Thymian. Der Thymian.*"

He picked another easy one.

"Chives," she said.

"*Schnittlauch*," he told her, but he had to say it several times before she could say it herself.

And so it went: parsley, coriander, basil, all three nearly dead, as well as rosemary and a plant that neither of them knew but which might have been oregano. Lydia wasn't sure.

He got up and stood with his back to her, scanning the perimeters of the garden.

"We need rain," he said. "We can't do anything here unless we get some rain."

"Perhaps we should do a rain dance," she suggested.

"A rain dance?" He laughed.

Then, before she knew what she was doing, she was standing up and dancing about, waving her arms up at the sky and then swinging them down towards the ground, chanting and hollering as if she were summoning the gods.

"Come on," she shouted. "You have to do it too!"

And to her surprise he did. They kicked at the dust and gravel and whooped like Indians, and for all too brief a moment she forgot herself entirely but just danced and laughed in the sun.

When she went back into the house though, there really was no water. What did dribble out of the bathroom and kitchen taps too quickly drooled away to nothing but an airless wheeze, and then not even that. She stood behind him, watching as he tried himself, turning the taps this way and that, and then furiously slammed his hand against the sink. He pushed past her and back into the garden. For half an hour she watched him, suddenly feeling worried, as he worked at the dead pump again.

"It's all right," he said. "We will fix it."

But she knew somehow that he wouldn't.

During the day, his memories of her came like trap doors through which he suddenly fell. He saw her now as he leaned over the sink, clinging to the dead taps, his knuckles pushing through his skin. A picnic in the Tiergarten. She always liked the parks. She would lie flat on the ground sometimes, as she now was in his memory, face down, her cheek to the ground. She liked to feel the closeness of the grass. She used to say that she could feel the earth's heartbeat. It looked as if no matter how the world turned, she would still cling on, while, if gravity suddenly ceased to exist, all around her the rest of them would fall away and fly off into space.

Play for me, he would say, in the dark nights of the garret room, and she would take out her violin. The sound of it would fill the room, every corner, cupboard, crack, and cranny, every chamber of his heart, every space in his head, so that he could hold it tight within his memory, so that even when the music was gone a sense of it remained.

He looked out the window. Once they had sat in the garret window, facing each other, their legs intertwined, Eva finding faces in the clouds or counting chimney pots. *Suppose we said every chimney pot is a note,* she said. *That first one, over there, being a "C," then the piece would sound something like this,* and she hummed it, thirteen notes in all, forming a funny little tune. She called it their "Chimney Pot Concerto." And when she was done she mapped out the notes on a piece of paper held to the glass. *So that we don't forget it,* she said. *It's quirky, don't you think.*

I'm not sure that the ministry would approve. It's a bit atonal, Heiden said.

And the two of them had laughed.

They walked through the wood away from Greyfriars, her holding one of the buckets, him the other two. She felt oddly relieved to be away from the house.

"Stay close," he told her. "Don't try to run."

But she had no intention of running. She felt safer with him near her. And anyway, where would she go?

The bucket was heavy. Shafts of light came through gaps in

the branches and it was dry and dusty underfoot. He had made her wear a tin hat that he'd found on top of a wardrobe. It kept slipping down over her eyes.

"No baths. This is for drinking and cooking, that is all," he said, as they stumbled on. "When the rest of the men come we will send them out to get more."

"There are streams across the marsh," she told him. "On the other side of the wood."

He nodded as if he already knew, and they pushed on through the bracken, picking their way over broken branches and bits of rubble, trying not to stumble down animal holes or catch their ankles on trailing brambles. She glanced behind her but the wood had already swallowed them, and there was no sign of the garden or Greyfriars. He could kill her in these woods, she thought, and no one would ever know.

He turned and waited. "What's wrong? Come on—keep up!"

She hurried to catch up to him and tried to smile but couldn't. She imagined her body lying half-buried beneath the bracken, a single bullet hole in her back.

They walked in silence, side by side. His eyes scanned the trees and looked up into the branches. Sometimes he stopped and turned his head to one side to listen.

In a small clearing they walked through a cloud of mites. She swung her bucket at them, but they seemed to swarm around her even more furiously, and yet they took no notice of him.

After a while they stopped. She was hot and tired and feeling faint, and they found an uprooted tree to sit on. Only now that she'd put the heavy bucket down did she see that inside it was crawling with baby spiders.

"In Norway I used to make up tunes in my head," he said, "whenever we had a long way to march. It was the only thing that kept me walking."

"Was it very cold?"

"Yes. Bitter cold and blizzards. I was trapped in the mountains for five days," he said. "A few of us got separated but we managed to find somewhere to hide out from the storm, but it was still bitterly cold. Some sort of shed: a concrete floor and a couple of windows. We had a smaller room too, just about big enough for a couple of men to lie in. From the window in there you could see the railway line across the gorge. We used to take turns to sleep there. We had some shelter quarters and some lining to lie on. You had to do whatever you could to keep warm."

He bent to push his finger into the top of his boot and rubbed at his ankle, and then rolled his wounded shoulder as if trying to loosen it. She let her toes scuff over the dried leaves and dead twigs and watched him. He was reminding her more of her father every day, making her longing for him to come home even more unbearable, wanting him to return and wrap his arms around her and tell her, *Hey, missy, don't cry.*

For ages they sat there until she started to feel afraid again, and then he said, "Look, there's a face in the branches up there, made out of leaves." He pointed. "Can you see it?"

But although Lydia looked she couldn't see anything.

"You speak very good English," she said.

"My grandmother," he told her. "I spent my holidays with her and my grandfather in Bavaria. She would only speak to me in English. She was born near Cambridge, I think. And then I lived in London for a while too. My uncle had an apartment in Bloomsbury and I stayed with him. He was a journalist for a German newspaper. I spoke no German at all when I was there—only English. I suppose I wanted to—how do you say?"

"Blend in?"

"Yes...exactly."

"What did you do in London?"

"I studied," he said. "At the Royal College of Music actually. It was rather good."

"Do you play an instrument then?"

"Of course." He laughed. "They would not have let me in if I didn't. I play the cello."

"Oh, Alfie wanted to play the cello but he ended up with the violin," she told him. "My parents said it was too expensive."

"They are," he said. "I was fortunate. My grandfather left me some money when he died. I bought mine with that. It was him that first taught me, in a way. He taught me how to play the saw."

"A saw?" she said. She almost laughed. "That you saw things with?"

"Yes," he said. "What's so funny? It has to be a special type, of course, not an ordinary saw, although you can still play them too. It's quite like a cello really. But...well..." He maneuvered himself so he was sitting sideways on the trunk and facing her. "A cello hums to you, you see, but a saw, a saw is different. A saw sort of...sings."

She smiled at the thought of it. She might write a story about it one day: a man with a singing saw.

"It's pretty here, isn't it?" she said. "Don't you think?"

"Yes," he said. "I'm rather fond of England. It's very serene and stately. The hills. The rivers and the streams and the woods. So pretty...the Home Counties, the Cotswolds...have you been?"

She shook her head. "How long were you in London?"

"Not long. Two years. There was a lot of trouble in Germany then. They were burning books at the universities. It wasn't a good place to study. Everyone thought there was going to be civil war and my mother thought I'd get caught up in it, just like my father had done. She wanted me to be safe somewhere, so I came to England. Even when she wrote and told me all that was

happening back in my homeland—the Olympics and the auto-
bahns, the air force, all that—she didn't want me coming home."

"But you did?"

"Yes. I felt I had to. They were recruiting. It was my duty.
And anyway, I felt cut off from Germany. I wanted to go home."
Then, as if he'd suddenly remembered, he pulled something
crumpled from his pocket. "Sorry, I have been meaning to give
you this," he said. "I found it in the shelter. I presume it's yours."
He handed her the story, *The Incredible Adventures of the Tiny
Princess.* She felt her face redden.

"Oh," she said. "I thought I'd lost that."

"Well, it was down the side of the bench," he said. "I hope
you don't mind, but I read it. It is very..." He fumbled for the
word. "...creative."

"It's silly really," she said. "I wrote it ages ago. I'm much better
now."

"My grandfather used to tell me stories," he said. "Fairy tales
and folk stories. He used to carve scenes out of wood..." He
trailed off and she looked at him, waiting, and then he said, "Do
you know the tale of Bearskin? About a young soldier who after
a war has ended makes a pact with the Devil?"

She shook her head.

"The Devil says that he will make the poor soldier rich if he
does not wash himself or cut his nails or his hair for seven years
and wears the skin of a bear."

"What happens? Does he beat the Devil?"

"You will have to read it and see. I think you might like it.
It's Brothers Grimm. It was my grandfather's favorite. He liked
magical stories like that."

"Do you believe in magic then?" she said.

He smiled. "That depends on what it is."

"What about angels?" she said.

"Angels?" He rubbed at his ankle again and tidied the bottom of his trouser leg. "You seem to have an obsession."

"You don't have to see them," she said. "Sometimes they're like a tiny light. Or you just know that they're there. They live in heaven and only come down when you need them. They leave something behind sometimes too, like a clue, so you know that they have been there."

"What have you run away from?" he said, the question coming from nowhere. "You ran away from something, didn't you? What was it?"

She picked up the bucket and tipped it on its side and started knocking the rim against the ground, trying to dislodge the spiders. She didn't want to carry it now in case they crawled up her arm.

"Where were you? Were you evacuated?"

She bashed the bucket a couple more times and then gave up. Six or seven tiny spiders still clung stubbornly to the bottom.

"What happened?"

She looked at him. She supposed it didn't matter now. "We all got sent to Wales," she told him. "Everyone from school. Even Button and he'd only just got here. I don't think they know what to do with children anymore. They keep shunting everyone around. It's like nobody wants us."

"Who is Button?" he said. "What sort of name is that?"

"I don't know. He's just a boy. He had to come with me. He's from Poland."

"So why did you run away?"

She shrugged. "I don't know. I didn't like them in Wales. They were mean."

"And this Button, where is he now?"

She shrugged again.

"You left him there?"

When she didn't answer he asked her again—*You left him there?*—and she nodded. She thought she might cry.

"They were horrid to him," she blustered. "All the Welsh boys."

"What do you mean?"

And she told him how they used to tie Button up, how they beat him with sticks, how they liked it when he cried, and how one time—the worst time—they'd taken him to the brook and pushed him in and held his head under until he almost drowned.

"And when I tried to stop them, they said they'd get me; they were going to drown me for real one day." And that, she said, was why she had run away. She had been scared.

"Boys can be animals sometimes," he said.

Lydia nodded. And now she'd left Button in Wales with them, and after everything she'd promised her mother. She hadn't looked after him at all; she'd left him there on his own.

Overhead came the chuttering of a plane. He lifted his hand for her to stop and they looked up through the branches, holding their hands up to the sun as it seared through the leaves. He pointed. "There," he murmured, but she couldn't see.

"Is it one of yours or ours?" she asked.

He said nothing. His eyes were fixed on the plane, following it between the gaps in the leaves.

"Come on," he said, "we need to go. No more talking."

They walked for a couple of minutes in silence, listening to the scrunch of their feet and watching a lapwing darting between the trees, disappearing, then zipping past again.

As they got nearer to the edge of the wood and the marshes, he made her wait, hiding in the ferns with one of the buckets, while he walked on ahead with the other two.

She watched him, his back arched, pistol in his hand, as he moved from tree to tree so quietly. She put her hands over her mouth. He had said once that he could hear every sound and every breath; he could hear the beat of her heart. She turned back to see if anyone was coming, straining to listen in case she heard footsteps that weren't his.

When he got to the edge of the wood she saw him crouching down, leaning forward with his shoulder against a tree, and holding a tiny pair of binoculars to his eyes. He scanned the thin stretch of marsh and the coast for what seemed an inordinately long time. She picked at the ferns as she waited, keeping her eyes firmly fixed on him. Now that they were still and silent she could hear crackling gunfire and distant booms far off, yet still quaking through the ground beneath her. She needed to pee.

She looked at the large clump of ferns and then pushed her way in, first just one step and then another, crushing some of the leaves down beneath. She could still see him through the mesh of foliage even if she squatted. She took another step in but as she did her foot stepped on something hard that shifted out from beneath her so that she fell. She looked to see what it was. It was the heel of a boot, and it was attached to a leg. And then she saw that it was a body, face down on the marshy soil.

Lydia shrieked.

He came running, scrambling, pushing his way through the ferns towards her and picking her up and onto her feet.

"What is it?" he shouted. "What is it?"

The body was covered in dried blood. It looked as if something had dragged it out from a hole in the ground. It had the same shoulder flash on its uniform as the Essex Regiment. The legs of it were torn where something had dug the body up and scratched and ripped at it; a hand still sticking up out of the dirt, the fingertips gnawed and frayed.

"Don't look," Heiden said. "Come on, we need to get the water and leave."

"No," she said. She wiped at her eyes. "No, I want to go back. I want to go now. What happened to him?"

"I don't know. It doesn't matter."

"Has someone shot him? Did someone shoot him?"

He bent down beside the body and carefully turned it over. He studied it for a moment, then stood up again. "He's had his throat cut," he told her. "Come on now, we need to get the water."

But she was already pushing her way through the ferns and running, stumbling, back towards Greyfriars.

He called out as he chased after her, suddenly, surprisingly, using her name. "Lydia!" he yelled. "Lydia, stop!" But Lydia would not.

She watched him sitting at the window, peering through the slit in the blackout fabric with pistol in hand. He'd been there for half an hour already and he hadn't moved, not even to stretch a muscle or relieve some cramp. He wasn't human. He was something else, made by German scientists. He looked like flesh and blood, she thought, but inside he was mechanical. He'd said himself that he could shoot a moving target at fifty yards. He probably had X-ray vision.

He'd easily caught up with her in the wood, abandoning the buckets as he ran after her so that now they too were lost.

"Now do you see why you mustn't leave the house?" he had said. "They are all around us. We have to be more careful."

And, indeed, he had even thought he'd seen a figure—a man in uniform, he had said—disappearing around the side of Greyfriars as they had returned through the wood to the house and were almost setting out across the lawn. He had made her wait, hidden way back in the trees, whilst he had gone to investigate, but after several minutes he had come back saying that it was nothing. And she wondered whether he was telling the truth, or whether there really had been someone snooping about, a German or a Brit.

Sitting in the dark again, she felt as if she'd been thrown back into her cage. She had cried herself out so that now her stomach hurt, all the muscles in her aching as if every organ was clenched and clasped tight. She kept seeing the dead body and those blackened fingertips. So Heiden had been right—there were men stalking through the trees; men with guns and knives who slit people's throats, men perhaps even coming right up to the house, up to the door and trying the handle, trying to see if anyone was there.

She now knew what Mr. Morton meant when he had said Britain was under siege. All the thrill and adventure of war that she'd dreamed of had emptied away. It was terrifying and lonely, and she wanted it to stop.

The leather squeaked as she hauled herself up in the chair again, but still he didn't turn from the window. Now that she knew that they had no water and no hope of getting any soon, she was desperately thirsty. Every time she tried to swallow her throat seemed to stick together as if she was drying up inside. Something else had been playing on her mind too since they'd got back.

"You said my name," she told him. "When you ran after me. I heard you."

He stayed quite rigid, staring through the slit at the window.

"I heard you," she blurted. "You shouted at me to stop. You shouted, 'Lydia.' How did you know that's my name?"

"You must have told me," he said.

"I didn't." She was quite sure.

But he still didn't move. She could feel the heat of the leather seat melting into her, her skin sticking to it.

"Perhaps I read it somewhere," he said without turning.

"Where?"

"I don't know. It was on the story, the one I gave back to you, that I found. It had your name on it."

She quietly slid it out from under her cardigan, turning the little homemade book over in her hands, but it was just as she suspected: her name was not on it anywhere.

For most of the time they sat in silence, one of them occasionally feeding the fire with the last bits of twig and stick they could find about the floor or moving to the window to watch the snow hurl itself against the pane.

Once, coming out of a dream, he had woken to find Bürckel sleeping wrapped around him, his arm around Heiden's waist and head nuzzled into him. He didn't move the boy away. Instead, in the darkness, there was some comfort in his warmth, in the smell of the boy's hair pushed up against his face, and his soft hushing breath blowing against his neck. When he looked out across the room he saw the whites of Pendell's eyes, watching.

Who will you go home to? Pendell asked. *When all of this is over. Me?*

Yes. Do you have a wife? A young lady? Children?

Heiden didn't answer.

I have a family. I have a wife and two children. My son thinks this war is an adventure, Pendell said. *Is that what this is? This generation's great adventure? Everybody wants to be a bloody hero. But heroes don't often come home, do they? They disappear. They leave a hole. When my daughter knows I'm coming home she sits on the stairs and waits for me. She's almost twelve years old and yet she still sits and waits. I think about her all the time, her sitting there on the stairs.*

Why are you telling me this? said Heiden. *Do you think I care? You know, my comrade wanted to kill you.*

Pendell nodded.

But I stopped him.

Yes. I know.

He'll keep trying, Heiden said. *He'll keep saying that we should shoot you. And I will have to keep stopping him. Every time I will have to stop him—do you understand?—until one of us wears the other down.*

I'm not asking to be saved or spared, said the man. *I'm just telling you that I have someone waiting for me and that at some stage—God willing—I would like to see them again. Is that too much to ask?*

That will be down to God, said Heiden, *if it's "God willing."*

He wished now that there had been more conversation in that dynamite room; it might have whiled away the hours faster, kept their minds off the cold and hunger. Instead, it was mostly silence as they sat facing each other, their backs against the walls. He never had been able to bear the silence. He needed to fill it with rhythms, tapping them out with his fingers.

The man Pendell intrigued him. He seemed to have no fear of Heiden's stare, or of the pistol that was trained on him. Heiden had studied the way he sat: one leg up, an arm draped over its knee, gently rubbing circles around the tip of his thumb with his finger, and head slightly tilted as if considering Heiden but only ever with the very vaguest interest. Heiden amused himself mimicking the man's moves: the way he sucked his bottom lip in and softly chewed on it, the gentle cough he would occasionally make deep in his throat, or the way he drew his finger along his top lip as if it were a new discovery, the chapped and peeling skin. It was a game that Heiden had played as a child, secretly mimicking strangers and playing copycat. Finger and thumb rub together. Head tilts, a gentle cough; the very vaguest hint of interest.

His mouth still tasted sweet. He and the girl, Lydia, had

cracked open a Kilner jar of preserved pears and had shared the juice, just like they'd shared the tinned peach juice in the dynamite room in Norway; but now in the house, and without water, he was thirsty again. He could hear her skulking around the rooms upstairs. He couldn't think what to tell her about the body—an unfortunate discovery. Nor had he told her what he'd seen in the distance, through his binoculars across the marshes—lines of tents along the shore and people running. He would of course have to go back for water, but he couldn't risk it, not yet. If they were coming, let them come. Let them put a bullet through him. He needed to be watchful. He needed to wait for Diederich.

In the attic she stood on her tiptoes and peered through the window. Small, white clouds languished in the sky, their shadows drifting slowly over the cornfields. Looking out across the empty fields reminded her of the nature studies classes they had in Wales—Miss Mountford taking them out over the fields, where they'd sit on sacks of straw and learn about photosynthesis and pollination and the different types of cloud. Sometimes they went high up into the hills.

It's not like Suffolk, is it, one of them had said.

No, it's not, said Miss Mountford. *But it's jolly nice, isn't it? Look at all the colors.*

Lydia had never noticed them before, all the tones of the Welsh stone, purples and blues and greens and grays, the shadows of the clouds passing over them like great flotillas of ships.

The soldier appeared from her father's work shed with a wrench in his hand. She had watched him earlier standing at the edge of the garden peeing into the hydrangeas. There wasn't any water to flush the toilet, and even the stench of her own pee still in the toilet bowl made her stomach turn.

From the tiny attic window the only sign of life was the scarecrow at Heathcote Farm, dressed as Mr. Hitler with a sagging sandbag for his head and a trench coat full of holes and nesting mice.

She lowered herself from the window. She could hear him banging around in the kitchen, the clank of him hitting pipes. All that was left in the house to drink now was her father's home brew, and not even her father had been keen on that. Heiden would fix it, he had told her—she didn't need to worry—but downstairs she could still hear him banging.

The man Harris woke up coughing. Bürckel offered him his canteen and the Englishman took a sip and handed it back. He had been deteriorating for some hours now, drifting in and out of consciousness and then jerking awake. On more than one occasion when Heiden had been bent over him, the man had grabbed at his arm, saying, *George, George*—

I'm not George, Heiden said, pulling his hand free, and then the man called Pendell had gone to him and had given him some water or held his hand or simply said, *Yes. Yes, I'm here.*

He watched Gruber in the snow as he stripped the clothes from the dead boy. He struggled with the body's dead weight, hauling it about as if it were a sack of corn, unbuttoning the shirt and dragging it off the shoulders and down over the arms, then unbuckling the belt, dragging the trousers off as well as the body lay on its back. He even took the socks and underwear, stripping the body completely clean. Then he gathered the clothes up in his arms and, with the boy's boots swinging at his side, he trudged back up to the store, leaving the body sprawled out at an awkward angle, porcelain white in the snow. And Heiden had done nothing.

It was easy to hate people in war, far easier than loving. He found it easy to hate Gruber, for example, for thinking Heiden a coward for not shooting the English officers or throwing them out in the snow; or for wasting matches, sitting beneath the window, striking them against the floor, and then blowing them out and flicking them across the room so that they bounced off Pendell's coat or caused sparks in the corner where there was still dynamite dust on the floor.

We've another box, he said when Heiden wanted to know what he was doing.

We don't know how long we're going to be here.

Not much longer, I hope. These Tommy sailors are boring the hell out of me.

Even the way he called Heiden "Lance Corporal" had a tinge of sarcastic resentment. He seemed intent on making everything difficult, challenging everything Heiden said so that they ended up bickering like children, chipping away at each other.

The man called Harris sat half-twisted against the wall as if he wanted to become part of it, the mortar to become his flesh, his face whitening, his bones turning to stone, his skin turning to dust. Pendell was silent at the window, sucking at one of the spent matches Gruber had tossed at him. He stood quite firm, legs spaced and solid, his arms folded and mittened hands pressed into his armpits, as if he were waiting for nothing more than for the storm to stop before he went on his way.

There was little left in the store to burn and all of them were starting to freeze. Heiden had been out in the storm with Bürckel, but the firewood they had brought in had been too sodden to do anything but smoke. He sent Bürckel out again anyway.

I'll freeze out there.

You'll freeze in here, said Heiden.

Yes, stop being such a baby, said Gruber.

Outside the store it had grown dark again. The storm blew

and blasted against the walls, whistling in through a hole in the roof. Gruber bent over his boot, trying to work out how best to position a flattened piece of matchbox and keep it in place so that it covered the split in the boot's sole. He fumbled irritably with it. He had tried the dead boy's boots on for size, but they had been too small and were split even worse than his.

Eventually Bürckel came back in shivering. He tossed an armful of frosted sticks on the floor and, without saying anything, went into the annex room and took his turn to sleep.

Let's make bets as to which one of us gets pneumonia first, said Gruber. *My bet's on him. If we're reduced to eating each other he'll barely be a meal.*

Heiden ignored him. He shut his eyes to it all and leaned against the cold wall, holding Eva's letters in his hand. *I miss you. I love you. I think about you every night.* Perhaps if he could imagine her still being in Berlin she would still be there. Perhaps she was still waiting for him—sitting on the bench of the hospital garden, waiting for him to come down the drive and take her home. Or maybe it was her and not the two nurses that he remembered passing through the double doors of the institute, Eva turning to look back at him, Eva raising her hand in a half wave, before she goes through and the doors slip silently shut behind her. *I miss you. I love you. I—*

The boot hit him in the chest. *For God's sake, stop it! That infernal tapping!*

He looked at Gruber, tossed the boot back, and went to the window where Pendell was still sucking the match and staring out into the dark. For a time they both stood there, watching, two faces in the glass. Then Pendell pulled the match from his mouth.

Can I borrow your knife?

Heiden glanced at him and laughed. *You want my knife?*

Yes. Don't you trust me?

Heiden laughed again, nervously this time, then looked at the man more closely, trying to see something in those calm eyes. Then he took his knife from his belt, unsheathed it, and laid it on the ledge. Pendell picked it up and turned it in his hands, running his finger along the flat of the blade and studying the tip; then, taking hold of the head of the match, he made three precise incisions in it and handed the knife back.

Is that it? said Heiden.

He watched as the man slowly prized open the slits he'd made in the matchstick, shaping it into something new. Then Pendell glanced at him and smiled. *What were you expecting? A blade in the ribs perhaps?*

She could hear the man moving about downstairs—an animal with a wound where someone had already tried to hunt him down. She wondered if she could love him, if everyone else was dead and she had no choice. She would have to learn to cook, and they would tend to the vegetable patch and put the garden in order. New chickens. A new Jeremiah. Maybe even a new name for the house—The Lair. War, if it lasted long enough, would eventually turn her into a woman. And he would make her love him as if it were a spell.

She sat in Alfie's bedroom and waited but Alfie didn't come. She had seen something all those months ago as he stood in the arms of the tree in his cricket whites: he had looked like an angel. She knew that he would protect her. And so, here in his room, she waited, slowly turning the button on her cardigan round and around, and shutting her eyes so perhaps he might appear. But there was no sign of him. She looked everywhere for a feather, a clue that he had been there, that he would come back—along the windowsill, under the bed, behind the backs of the books on the shelf—but there was nothing there.

She sat on his bed, her hand gently smoothing down the blanket where he used to lie. She thought she had heard his voice, just once, that morning. *Lydia,* it said.

She closed her eyes and saw him in the garden with Eddie bowling a few overs. The *twack* of their grandfather's cricket bat. The ball wedging itself into a tree. Eddie running with him across the lawn on his shoulders, and them falling and laughing and tussling on the lawn until Alfie was sprawled on top of him, pinning Eddie's arms down and shouting, *Submit, submit!* Then she was struck with a memory, quite clear and sudden now in her head, of Eddie straining his head up and kissing her brother, there—quite purposefully—on the lips. And Alfie had let him: a kiss that had lasted no more than a moment, and yet, in that moment, before he turned his head and caught her eye, Alfie seemed to forget entirely where he was or that Lydia was even there.

Can I tell you something? A secret.

The whisper was there in his ear; a sudden draft of sound, Bürckel's soft voice. Around them the others slept. The room was dark but for the faint glow of the fire and its occasional flitter of sparks, a fragment of explosive dust in the air suddenly igniting.

Bürckel pulled himself closer until he was pressed against Heiden, his warm breath against the side of Heiden's face.

I've been thinking about it ever since we got here. I can't get it out of my mind. You promise not to tell Gruber. You mustn't tell him.

Tell him what? said Heiden.

The boy was paler than usual, his eyes wide and wet.

What happened was my fault. I'm sure. I'm going mad with it, thinking about it. I'm quite sure it was me. I'm going to hell, aren't I?

What are you talking about?

The shooting. In the clearing. It was me that started it, me that started firing first. It was my fault.

Are you sure? said Heiden.

No. I mean, I don't know, said Bürckel. *I think it might have been. It was. I mean, it must have been.*

Why must it?

Because I was so scared. I was terrified.

But you were in that ditch, with me and Gruber. You were there. Don't you remember?

Yes, I know, but before then I was firing. I can still feel my finger on the trigger, even now.

He lifted his shaking hand as if to show Heiden.

I can still feel the pulse of it firing.

It was then that Bürckel had started to sob, and Heiden put his arms around him.

Everyone was scared, you know, he said. *It might have been any one of us.*

But it was me. I know it, said Bürckel. *Oh God. I am going to hell.*

She had been watching him from the kitchen for almost an hour: her father's shirt off and his braces hanging down around his legs as he worked at the pump, jabbing iron wires he'd found in the garage up into the spout to try to clear out the silt. He pumped at the handle, the muscles in his arm flexing in the sun.

The leaves of her mother's mint plant were now dead and crumbled when she touched them, scattering their bits over the sill. She wondered how long she could go without water before she herself turned to dust.

If God was real and he was a good God, he would give them water. But, with the war on, how could he be everywhere, watching everything, knowing that she needed him? With so many people to worry about, how could he save them all?

She would store every memory she had, she decided, so that no matter what happened in the hours and days to come there would always be a part of her, secrets, that nobody could take.

One Christmas, not so long back, while the rest of the family sat about in the sitting room examining their opened presents, her father had called her over and whispered in her ear that there was something else waiting for her in the hallway if she would like to find it.

She had gone into the dark hall and at first found nothing; then she saw in the lamplight a pair of yellow wooden camels side by side on one of the steps, and, three or four steps higher, a pair of blue elephants no more than an inch tall.

She laughed as she gathered up the camels and the elephants and then the two gray penguins that were waiting for her on the top step. She looked down the corridor and saw the trail of animals laid out before her. She collected them together in her jumper as she gathered them up—giraffes, hippos, antelope, and crocodiles—all the way to the steps to the attic, and then up those too—parrots, lions, and polar bears—until she was in the attic and there in the middle of the floor had been the most beautiful painted ark. A wooden Noah and his wife stood waiting outside.

The front door swung open and the man came down the hall, almost running.

"Lydia! A glass! A glass!"

Moments later, out in the garden, she held it beneath the spout of the pump as he worked at it, and eventually the water came out, trickling at first and then coming out faster and faster. She looked at it, cloudy and dirty, and he took it from her and emptied it into the grass. Twice they filled the glass and tipped it away until finally the water ran clear and clean, and she held it up to the sun and saw how it sparkled. Drink it, he said. Lydia did, and it tasted cool and good.

★　　★　　★

He could not decide. A 1938 Merlot or a 1936 Cabernet Sauvignon? He had taken all six bottles down from the top shelf of the larder, but they were all French and he had never been fanatical about French wine, much preferring a Spätburgunder or even an Italian Barolo. In the end he chose the Sauvignon because it reminded him of Dieppe and the café on the beach and the seven or eight of them from the Pioneer Group sprawled out on the pebbles that night, passing the bottles around. Though it had only been a few weeks ago, it didn't feel like something that he had experienced at all—but rather someone else's memory.

He found a corkscrew in a drawer, two packets of cheese biscuits in the larder, and a tin of Skipper sardines. The tin of ham he found reminded him of Norway, and he opened it and dragged the processed meat out onto a chopping board with a fork; then he cut it into slices and displayed it in a swirl on a plate that was chipped but pretty, with cornflowers painted around its rim.

His thoughts slipped back to the dynamite store and the man called Pendell.

Heiden had been sorry about what Gruber did to the boy. *He thinks we need the clothes.*

He had dignity, Pendell had told him. *Do you people understand that? Your comrade has even robbed him of that.*

Heiden gave him the identity disc he'd taken from his pocket. *I got you this,* he said. The other half he had left on the chain around the boy's neck.

Pendell took it but said nothing. He was crouched outside the store, scooping up handfuls of snow and trying to wash his face with it. He had balanced his grubby uniform jacket on the end of a broken branch that he'd wedged into the frozen ground.

Heiden watched over him from the doorway, his pistol loose in his hand.

He remembered quite vividly now looking down the slope to the clearing where the young English officer's body had eventually been buried beneath snow. When he had trekked down there to retrieve one of the discs, the boy had looked white and brittle, clumps of frost caught in his hair. He had to keep shooing crows away that were intent on pecking at the bloody bullet wounds in the boy's chest. He had closed the boy's eyelids and then snapped one of the bootlaces, now wet and rotten, from around the boy's neck and pocketed the disc, leaving the other there with the body. As he walked back to the store, he had heard the crows landing again behind him, squabbling over their find.

That morning the storm had stopped, and he and Gruber had known that if they were going to try to reconnect with the remnants of the platoon, they would need to move soon while it was still calm and light. In the store the man called Harris kept pulling at his collar and trying to kick off the coats and blankets around him. He was delusional, mumbling that he was burning up, his tongue thick in his mouth.

In the kitchen Heiden opened the sardines and breathed in their sea smell. He drained the oil into a cup for later, and as he picked one of the fish out with a fork he tried to remember the song the man called Harris had kept on murmuring. Something about a rabbit and a farmer and a gun, but now, thinking back, he couldn't be sure. Nothing in the past seemed real anymore. He slipped the sardine into his mouth and held it on his tongue, savoring the taste before he chewed it and let it slide down into his throat.

He remembered offering Pendell some chocolate he had been saving. He had opened the small round tin and offered the man one of the chocolate triangles inside, and Pendell had said, *Are you going to poison me?*

And he had replied, *It's Scho-Ka-Kola. Standard soldier ration. Not very good, I'm afraid.*

Pendell had thanked him and reached out to take one of the slices, and Heiden had done the same. He had sucked on the chocolate, which had been thick and warm and deliciously sweet. Together they had watched a grouse rummaging around for food in the frosted brambles and snow, and Heiden had thought about shooting it but too late—the grouse had gone.

Now, in the kitchen, he collected the jam jars and scraped the waxy remnants from inside and then set to chopping the ends off some candles. Initially, for some weeks, he had put the conversation with Pendell out of his mind, had forgotten it entirely; and it was only later, when it had mattered, that it had returned to him as if all of a sudden it was fresh and new again.

We've a house, back home, on the edge of the marshlands, Pendell had said, *half a mile to the beach. It's pretty, very pretty. We get grouse there too, you know. It's jolly good for bird watching.*

He had told Heiden about the Suffolk marshes, about the different types of waterbirds they had there: oystercatchers, avocets, spoonbills, all sorts of warblers on the heath, woodlarks, and stonechats whose call was a tack-tack-tack and sounded, he said, like gunfire. *We live midway between the village and the sea. A sort of outpost,* he said. A village called Willemsley. A house called Greyfriars, the land having belonged to a grey friar monastery once. *So peaceful and quiet,* he said. He had laughed, perhaps at how sentimental he was sounding, but he carried on nevertheless, talking about the lavender in the garden, the buddleia, their chickens, a rabbit . . . *We have a terrace that we have tea on in the summer,* he said, *and a piano. My wife loves to play. Have you ever been to England?*

London, Heiden had told him; he had studied there.

London? Oh. Dreadful place, that.

Pendell had taken off his shirt and draped it over the stick. His skin was pale and he had a dark pink scar on his shoulder. He took a handful of snow and rubbed it into one of his armpits and then the other, grimacing. Over the hours they had watched each other; and yet there, seeing him outside with his shirt off in the brutal cold, Heiden realized how thin the man was. The muscles in his arms were prominent but not large. A hard worker, and yet his hands had the delicacy of a craftsman: long, thin fingers.

A septic shot pellet, the man said, tilting his shoulder so Heiden could see the scar.

A battle wound?

Pendell smiled. *No. An overzealous new recruit on training actually. Happened just before we were sent out. We got it out in the end, but the little blighter's left a bit of a hole. I've never had a scar before. Jolly lucky really. They say, don't they, that every man should have a scar somewhere, a distinguishing feature. Well, now, I have mine.*

He took two glasses from the cupboard and held them up to the light to see if they were clean. He had found apples in a muslin bag in the larder, next to a string of onions in the knotted leg of a stocking, and a jar of pickled cherries that had a handwritten label that was now yellow and peeling away from the jar. He listened for sounds of the girl. She was upstairs asleep on her bed. He wanted this to be a surprise. He needed her to trust him, and quickly; they were running out of time.

He lit the candles and let them ooze wax into the bottom of the jars so that he could stand them inside, blowing them out once they were ready. Then he pocketed all but one of the spent matches for later.

He sucked on this last match, softening the wood, as he went about preparing the rest of the food. He'd leave one in the kitchen window, just as he'd left one in the air-raid shelter. Perhaps one more in the work shed or in a bedroom window. Three cuts and the split wood edged apart to form the figure. The simplicity of it pleased him. The simple transformation.

Now, I have mine. Yes, that was what the man had said, and it was then that Gruber had appeared in the doorway, leaning heavily against it, pistol in hand. He glared at them both. *You two are getting friendly. Don't think I don't understand what you're saying. I'm watching you and I'm watching you.*

He had pointed his pistol at Heiden and Pendell in turn.

If you're going to shoot us, then shoot us, Heiden said to him in German.

Oh, I will, said Gruber, and he pretended to fire at them— *Pop. Pop.* —and then laughed. *You two have lost your sense of humor.*

He had laid it all out while she was upstairs. Now he watched her face as she stood awkwardly in the doorway and looked at everything spread on the blanket. Though he had opened the windows as much as he could to try to let some air in, the shutters were still closed and the evening remained hot and damp. Enough daylight still filtered in that the candles glowing in the jars on the floor now seemed a pointless gesture.

He watched her taking it all in—the green and blue tartan blanket from the back of the Crossley, the cheese biscuits, the plate of ham, the tomatoes, the sardines, the bowl of pickled cherries and wicker basket of apples, the Cabernet Sauvignon and two glasses.

"Well, sit down," he said. "I thought we should celebrate, having water again."

He had put a cushion on the floor for her, and he sat cross-legged on another. The chairs were pushed back against the wall to give them ample space. His shirt stuck to his back and across his shoulders. He tried to pull it free but it kept clinging to him like another skin, wrapping its damp heat around him.

She sat down and he waited for her to say something—something about the picnic, about the effort he'd gone to, or just a thank you—but she only looked at him and at the spread of food and, in the end, said nothing.

"Would your parents allow you some wine?" he said.

She shook her head.

He put the bottle back down and then changed his mind and poured himself a glass anyway. He handed her a plate, thinking of the picnics he and Eva had enjoyed in the garret room, or the parade days in the Tiergarten or Tempelhof Field: paper bags of lemon tarts that they had got from the Wertheim department store, Eva lying with her head in his lap, the sound of children shouting and laughing, the smell of cut grass.

He sipped at his wine and opened the cheese biscuits and offered them to her. She took just one. He put a handful on his own plate, along with a couple of slices of ham.

He watched her as she nervously bit into the cheese biscuit and it cracked into pieces between her teeth and fell into her lap. She collected them and, keeping her head down, piled them on her knee, and then took another from the packet and studied it as if assessing the risk of another crumbling.

"Aren't you hungry?"

She shook her head.

"What about some tomato?" They had been a last-minute addition to the picnic, found growing in a pot outside the back door. Only a few had been edible and he had picked them, cut them into quarters, and displayed them on a plate. She nodded and slowly reached out to take one and put it in her mouth. He took a mouthful of wine. Outside he could hear crickets twitching.

"I have always liked to picnic," he said. "It is a very English thing to do, isn't it, and everyone does it, everywhere you go. People picnic. It makes them happy."

He waited for a response, but she lowered her eyes and slowly reached across for another piece of tomato.

"Do you want some ham with that?" he said, offering her the plate.

She shook her head. She put the tomato in her mouth and dragged the flesh from its skin with her teeth; then she laid the skin out on her knee next to the pile of broken biscuit. The skins were tough, but it was little wonder she was gangly if she was going to be this fussy.

He tried her with a smile. They'd had conversations before— she'd interrogated him about God, for heaven's sake. Why wasn't she eating anything when he'd gone to all this trouble?

He took another gulp of wine. What he wouldn't give to be drunk now: deliriously, ridiculously drunk.

"I used to have an apartment in Berlin," he said, trying to come up with a story. "We used to lay a blanket down and have picnics like this on the floor. Put a blanket down anywhere and some food, and suddenly everything is all right because you're picnicking."

He looked at the girl. She was still offering no conversation. He tried again.

"Do you like school?"

She nodded.

"I wanted to be a teacher once," he said. "But it was not to be. War changes a lot of things. Plans get changed."

He took another mouthful of wine. He tried to imagine her as a woman, redrawing her in his mind with generous curves and another four or five inches of height. She would always be a slight girl. She hadn't the frame to be much larger. Eva had been slight too.

He could feel the alcohol now, thick like an oil spill over his thoughts, and heavy in his head. He went to the gramophone and lifted the lid, then raised the arm to inspect the needle.

"What shall we play?" He opened the cabinet beneath and took out the collection of shellac records. He looked over his shoulder at her. "Do you have any favorites?"

"I don't know."

"You don't know? Then I shall have to decide."

It took a few minutes, flicking through the selection several times before choosing one called "Summer Classics" because it seemed the most apt. He removed the record from its sleeve and lowered it through the spoke. He slowly turned the winding lever, feeling the tension tightening, and placed the needle in its groove.

There was a crackling anticipation before a scratchy recording of Vaughan Williams's "Fantasia on Greensleeves" started. He smiled at how contrived the selection was, how patriotic of the English to put an English composer first when Bach, Beethoven, or Mozart would have made for a much more appropriate opening.

"Germany has produced more of the world's finest composers than anywhere else. Bach, Beethoven, Handel," he said. "Pachelbel, Mozart, Brahms, Strauss, Mendelssohn, Schumann, Wagner, the list goes on."

"We're not supposed to play German music," said the girl. "Father won't allow it."

"Well, that's a shame," he said. "You take away the German composers and there really isn't much worth listening to."

He emptied the rest of the bottle into his glass. The music sounded distant, as if coming to him through a dream, and the room was hot and clammy, the wine slowly unpicking him. He wished he could break her open and see what she was thinking. He wondered if she hated him, if she was still scared. He could

barely imagine the house without her. There was some comfort in knowing someone was with him, in hearing her footsteps
overhead, in finding telltale signs of her in the rooms—an un-
made bed, a kicked-off sandal, a glass over a dead fly.

He thought of Professor Aritz's house in Pimlico, of Baxter
pawing at his shin with his disgusting bit of bone between that
shaggy-haired jaw and wanting Heiden to toss it down the hall
for him to fetch and slide and skitter back over the tiles with.
He had only visited the house three or four times, but each time
they had gone out to the local park and took a turn around the
lawns as Baxter pelted up and down, scattering the pigeons and
small children.

It had been no surprise to the professor when Heiden decided
to abandon his studies in London and go back to Germany. He
knew that Heiden felt it his duty.

So . . . you are lost to us, the professor said.

I am not lost, Heiden said. *We all know that I was never going to
be one of the great musicians.*

*Perhaps not, but better than most. You sell yourself short. And I'm
afraid I shall rather miss our squabbles.*

The professor had laughed and taken a folded piece of paper
from his pocket. *If you are ever back and need somewhere . . .* He
handed Heiden the address. *You never know how these things pan
out. The cottage is empty most of the time—too cut off for me so I never
use it myself, but you might find it to your liking. I suspect it's a cottage
that likes visitors, and unfortunately I've rather neglected it on that front.*

He remembered the watercolor of a cottage hanging from a
bent nail at the end of Professor Aritz's hallway. Lightly dabbed
flowers growing up a trellis, window boxes at every sill, caramel-
colored stone, the thatched roof and lead-lined windows, the
peaked top of the red, slatted front door.

He got another bottle of wine and a box of chocolates from

the larder in the kitchen. They'd been hidden on the top shelf in a sleek black and red box. The professor had been right. He could have been a musician, but never one as talented as Eva. It was hard to admit, but he was jealous of her for that.

He took the bottle of wine and chocolates into the sitting room. He opened the box. Around them Mahler's Adagietto from Symphony no. 5 was simmering, the slow swell of strings sifting through the air.

"Here," he said. "Have one."

The girl hesitated and then nervously picked out one of the chocolates and put it into her mouth. He looked at the inlay card and chose one himself with a swirl on the top. He bit into its soft shell. The chocolate coating was rich and dark. Inside was a sickly sweet fondant that tasted vaguely of orange.

"Black Magic," said the girl. "They're my mother's favorites. We're not really allowed them. They're for emergencies."

"Emergencies?" He laughed. She leaned over and took another. "Do you think this is not an emergency?"

"I suppose so," she said. "I like the caramel ones best."

He uncorked the second bottle of wine—he'd gone for the Merlot this time—and he poured a glass and took a sip, then picked out another chocolate. Already it was soft and tacky in his fingers.

He looked at the girl. "We can't stay here, you know, like this; not for much longer."

"Why not?"

"People will come. We've already had someone snooping about."

He put the chocolate in his mouth and licked the melted smears from his fingers. It reminded him of Norway, that peace offering of sorts that he had made to Pendell.

"Will you promise me something?" the girl said. "If you leave, don't leave me here on my own. I don't want to be on my own."

He could feel the chocolate liquefying, spreading out over his tongue as it melted and spread between his teeth.

"I'm sorry we're not outside," he said. "It's not a real picnic unless it is outside. I told Eva that."

"Will you promise, what I said?"

"No. I can't," he told her.

"Why not?"

He stood up. "Why don't you play something on the piano for me?" He went over to it and lifted the dust sheet from it. "I'd like to hear you play. What was it you said you knew?" He opened the lid and pulled out the stool, but she shook her head.

"Why not?"

The girl said nothing.

"Then I shall have to play for you."

He sat down on the stool and theatrically flexed his fingers, then started to play all the wrong notes, a dreadful racket, so that she had to laugh and he laughed as well.

He turned on his stool and lifted one finger to her—a *wait*— then disappeared from the room. She heard him leave the house, going across the gravel to the garage and opening the doors. She sat waiting on the floor, suddenly feeling awkward, as if she shouldn't be there, living with a strange man who wouldn't even tell her his Christian name.

When he came back he had her father's long saw and Alfie's violin bow that she realized, with a brief wave of anger, he must have taken from Alfie's room. He perched on the piano stool facing her, holding the handle of the saw between his legs and the other end in his hand. He looked up at her as if to see if she was ready. He surely wasn't going to play it. You couldn't play a saw.

Then, as if to prove her wrong, he rested the bow against the side of it and gently pulled out a note that was long and slow and seemed to wobble in the air. He bent the blade into a curve, shaping it like an *S,* then pulled out another note that seemed to vibrate. As it sounded he bent the saw more and the note traveled up the blade, rising higher and higher in pitch and then down again. His eyes glanced at her, seeing the amazement in her face. He smiled. Then he pulled the bow across again, bending the saw this way and that and wobbling the end of the blade a little so that the note quivered, swelling high and then low, rising up and down as if on air currents.

"It's beautiful," she said, "but sad."

"My grandfather said it was the sound of tears, but they don't have to be sad."

He repositioned himself, getting himself comfortable. "Massenet's 'Méditation' from *Thaïs,*" he announced quietly under his breath. "Performed on bow and saw."

Lydia giggled, and he started to play again.

Whole days and weeks now he could not account for. Somehow though he had marched and fought and clawed his way across Europe. Everything he had since become had grown out of one moment—a hole blown into a body that might just as well have been his. He had tried to shut himself down, to not allow himself to think or feel or reason or rage. But now, in this house and with this girl, he did feel and he did hurt and he did remember, every memory leading him back to that point, that shot, that day that had started so simply: a line of trucks being stopped at a junction west of Berlin on their way back to the barracks, and Metzger's head appearing at the back.

I want volunteers. They'd been ordered to send a truck out to a medical institute. *Near Brandenburg,* he told them.

Heiden's chest had tightened. *I know that place,* he said. *I'll go.* His heartbeat had quickened at the thought of seeing Eva.

He had scrambled out, regrouping in another truck with a

handful of others. Then, as the rest of the convoy had set off again, they had turned off the main road on a new course heading north.

The truck had sped away along the narrow road through the fields, the soldiers in the back jolting around inside as it splashed through the puddles and lurched over the bumps, the rain blowing in through the open back and hammering against the canvas.

When they eventually pulled off the road and started down a short drive, he looked out of the back and saw the familiar-looking lawn. As the truck pulled up he could hear footsteps crunching through the gravel and voices nearby, barely audible over the thrum of rain on the roof.

He ushered a soldier out of his corner seat at the front so that he could pull the canvas roof away enough from its fastening to stare out and try to see her. Through the narrow gap he saw the dented side of the truck, Major Metzger's jawline in the wing mirror, the thick rolls of his neck barely contained within the collar of his uniform. There were scuffed arcs in the gravel where a car had skidded or something had been dragged. He recognized the long line of windows. The fanned brickwork at the top of each, and the Grecian pillars and part of a double door. A nurse hurried past, almost running; but it was not Eva. He strained to look but he couldn't see her anywhere.

As if in response Metzger appeared at the back of the truck. *Spread out, and make yourselves seen.* He stood aside as they clambered down and fanned out across the grounds in front of the building. The rain fell steadily.

Two gray postbuses were parked over by the west wing, where the drive turned in on itself and fed back up to the road. Their windows were blackened out, but he could see the vague outlines of people inside the first one, sitting in the seats or standing in the aisle. A ragged line of women were being held in a queue alongside the second bus. They were still in their hospital gowns despite the downpour. Most of them were thin and their hair was stuck damp to their skulls. Some of the women fidgeted and fingered their gowns, pulling them up at the front so that their pale legs showed, whispering to each other or themselves. Others were silent. Something about the sight of them made Heiden's stomach tighten. Why didn't they get them out of the rain, or at least put them in some clothes? He glanced about trying to catch the eye of another comrade, but none of them seemed bothered by what they were seeing, or if they were they didn't show it. Surely Nurse Hartmann or Eva, if they came, would do something about it.

A medical practitioner walked down the line and checked his clipboard. He lifted the page and looked at the gaggle of patients, then wiped a raindrop from the paper with the sleeve of his white uniform. The line jostled.

Heiden turned his attention to the building, but although there were a lot of staff milling about, he could not see her. Metzger watched from the lawn, frowning as the rain slapped against his face. Foerster, a bald-headed factory worker from Mannheim, and Eberhardt—who in another lifetime, before the war, had been a prodigious accordion player—strolled up and down along the line of women, their fingers on the triggers of their rifles. Aachen and Rosenheim, two farming boys from Eberswalde, stood near the double doors of the entrance. The rest of the men were spaced out along the length of the building and around the drive. Nurse Hartmann came out, and he instinctively lowered his head and glanced furtively across at the buses. Foerster was making deranged faces at the women, trying to antagonize them. He grimaced at them and yapped like a dog. *Stop it, you idiot,* Heiden said under his breath, but Foerster did not stop.

The man with the clipboard called Nurse Hartmann and one

of the doctors over. He scratched the back of his head with his pen and spoke quickly to them, seemingly agitated. Nurse Hartmann rubbed at her forehead and called two nurses over, who she sent running in opposite directions. The man with the clipboard approached Metzger and showed him the list, running his pen up and down it and pointing at the line of women. Heiden saw a familiar deepening in the Major's frown. Metzger pursed his lips and sucked his cheek in, and then with a raised arm and a commanding glare, he summoned the men over.

Sometimes it felt like a dream, endless corridors and endless doors. Their heavy boots echoing. The half-lit wards, the terrified faces. *We've done nothing! Please. Please, don't shoot!*

We appear to have misplaced six retards, Major Metzger had explained. *And our good doctor thinks they might have got wind of where the buses are taking them, and that perhaps they don't want to go. I want them found. And quickly. I don't care how.*

The familiar entrance hall. The marbled floor and wide staircase. The brass light fittings hanging from the ceiling on long rusty chains and portraits lining the stairwell. It wasn't much more than six months since he had last been there. Eberhardt and Rosenheim sprinted up the main staircase, leaving Heiden and Aachen, one of the boys from Eberswalde, and the bald-headed Foerster, who had wasted no time charging into the main ward to the right of the entrance, waving his gun at the patients and yelling. Heiden and Aachen followed.

We've done nothing! Please. Please, don't shoot!

It was the same ward he'd walked through with Nurse Hartmann and Eva, although it looked smaller and darker now that the sky outside was thick with rain. Pale-white faces peered out from within each bed, fingers clasping at white sheets.

They went through a doorway into another ward, hurrying

through it almost at a run, and then into a third, with more beds and more wide-eyed men. As they passed, Foerster yelled *Boo!* at one of them and the man started shrieking. There were cupboards, cabinets, small empty offices, a tiled bathroom with a single bathtub and nothing else but a chair and a towel; another corridor, and more doors, two nurses pressing themselves against the wall as they passed. *They can't be far. A handful of retards . . .* said Foerster. But Heiden didn't care about the missing women. He just needed to find Eva.

They pushed into offices and surged through another ward of men. Upstairs, children were crying. One of the soldiers was yelling, *Shut up! Fucking shut up!*

They found their way into the dining room and then into the orangery. There were wicker chairs around small wooden tables which Foerster kicked aside. At one of the tables on the end an elderly doctor in a white lab coat and another man in a suit stared blankly at them.

Six women, said Foerster as they hurried through. *Have you seen them?*

N-no, said the doctor.

You? He pointed at the other man, who quickly shook his head.

They piled out through the far door; at the end of the corridor in front of them was the main entrance again. Through the open doors, Metzger was out on the lawn firmly holding a nurse by her elbow.

This is useless, said Aachen.

Up above, the heavy feet of jackboots thundered across the ceiling. People running. Shouting. Somewhere a woman was wailing.

Heiden could feel a sickness sweeping through him, a sudden emptying inside. Was this what they had been reduced to? What the hell was it they were doing?

Then Foerster found a door to a set of narrow steps that lead them down into the dark. Perhaps she was down there. A dampness pervaded the air below in the endless corridors and dimly lit storage rooms full of cupboards with paint pots and petrol cans, and piles of blankets caked in clods of earth. They kicked them about to see if anyone was hiding within them. Foerster kept walking into the light bulbs, which hung low from a sinewy cord, and the dim light slapped and splashed across the dank walls.

They made their way through another door and down an unlit corridor.

Come out, come out! Aachen muttered to himself. *We know you're down here somewhere.*

They found themselves in a laundry room. Everything was dark. There were two wooden tubs and a sink, a mangle nailed to the wall, and a bucket of grubby water. He remembered Eva's complaints about not being allowed to send clothes to the laundry until they'd tried to scrub the dirt from the clothes themselves. Now here on a shelf an opened box of washing powder was still spilling its contents. He could hear the hush of the powder emptying. Someone had left in a hurry.

They went down a corridor. Aachen took the lead and Heiden turned every now and again to see if anyone was following them. He had lost sight of Foerster and could hear only his voice somewhere down another corridor. Above him, from the wards, came shouts and muffled sobbing. *Come on,* he said. *We have to hurry.*

The corridor opened out into a large room whose walls were lined with pipes.

Then above them came feet pounding across the ceiling, and trails of dust issued down through the cracks. There were shouts and a shriek; more footsteps running.

They must have found them, said Aachen. *Come on then. Let's go.*

At the far end of the room was another door that looked heavy and made of iron, and when they reached it they felt a bitter draft blowing in from under it; outside they could hear the rain.

Let's go this way, said Heiden. He was desperate now to get out.

The bolts were stiff and it took both of them to haul the top one across. He kicked the bottom one back with his boot. The door was warped and swollen, but after several attempts they managed to push it open.

She had put a clip in her hair at first, then changed it for an Alice band, then to a red ribbon knotted around her head, and then knotted around a ponytail instead but her hair wasn't long enough. Now she was trying to fasten the hair clip back in again and wishing that she had never taken it out in the first place. Her hands shook and the clip kept sliding out of place.

She tried fixing the clip one last time until finally it clicked, and she looked at herself in the mirror of her mother's dressing table. It had three sides to it, and there was no hiding from her reddened eyes and the nervous pallor of her skin. She had never considered herself pretty. She opened the drawer and rummaged around, pulling out a lipstick. She took off the top. Salmon pink? Perhaps not. She pulled another one out, taking the lid off and winding it up. That was better: a bright scarlet. She leaned in closer to the glass and opened her mouth. She had watched her mother countless times and yet now she wasn't sure how to apply it. Straight along the lip or in little dabs? She tried the former but it was rather wobbly and she couldn't keep her hand still. She then dabbed in the gaps, but she was only making it worse. She sat back and tried to calm herself, and then turned her attention to her bottom lip, this time with more courage. When she was finished, she pressed her lips together as her mother always did.

She opened up the jewelry box and wound it up. With a click, the three porcelain fairies inside pirouetted and turned to the whirr of the mechanism and its rickety chime.

As she listened to the music she slumped back in the chair. The white summer dress was not wholly appropriate, but she liked the lace flowers around the cuffs, the collar, and the hem. She had tied a long white ribbon around the waist to give her some shape. Just dressing up. Nothing more than that.

She shut the lid of the jewelry box and took out the rouge and opened it up. A soft rose pink. She dabbed some onto her right cheek with a pad. She added some more and then some more. Then she did the other cheek. With every passing moment she looked less and less "Lydia." She tried a smile that almost worked. She wished she didn't feel so hot. She wished she could stop her heart from bumping so hard against her chest.

This is what happens in a war. These are the things that need to be done.

She listened. He was still in the sitting room. The picnic had been tidied away. He was perhaps in the chair or on the floor studying the maps, or watching through the window. It was dark outside. Quiet. Beside her the oil lamp flickered.

She remembered her and Rosie and a handful of others once running through the fields, shrieking as they ran across the lane, laughing and shouting. *Quick! Quick! They're coming! They're coming! The Germans are coming!* Up the drive and across the lawn and into the house, hot and sweating and barefooted.

You'll make them come, you will, her mother said. *All that hollering and blazing. You go running around crying wolf, and no one's going to believe you if one day they're really here.*

And now he *was* here, and it was all her doing—she had cried wolf and the wolf had come.

She stood up and looked at her reflection. She would not

cry; she would not let herself. She wouldn't think anymore. She imagined her body filled with pebbles, like the people in the half-buried bungalow on the beach—a girl now made of stone.

She found him in the sitting room in her father's chair, still drinking her father's wine. He didn't look up and at first she thought he was asleep. She waited in the doorway. She wasn't quite sure how she should stand and she found herself fidgeting. He must have known that she was there. He must have heard her breathing. She could feel her heart quickening. Should she take another step in, say something, do something?

He lifted his head and looked at her.

"Scrub that off," he said.

She stood quite still, thinking he might change his mind, then felt the blood drain from her. He got up and walked towards her, standing closer than he'd ever been before.

"I don't know what game you are playing," he said, "but you are out of your depth, so stop it. You haven't the slightest idea what you are doing."

She turned her head, holding it still, and waited for the slap, but it never came. And that was when she finally burst into tears.

The door was warped and swollen but after several attempts they managed to push it open. A steep bank rose up immediately from the door, and he and Aachen scrambled up it. The rain fell heavy, soaking through their greatcoats. Over to the right were some old, dilapidated stables. To the left the institute building stretched on until it reached a perimeter wall. There were vehicle tracks and broken plant pots spilling their earth and dead roots. The lawn had been made muddy with the tramping of feet, and Aachen slipped in it, cursing. Heiden searched the institute windows but there was still no sign of her.

They walked a short distance away from the building, trying to find their way back to the front. Heiden sensed something and stopped—eyes watching him perhaps. Was it her? He turned and looked towards the woods, and then signaled Aachen to follow him as he cautiously moved closer. Something was filling him with a sense of unease. For a moment they both stood at the edge staring into the darkness, to where the trees grew thick and close, and then Heiden took a few steps in and held still, listening. The rain poured down but beneath its torrent he heard a sound like a whisper being muffled. Aachen didn't seem to notice, but Heiden glimpsed movement there in the brambles—something had shifted.

He stepped in further, ushering Aachen to follow and pushing branches aside with the tip of his gun as he quietly picked his way through. His eyes caught another movement, a shuffling up ahead where the trees in the copse were clumped thickly together. Another sound. A *ssshush*. He raised his gun and took a few steps, then signaled to Aachen to take them from the other side. He didn't want to hurt them, just drive them back to the building. But something made him hold still. His hand was trembling. He could see Aachen edging closer to them, his gun held ready, finger curled around the trigger. And that was when Heiden called out, before he knew what he was doing and before he could stop himself.

Eva?

Aachen looked at him, confused, and for a few moments there was nothing—no movement, no sound—and then slowly, very slowly, she rose up out from the brambles, wet through and covered in mud, her face pale and washed with rain, her eyes wide with fear.

Eva. My God. Eva. What the hell . . . ?

She signaled with her hand, and then, cautiously, one by one six other women, dirty and dazed, still in their drenched bed gowns, eyes red and bewildered, staggered up from within the brambles around her, two of them taking hold of her hands.

He lowered his gun and glanced at Aachen but Aachen didn't move, his gun still pointing directly at the women. He looked at Eva and at Heiden and then at Eva again.

What's going on? he said. *What is this?*

One of the women tittered. Eva looked at Heiden; a look of desperation. What in God's name was she thinking? What in God's name was she trying to do?

It was then that he had been aware of Metzger behind them, and Rosenheim and Foerster too, all three standing at the edge of the wood looking in, their pistols pointing.

Do you know this nurse, Lance Corporal? And even now he couldn't quite remember what, if anything, he had said or tried to say.

These aren't criminals. Eva's voice was suddenly strong and defiant. *These aren't murderers. These are good people,* she shouted. *Good German people.*

They are nothing, Metzger said. *Retards and lunatics. A drain on our resources. We're fighting a war, Nurse. We have to flush out the waste. Take them back to the bus.*

But Eva wouldn't, she couldn't, she said, shouting that they were taking them to Brandenburg, that they weren't ever coming back, not ever.

You take them back to the bus or God help me, Metzger yelled.

No, she said. *I won't,* even though Heiden begged her, pleaded with her.

For God's sake, just leave them.

I can't, she said.

Please, Eva!

No, she said. *Can't you see? It's not right.*

And he *could* see, but he couldn't stop it. Out of the corner of his eye he saw Rosenheim and Foerster, both with their guns pointing at the group of patients, and Metzger next to them. Not far from him Aachen stood, his own pistol shaking in his hand. He didn't seem to know who to point the gun at first, Eva or the women or even Heiden. Heiden didn't dare move.

What happened next, he could not be certain; only that in the midst of the commotion that followed—as Metzger raged, and Heiden pleaded, and Eva cried, and neither Aachen, Rosenheim, nor Foerster seemed to know where to point their guns— Eva had suddenly made a move and two of the women scattered as well. In the confusion as Metzger yelled *Stop!* and Heiden shouted *Don't shoot her! Please don't shoot!* still Eva had run to him and a single shot had fired.

He had woken with a gasp and now he sat on the floor, his back resting against the side of the bed with his knees pulled in to his chest. The wooden floorboards were warm on the soles of his bare feet. The house still held the heat of the day, clinging to it in every pore. His eyes were swollen and he could feel a pulling in his head like tendons tightening; all he wanted to do was sleep. The same line would play over and over in his mind, the only words he remembered from that day with any clarity— him shouting at Metzger, *Don't shoot her. Please, don't shoot.* But Metzger shot anyway.

In the dynamite room in Norway there had been nothing to do but run it on a constant reel, to see her face and that of Metzger. He hadn't been able to shake it off, and he had wanted to scream, to go out into the snow and scream out the words just to get rid of them, but they were always there trapped inside him. *Don't shoot her. Please, don't shoot.*

He had played the line so many times now that it was worn

thin, almost indecipherable, a lie perhaps that he'd told himself so often that it now felt weighted with truth, because perhaps he had said no such thing. Perhaps, in those few moments, he had only thought it and managed to utter nothing at all to stop Metzger. Perhaps, in fact, he hadn't even thought it but had dropped it into the memory later as an attempt to redeem himself, and maybe there had been no time to stop it. *Don't shoot her. Please, don't shoot.* But Metzger shot anyway.

It had been waking him like an alarm call—this shot, always the shot—and beneath that now was the soft undertow of the girl's breathing. He didn't dare turn and look in case she wasn't there. He tried to imagine that it was Eva's breath, Eva sleeping so peacefully in the bed behind him, that there was no girl called Lydia, no Norway, no Pendell, no Gruber, no war. He was in the garret room in Berlin and Eva was safe and sound.

He smelled the burned tinge of gunpowder in the air sometimes, and often he woke feeling the blast still resonating in him, the rumbling aftermath of a dream. And for the briefest moment he thought Metzger had missed, or just fired into the trees to scare them, but her legs had slowly buckled from under her, collapsing as if from inside, and she slipped, almost graceful, to the ground. For a moment there was no sound but the rain coming down through the leaves, and then the two women who had been holding Eva's hands opened their mouths and shrieked.

He had tried drowning himself once, without even knowing it. The memory was there again: him walking out and out into the sea, and it was only when some soldiers pulled him back—*Hey, sir! Where are you going?*—that he realized what he was doing.

It was a wonder he remembered anything of the campaign. He had passed through it like a hollow man, devoid of feeling, thought, or emotion. Perhaps he did rape the woman in Narvik. Perhaps they all did. Perhaps that was why he had staggered out of the railway administration building and retched into the snow, his cock still sticky with other men's cum. Or it was the sight of them doing what they did and him doing nothing that made him sick. Or something else. Something different. The war had found its way into his head somehow, like a raindrop trickling into his ear.

In his sleep he still searched the corridors of the institute as if one day he might find her, cowering there in the depths of the boiler room, or sitting on a bed in an empty ward. *I've been waiting for you,* she would say.

The girl slept behind him. The bedroom was pitch black.

He had tried to haul Eva's body up because her eyes were still open and looking at him and her skin was still warm and he was sure, so sure, that he could still hear her breath. He kept shouting, struggling with her rag doll limbs—*Come on! Get up! Get up!*—but she was too heavy, a deadweight, and she slumped to the ground.

He slipped down beside her on his knees and took her hand in his and squeezed, squeezed it hard, saying, *Please,* and, *Eva, please,* and, *Eva. Please get up.* He was aware of Metzger standing behind him as he crouched, the tip of Metzger's gun tapping at the back of his shoulder, and Metzger saying that she had made him do it, that it was an accident. Wasn't it?

Wasn't it?

He lowered himself down onto the bedroom floor and felt the side of his face press against the floorboard. He wrapped his arms around himself and brought his legs in tight. If he folded himself in tight enough perhaps he could disappear.

He had stroked the back of Eva's hand, the fine soft skin, the warm nubs of her knuckles. He had held it up to his lips, still warm, fading but still there.

And maybe without thinking he had nodded.

Metzger said, *Good. Now get these pathetic creatures on the bus.*

He stared at the damp earth, the rain coming down so heavy now that it was disturbing the leaves and splashing off the branches. He was vaguely aware of Metzger walking away, Rosenheim and Foerster following, and then, after a while, Aachen too. He felt numb to everything around him, barely existent at all, as if, like her, he were lifting up out of his body. He slowly hauled himself up, and shut his teary eyes, trying to press it all away, and feeling everything swaying around him. When he opened them again the women were still sitting or standing around in the mud, wet through in their filthy gowns. They stared at him with their bewildered faces.

Come on, he said, unaware that the voice was his. *Please. Come on. Get up.*

He rested his head against the bed, and when he closed his eyes he could see the small annex room of the dynamite store. Outside, the storm was quieting. Snow was falling softly now and there was a low whistling of the wind as it coursed through the gorges. It was midafternoon. Even if the snow stopped falling, they should wait until morning before they moved on. He stretched his arm out along the cold floor and tapped out a rhythm on the concrete. *Tap-tap-tappity-tap.* In the main room neither Gruber nor Bürckel spoke. The fire crackled. The damp twigs spat. He drew circles and treble clefs on the dusty floor with his fingertips. He imagined the concrete away, until it became the warm skin of her back, and his fingers were trailing over her body, feeling its softness, its warmth, its life, and when he lifted his hand to his nose, he was sure that he could smell her. She was still there on the tips of his fingers and in the cold curl of his hand.

*   *   *

It was two in the morning. He couldn't sleep. His mind was heavy with tiredness and yet thoughts still crawled back and forth. The voices and images were out of sync, an incessant noise in his head. He had been sitting in the chair watching her—the flickering of her eyeballs beneath the skin of her eyelids suggested that her sleep was perhaps not as peaceful as it looked. He wondered what she had been thinking, making herself up like that. Did she think he was an animal?

He quietly picked her dress up off the floor and folded it, laying it over the foot of her bed, then placed her sandals side by side beneath the dressing table, undoing the buckles so that in the morning they would be easier for her to put on. Then he picked up the toy bear she had left on the floor and shone the faint light of his torch on it. The bear was saggy and moth-eaten, its fur worn away in patches. He had a hole in one of his armpits, and when Heiden gently squeezed him a faint breath-like puff and flecks of stuffing dispersed like dust into the air. Mr. Tabernacle, she had called him. Hardly a name at all. He had an old school tie around his neck and a couple of threads were still hanging out of the socket where one of his eyes was missing. He needed a button sewn there, or a patch.

He sat the bear on the chair and made his way down the stairs, shining his torch on ahead of him. He opened the front door and stood on the step for a moment, feeling with relief the freshness of the summer's night cool upon his face. He stepped out onto the gravel, taking his pistol from its holster, eyes and ears suddenly alert as his feet crunched over the chippings. For a few minutes he stood watching. There were very few stars out. Thin clouds pulled across the sky, moonshine trying to find a way through.

He pulled out the piece of paper from his pocket, unfolded it, and read the scrawled address. He would have liked to have seen Professor Aritz again. He had thought often of the cottage in the painting that hung at the end of the professor's hall. When he envisaged it in his mind now, it was difficult to tell what was real and what were embellishments added over months of dreaming: roses over the doorway, the small four-paned windows, the window boxes, the soft, warm stone. The professor had said nothing of a garden, but in his mind Heiden had given it one—slightly overgrown, and everything in flower and bursting with color. He could smell the fragrances and hear the bees bumping against the windows. A little sanctuary, so far from anything that not even a war could find it.

In the store in Norway he had stood for hours at the small window, trying to see through the impenetrable mesh of frost and snow. If he stared long and hard enough he saw things in the ice, just like da Vinci had said: shapes and patterns, connections forming, fractures that he would follow like trails. Images lifted out of the frost as well: a boat on a sea, silhouetted birds flying, and faces and figures. He had seen himself once, in a field, or at least a figure that could have been him, sitting all alone on what might have been a log—it was difficult to tell.

He sometimes imagined he could bring her out of the snow, make her walk out from between the trees, across the clearing and up the bank to the door. He would open it and there she would be, the blizzard blowing around her. Metzger's bullet would have gone right through, in one side and out the other, and done not a fraction of damage but for the smallest, most ridiculous of holes. She would stand there, beaming at him, and say, *Ah, so this is where you've been hiding. I've been looking for you.*

It had been impossible to think forward, only, it seemed, to think back. If he had been able to turn himself off, to shut himself down, he would have. Thoughts and memories clamored and clawed at him, an endless rabble of voices, images that flickered and flared. He scratched at his head to try to get them out, and covered his eyes, and buried himself beneath his arms. He scrawled lines in the concrete floor with his knife, over and over, digging out channels.

You'll make it blunt, Gruber had said, but Heiden ignored him.

He kept thinking back, always back, this time to the field in Voreifel close to the Luxembourg border. He wondered if this was what he had seen in the frosted window—the image of himself sitting not on a log but an overturned tin drum, resting his foot on a drag harrow and having his lunch; he had liked to take it at a peaceful distance from all the rabble of the boys. This must have been November, because the 3rd Mountain Division had been on training there at that time, practicing maneuvers through the open country—November and the first mention he'd heard of the Pioneer Group. The afternoon was sunny and bright but with an autumnal nip in the air, and the ground was damp, the night's frost still wet in the grass. He was sipping from his field flask when Lieutenant Ziegler joined him. Ziegler was in his thirties but looked older, the war already graying his hair at the sides. His ears stuck out wider than most, and whenever Heiden saw him he had an almost irresistible urge to pick him up by the ears and give the platoon leader a little shake. His funny looks were a contrast to his fierce temper, but Heiden had always considered him a fair and tolerable man.

It's Heiden, isn't it? he said. *You're one of the General's Bavarian crowd.*

I've spent time in Bavaria, yes. My grandparents . . . But I'm from Berlin.

Ziegler nodded and opened a linen bag he had with him,

pulling out some black bread wrapped in cardboard. He took a bite and thoughtfully chewed on it before he said anything more. Had Heiden heard of the Brandenburgers? They were looking for a certain type of soldier.

Heiden had asked, *What for?*

Espionage. Sabotage. All very exciting, I'm sure. I've seen your ways, Lance Corporal. I could make a recommendation.

No, thank you, Heiden said; he was happy doing what he was doing.

Fine, Ziegler said. *I'm glad to hear it. But if you change your mind . . .*

He had put this conversation out of his mind. After all, there had been Eva to think of then. He would put himself at no more risk than necessary. He needed to make it home. But now she was lost—gone—and in losing her he had lost himself, too. What was there to go home to now? Who was there for him? Who was he anyway? He no longer seemed to know.

In the dynamite room he stared blankly across at the figures he barely knew huddled and sprawled around him.

We're out of matches, Gruber announced, and he tossed the empty box at Heiden's feet. He had been trying to relight the fire.

You fucking idiot, murmured Heiden, standing up. *You've fucking wasted them, that's what you've done.*

Oh, stop your whining. I wasn't planning on us being here this long.

Well, we have been. And who knows how much longer we will still be here.

In that case, it looks like we're going to freeze.

Shut up.

Well, stop your bloody whinging. I've had enough of you and your goody-goody attitude. What do you think you are, some sort of fucking crusader?

Before Heiden knew what was happening he had launched himself across the room and had shoved Gruber hard against the wall, his arm held against his throat and his knife pressed against Gruber's side.

Don't fucking speak to me anymore, he said into the man's face. *If you say another stinking word to me, I'm going to gut you like a pig. Do you understand?*

And it was only when Heiden finally released him and stepped back and stared at the startled faces of Bürckel, Pendell, and Harris that he realized there were tears on his cheek.

He rushed into the annex room and stood there, arms outstretched and palms pressed against the cold of the wall. He took several deep breaths, his eyes squeezed shut, his head between his arms, and tried to compose himself.

If Ziegler and the Brandenburg battalion were looking for men with nothing to lose, let them take him, he thought, and erase him completely, because it was this—his identity, everything he had ever been—that he now realized he most wanted to be rid of. Without Eva, there was nothing left for the man he had once been. She was all that he was holding on to, everything, and now with her dead he was null and void.

As he opened the attic hatch he came face to face with an army of animals, each no more than two inches high. They were spaced out in their pairs around the opening in lines of defense: lions, tigers, penguins, rhinos...As his torchlight shone through their formation, their painted skins gleamed. Each was exquisitely carved, presumably by the same hand that had crafted the boat on the windowsill. He quietly climbed up through the hole into the attic, carefully picking his way through the barricade of toys. He looked about the room, at the small window high up in the roof, and the wooden box beneath it that had probably been put there to stand on. Beneath the window was a wooden ark, Noah and his wife standing outside like generals behind the serried ranks of animals.

He sat on the floor beside them, picking up the wooden figures and holding them in his torchlight. They reminded him so much of his grandfather's wood carvings, the fairy tales etched into strips of oak, maple, and ash; tales of heroics and magic and beasts, and of the man who had turned into a bear.

He took a matchstick from his pocket and put it in his mouth and sucked, gently softening the wood. He would shape it with his knife and leave it in the ark. A sign perhaps. A message. A little bit of Norway that he had brought home to her.

Sometimes when he closed his eyes he saw Pendell's face as if it were his own reflected within the glass window of the dynamite room. There was more than a similarity; there was an understanding.

Resting the match on the floor he made the three incisions, one up the middle forming the legs, another on each side; then he opened it up to form two arms and two legs. He took the lid off the ark and propped the matchstick man inside so that one day it could be found.

When he had managed to get himself out of the mountains and back to the burned wreckage of Narvik, he sent a message to Ziegler: *I've reconsidered our discussions in Voreifel. Please put me forward.*

The Brandenburgers, he was soon to discover, were a special commando force led by Admiral Canaris—a former ship commander with considerable experience in espionage. It was within this division that a new sabotage unit was being formed, one that would in time be called Pioneer Group 909. This phantom unit would consist of a handpicked selection of multinational soldiers who would be trained for a landing on British soil ahead of the planned invasion. Secrecy would be the main tactic. Any missions would be carried out deep within enemy territory and should pass by unnoticed and without any use of weapons.

The weeks of training at the battalion's training grounds near Brandenburg were brutal and intensive, but by early July he was in Aachen as part of the 11th Company under Lieutenant Schöller. From there, while the first and third battalions of the Brandenburg Division were being sent to train on the Heligoland rock in the middle of the North Sea, he and the rest of his company were sent on to Dieppe.

He remembered the first night there well: men sprawled out on the pebble beach passing the bottles around. Had that really only been two weeks ago? There had been a sense of euphoria among the boys that night. The Channel Islands had fallen—the first chink in the British armor. Quartered in the château of La Chapelle, they had gathered around the wireless, cheering as the Führer's final offering to the British was broadcast from the Kroll Opera House. Churchill would surrender. The men could sense the end coming, as if all that was left to do for the war was a bit of tidying up around the edges. There was singing, dancing, everyone getting drunk. Even Lieutenant Schöller was seen staggering about with a half-drunk bottle of claret in his hand.

For several days the hundred or so men there relaxed, sunning themselves on the beach and swimming in the sea. Heiden tried teaching a young Austrian called Leibnitz how to swim, but despite the boy's best efforts he couldn't keep his head above the surface—and he swallowed so much water that he ended up being sick. Like many others before he had arrived, he had no idea that the sea was salty. Men play-wrestled among the pebbles and sand or jumped on each other's backs and raced along the shore, tipping each other into the surf and laughing. They drank and smoked and lolled around, sprawled like basking seals. They played card games or told filthy jokes or just dozed in the sun. The beach was littered with bottles they'd raided from houses, cafés, and bars.

One night, as the sun finally began to fade, he sat for a while on his own, swigging from a carafe of Bordeaux. The horizon was beginning to blur, his drunkenness and the rippling of the sea making him feel unsteady. Something made him stagger to his feet; a thought, or a decision. He couldn't remember now but he had stumbled down the beach, between the drunken layabouts and sunbathers, still clutching the half-empty carafe in his hand, and he had walked, fully clothed, into the water. He pushed his way through the waves, feeling the swell of the sea slopping against him and splashing up into his face, and it was only when he felt hands grabbing at his arms and pulling him back—*Hey, sir! Where are you going?*—that he had realized where he was.

His thoughts slipped back to that blown-out beach café, its shattered windows and the sand blowing in, the broken chairs and light fittings, the bar already raided. It was a Thursday when they had gathered around the table looking out at the rubble strewn across the patio. Six men were being sent on a mission. Lieutenant Schöller had said, *I want you to be one of them.*

She sat on the edge of the bed in the darkness, her toes barely touching the floor. If she could conjure Button out of the wardrobe she would, just to have someone with her. There were strange noises about the house, creaks that should have been familiar but weren't, the man prowling in the night. She sat quite still and waited for the door handle to turn, for the door to quietly open. It had not crossed her mind until then that she should have something to protect herself with. He had told her that in

Norway they had raped a woman. If more men came, how could she possibly defend herself? She might scream and scream and scream but nobody would come. She got up and wedged a chair under the door handle, then piled all of her heaviest books on the seat. She sat back down on the bed and pulled the end of her nightdress firmly over her knees. She stared across the room at the door handle and quietly waited.

They had all spent time living in England: Lehmann as a doctor, Kappel as a journalist, Diederich and Pfeiffer, like Heiden, had studied in London, and Theissen had worked as a German lecturer for one of the universities. The men enlisted in the Brandenburg Division were mostly fanatical nationalists or idealists or, in the case of Theissen, just sharp-witted adventurers. Others, such as Heiden, felt they had nothing left and simply wanted to lose themselves somewhere within the chaos of the war. As with all the division, their command of English was impeccable, particularly Lehmann, who had been in England since he was twelve and, like Heiden, had a number of English relatives.

A bucket car would pick them up and drive them to Zeebrugge, Lieutenant Schöller said, where an S-boat would transport them across the Channel, weather permitting. It was a night raid, and it needed to be swift. It should take no more than a few hours, he told them.

The British, it was believed, had also developed a way of detecting aircraft using radio waves; some examples of their rather inferior technology had been found during the British retreat from France. If the invasion was to be a success, a coordinated attack on British airfields first needed to be executed, to take out their listening stations. Schöller showed them on the map spread across the café table. There were tall masts along the coast: Hopton, Dunwich, and here, at Bawdsey Point. He circled it. *This is your target,* he said. *You land here—Shingle Street. Bawdsey Point is a mile or so away.*

Heiden stared. It wasn't the target or the beach with the odd name that had caught his eye. It was the village a short distance northwesterly from their landing point. The name, Willemsley, seemed to be singed into the map, drawing his eye to it, no more than a mile, a mile and a half at most, away from where they were to land. It couldn't be the same place, and yet he knew that it was. Schöller was still talking. A manor house. High security. Previous air raids on it over the last two weeks had done little damage. So they would go in by water this time, he said, right under their noses—scale the cliffs directly below the east wing of the main building, find the transmitter block and disable it, and then leave. There should be no sight or sound of them. No gunfire. The raid should be silent and secret.

Schöller eyed them one by one over the rim of his pince-nez. *All of you on joining have surrendered your personal belongings: wedding rings, pay books, photographs, identity documents, etcetera. You will be receiving new documentation in due course. Nothing should be retained that might identify you as German. Is that understood?*

Lehmann, Diederich, Kappel, Pfeiffer, and Theissen. An hour later, with Lieutenant Schöller gone, they were still mapping out the details of the mission, the sunlight burning bright through the shattered windows of the blown-out café as outside the waves broke on the shore.

It's a suicide trip, said Theissen. *I know that coastline. They're not going to leave it wide open. It's too obvious a landing point.*

That's why we swim the last stretch, said Kappel.

Diederich, the youngest, sucked on his cigarette and casually blew the smoke through the broken window. *With all our gear? We'll drown before we get there.*

Not if we only take the absolute minimum, said Heiden. *We swim from the boat, we fan out, no communication. As Schöller says, the whole mission needs to be silent.*

He spent the rest of that afternoon trying to sleep but the château had been too hot and noisy, and his room had twenty camp beds or more squeezed into it. He lay sweating on the top sheet. The sun belted through the window. A group of men argued at the far end of the room about which one of them had left a bottle of Calvados on the beach and had to go back to find it, while halfway along the camp beds another group were sitting with a pack of cards, playing a boisterous game of Skat. Dieppe was infested with flies. Every time he opened his eyes he could see a cloud of them above his head. Outside were shouting, voices, gun blasts, laughter, and, in the distance, great chundering booms. He lay for several hours in a state of semi-shutdown, but in the end it was impossible to sleep.

Later that evening, he stood at the water's edge with the soft foam swilling around his jackboots. He watched the white sea wash up the beach, the water hissing as it dragged the shingle out from under his boots. He looked out across the water in the fading light, staring at the murky horizon and the vague promise of another not-so-distant coastline.

She was standing in Alfie's room, just standing, and it was dark. Model planes lined up along the shelf. The carved wooden soldier. The poster with the pointing finger. All of Alfie's things. The picture frame above the bed with butterflies, moths, dragonflies, and bees. There was now even a silver-studded blue in the center and, although it was pierced through its body with a pin, it was still alive and flapping, trying to wriggle free. She walked across the room to pick the wooden soldier up from the desk, but when her hand went to it, the soldier wasn't there but a few inches away, as if by the blink of her eye everything around her had shifted. She turned then and saw him: Alfie sitting on the sill with his feet on the bed, as if within that same blink, he had appeared; her Alfie but different, for he had such glorious wings that reached almost to the ceiling. The feathers were so fine and white as to hardly be there at all but for a shimmering of light. They spanned out in three layers, turning tawny brown where they joined his shoulder blades, while the lower feathers at the end were torn and ragged but glowed a soft-hued silver, and within them the bones burned bright white. He wore his cricket white trousers but his feet and chest were bare. Alfie, her Alfie, and yet more perfect. He had muscles in his chest and stomach and arms that she had never seen before, and he gave off a vague light so that even from within his cricket trousers she could see the glow of his skin. His hair was longer than she had ever known it, falling across his eyes and down to his nose and hanging in wet, dripping threads. He tilted his head as if to take her in and his cheeks swelled as he smiled at her. And she was not afraid; she was happy and safe—and even when, in another blink, he was gone and the room was dark and empty again, she could still feel his smile wrapped warm across her face.

MONDAY

SHE SKULKED AIMLESSLY about the house, slumping heavily into chairs or slouching against door frames. Once, a long time ago, after a bad dream, her father said, *missy, you can't be scared forever,* and she was only now beginning to believe it. Boredom was something else though; there was no limit to it.

She watched him from her bedroom window, filling her mother's watering can from the pump and walking up and down the vegetables with it, trying to bring them back to life. Eventually he came back in and she lolled about on the four-poster bed, listening to him downstairs. She imagined him lying next to her, his arm around her waist and how it might feel. If, in years to come, she had to marry him, she supposed that she would. He had wrists she wanted to curl her hands around, a face that she wanted to touch. She wondered if thinking things like that made her a traitor. Perhaps God would send her to hell. After all, she had spied on him in the bath. She had seen his naked body and had even caught herself thinking about it since: his pale white bottom, the scratches and cuts on his thighs, the wound in his shoulder that even now still looked sore.

In her bedroom she bent her hair clip in such a way that she could sit on the floor and flick it across the room at the window and hear it go *tink* against the glass. Every time she went to retrieve it she glanced down into the garden and hoped to see soldiers coming through the woods and across the lawn, half crouching, rifles at the ready, but the garden was always sunny and empty. She wondered if Rosie or any of the others were missing her, whether Miss Mountford was worried, whether any of them cared. Perhaps someone had come looking for her, whilst they had been out in the wood—searching for her, but she hadn't been here.

She tried walking on the paint pots, but her feet kept slipping out of the handles and she wasn't in the mood. She did handstands against the landing wall because there was no one there to tell her not to, and it was only when her dress slithered down over her head and she realized that her underwear was showing that she got embarrassed and tipped herself upright again. It was too hot and tiresome anyway. All she really wanted to do was sleep, but she didn't dare in case he was no longer there when she woke again.

She took another turn of the house, this time taking Mr. Tabernacle with her for the ride. Occasionally she would catch the man's eye as their paths crossed. Or she would walk into a room and see him there, hunched over his maps again, or repacking his kit bag, or sitting on the front doorstep, relacing his boots.

"Will you play cards with me?" she finally asked. "I know Snap and Beggar-My-Neighbor. Or we have Happy Families."

"Later," he said. "I have to concentrate. I don't want you playing by the windows either. I don't want you being seen."

She nodded and hung about in the hallway for a while, sitting on the bottom step of the stairs and watching him on the doorstep.

He had told her that they were to get the house ready for when the rest of the men arrived, and now the house was as ready as it could be—but nobody had come. Together they had pushed the beds in her parents' room and the spare room against the wall to open a big space where they would lay down blankets, towels, and coats for the soldiers to sleep on. With all the furniture pushed to one side, the bedrooms echoed and seemed emptier than ever. There would be tents in the garden, he told her. Stolen cars and trucks parked on the gravel. They'd need diesel, oil lamps, torches, food. They would have to loot the houses in the village for anything else they required: extra plates, bedding, toothpaste, shampoo, socks, towels...

They would come when the rain came. Or in the early hours of the morning when everything was dark. Not on a bright, hot morning like this at the end of July. She wished they would come now, if only so there would be a change. On the horizon puffs of clouds stretched out in woolly ribbons across the sky. Seagulls were coming inland. She could hear their cawing as they circled the house. Through the shutter slats she looked around the garden for the bobbing tail of Jeremiah, but the rabbit was not there.

She was hesitant about entering Alfie's room again, but she wanted to know if he might come back for her. It wasn't a dream, that first time; it was too vivid for that. She pushed the door open and stood in the doorway. Then she stepped in and shut the door behind her, leaned across the bed, and, pushing her fingers between the slats at the window, opened them as wide as she could so that he could come in. She stood where she had been standing the night before, her eyes firmly fixed on the wall ahead, the chest of drawers, the bookshelves. She wouldn't look at the window ledge. She would close her eyes and see if he would come back to her, sitting there as he had been, his wings tucked in, his skin faintly glowing. She pressed her eyes shut.

"Alfie," she said. "Alfie..."

A soft breeze found its way in through the shutters, and there was a gentle ticking somewhere in the house, coming up through the floorboards like the beat of a wooden heart.

"Alfie?" she said, and she turned and opened her eyes but the bedroom was still empty. The only movement came from mites of dust blowing about in the air.

They found Eddie's body in the mudflats just three days after the news of Alfie's death. His clothes had been neatly folded and placed on the dry ridge—a pale white heel and the crook of an arm sticking up from the mud that he had given himself to, opening his mouth to it, his throat to it, his stomach, disappearing in the night and being taken by the mudflats and marshes like many before. No one spoke about why he had done it.

His mother had not gone to pieces like Lydia's mother had. Instead, she had driven to Wales herself in an old Austin Six to tell Eddie's brother, Arthur, who was lodging in the same street as Lydia, next to the working men's club. She stayed with the family for two whole days. Lydia saw the both of them out walking on the hills and had felt bitterly jealous.

She listened to the quiet, then closed her eyes and tried to imagine her mother clattering around in the kitchen, Father reading the paper and listening to *Henry Hall's Guest Night,* Alfie swerving on the gravel as he pulled up on his bicycle. She thought of Button coming down the corridor, the sound of his soft footsteps and the rattling of the lamb as it trundled over the floorboards with squeaking wheels. She imagined him at the end of the hallway, wet and dead now from a drowning; the silhouette of him and the lamb, the gas mask over its head. *You've got to take care of him,* her mother had said. But she hadn't. She had left him. She wondered what the boys were doing to him now that she wasn't there to protect him, to say *No* and *Stop it* and *Leave him alone.* He didn't have the words let alone the voice to defend himself. They would taunt him worse than ever. His face seemed to ask for it. His arms and legs begged to be bloodied.

In her own room she hauled her suitcase out from underneath her bed, then clicked open the catches and lifted the lid. Boys can be such animals, Heiden had said. And he was right. She couldn't go back to Wales, but she needed to go somewhere.

She put in clean underwear, socks, and a change of dress, then took a small towel from the spare room where it had been put aside for the soldiers and her toothbrush and toothpaste from the bathroom. She collected a bar of soap, lipstick, blusher, and a brush from her mother's drawer. For the time being, she shut the case and pushed it under her bed. At the window she looked at the line of seashells laid along it: the rose petal tellin with both halves still attached to each other like a pair of pink wings; half a cockle that her father had varnished for her so that the smear of brown in its ridges looked like caramel. There was a king's crown, a Florida cone, a Scotch bonnet, and beaded periwinkle, all of which she had found herself somewhere along the shore. She picked up a giant conch that her father had brought back for her from one of his trips abroad and held it to her ear. From within the smooth shining twist of the shell she could hear the breath of the sea.

On Shingle Street she and Alfie had once found a line of white cockles leading down to the water's edge. They had followed it over the shingle as it arced around the spreading mats of sea pea and campion, and in between the clumps of kale. With the late afternoon sun still shining, the line of shells had been bright against the shingle, as if glowing in the heat.

Alfie told her that they'd been laid out by sea nymphs in the dead of night, and for a moment or two she had believed him, or at least had wanted to.

The line stopped abruptly several feet from the lap and swilling of the waves.

The tide's gone out, Alfie said. *The nymphs won't be able to get out onto the shore unless we take the line down to the water.*

So for an hour they scoured the beach for cockles, then laid them out, extending the line right down to the surf so that under the night sky the sea nymphs could follow it up onto the beach and sing and dance on the sand.

He held the six metal dog tags in the clench of his hand and blew into the curl of it as if he was blowing them good luck. The tin was some distance from the doorstep, nestled into the scuffed gravel, and he had been flicking the tags for almost half an hour but only got one in. He could sense the girl behind him, sitting on the stairs, watching.

He opened his hand, and with his thumb he positioned one of the tags and flicked it so that it pinged off the side of the tin and into the gravel.

Lehmann, Kappel, Pfeiffer, and Theissen. If you said the names in order it gave them a rhythm that he would never now forget. The faces of all but Diederich were burned against the back of his head. Five men, with Heiden the sixth, blacking out their faces in the cabin of the S-boat as it had sped out from Zeebrugge. How long ago had that been now? Four nights? Five?

They had packed and repacked their kit bags, ensuring everything was tightly wrapped in oilskin, then huddled around the table beneath the deck, poring over maps and photographs. Shingle Street. Bawdsey Point. The manor house and radio masts, the fenced perimeters and pillboxes. From behind the twin mounted guns and the cannon, men up on the deck studied the sky for aircraft and the sea for British torpedo boats, binoculars held to their eyes as the boat cut its channel through the water.

Lowering his head so only the men at the table could hear, he had drawn a tiny cross on the map with the tip of his pencil. If anything untoward happened and they were split up, he told them, he knew of a place near to the landing point where they could reconvene: a house on the edge of a village, nearest the shore and beyond the marsh. He wrote the name lightly on the map and left it long enough for them to read it before he rubbed it out.

The idea had been like a growth, getting larger and clearer and making him believe in it. He sometimes found himself wanting to laugh at it, at its sheer audacity, because—despite everything—he was here and still alive. Perhaps he had suffered enough and deserved a second chance. When he stepped out of this house again he would have a new skin, his old self rubbed out. Heiden would be dead.

He stood up from the doorstep and listened, then quietly pulled the pistol from his pocket. He had heard something crack, and something was moving the branches in the undergrowth between the garden and the narrow country lane. His eyes scanned back and forth, until a blackbird burst from the bushes. He raised his pistol as it took to the sky but he did not fire.

"What was that?" said the girl.

She was still on the steps behind him, now standing anxiously.

"Nothing," he said. "A bird."

He sat back down again and rested his elbows on his knees. He could hear the girl edging a few steps lower down the stairs. Her nervousness was making him uneasy.

It had started with a name on a map and a memory of a conversation held with an English naval officer. A village called Willemsley. A house called Greyfriars. Sitting with Lieutenant Schöller and the others in that blown-out café on the beach at Dieppe, he had barely been able to take his eyes from the map.

How close would they be to this man's house? A mile maybe? Two at most?

Greyfriars.

He picked out another dog tag and flicked it at the can, where it hit the rim and pinged off. Five tags in the gravel. He was beginning to wonder himself why no one had come. He had been here for four days and there had been no sight or sound of anyone but the one single soul wandering around the side of the house and halfheartedly trying the door. The boredom was eating at him, just as it had done in Norway, his mind wandering to places he didn't want to be taken, to faces he didn't want to see. A naked boy half-buried in the snow. Vomiting into a gutter outside a railway administration building in Narvik. A knife going deep into a man's neck. Eva's dead eyes.

In the S-boat coming over they had been too caught up in their own personal anxieties to talk much. It would be easier to blank these men out of his head if he knew nothing about them. He didn't even want to see their faces and yet now there they were, scratched into his mind. When the man called Kappel tried to show him a photograph of his girlfriend in Koblenz, Heiden had looked blankly at the face but said nothing, as if nothing had registered with him at all. Then he turned back to sorting his kit bag.

I'm just trying to make conversation, said Kappel. *That's all. Fucking asshole.*

They had gathered on the deck—the night was cloudy but serene—and carefully lowered themselves over the side of the boat, slipping into the water. The sea glistened and prickled through their uniforms, catching at their breath. Lights off, engines still and silent as the huddle of hooded silhouettes watched from the side. Then, with a nod and a hand signal, one by one they peeled away from the boat, six men fanning out, their breaststrokes barely etching a ripple. Their rucksacks, strapped to their chests, clung like limpets, their ammunition boots, tied and hanging from their necks, dragging beneath them through the water.

Heiden looked up again. The storm was closing in; a darkness filling the sky.

He flicked the last tag and it clipped the edge of the tin and fell, rattling in. He got up and collected the tags from among the gravel and then fished the final one out from inside the can. He shined it against the thigh of his trousers and read the soldier's number and unit. It was the young German private he'd been with in the dynamite store: Alexander Bürckel.

It was from the awkward height of the attic window that she saw the bicycle. She doubted herself at first because although the clouds were thickening over to the east and a grayness was creeping across the land, the road itself was still bathed in sun and prone to shimmers and mirages. He might have been a shadow. But as he came closer there was no denying it. It was a man, and he was cycling slowly down the lane towards the house.

She clung to the lip of the window. The backs of her calves were starting to quiver and the balls of her toes beginning to ache. She lowered herself and then pushed up again to look. As he drew nearer he became clearer, and she became more certain that it was Old Mr. Howe, panniers on either side of the back wheel for his letters, and the basket at the front. There was the gait of the bike as well, the effort of turning the pedals show-ing his age, and the bike swerving this way and that across the lane as he tried to keep it steady in the heat. She could imagine him puffing and panting beneath his cloth cap, the sweat running down the back of his wrinkled neck, the heat blasting up off the road. She watched him as he came closer and she banged on the window, knowing that from so far away he wouldn't hear, but she willed him to look up anyway, and see her.

His progress was slow and the bike wobbled from side to side. As she watched him grow nearer he kept vanishing behind the lines of trees. When he reached the point of the road that disappeared completely from sight, she hurried down the attic steps and then stopped, listening. She couldn't be sure where Heiden was. She ran to the top of the stairs and leaned over the banisters. The front door was ajar but she couldn't see him anywhere.

Her parents' room offered the best view of the drive, and she ran in and pushed two of the window slats apart so that she could see. She watched the lane, trying to glimpse him through the trees at the edge of the garden, and then he was at the gate and getting off his bike, propping it against a tree, and coming through, his cap deep over his eyes so that she could barely see his face. The sky above him was darkening as he came down the drive. There was something odd about him, about the way he walked in his heavy boots, and it was then, when he was halfway down the drive, that the shot suddenly fired, and his body jerked and turned and fell.

She pressed herself back against the wall and clenched her eyes shut. Not him. Not him as well. Not Mr. Howe. She felt sick to her stomach, everything tightening to a fist. She could hear Heiden coming from the sitting room downstairs, his footsteps out the door and across the gravel. By the time the second shot came, she was already running down the stairs.

The branches snatched at her as she pushed through the wood. The sudden rain fell in torrents, soaking her dress to her skin. The storm clouds were so dark that it seemed like nightfall. All she saw through the rain were the dark figures of trees. The man was a murderer. Why had she let herself think he would protect her or care for her, why had she allowed herself to see a gentleness in him that she now knew wasn't there?

He'd been crouched over the body on the drive. If he'd seen her or heard her leave, he had let her go; but now she could hear him coming, slipping and stumbling in the darkness behind her. *Wait!* he shouted. *Wait!* He would shoot her down. She knew it. A bullet through the back. Or he would slice open her throat, just like the dead soldier they'd found. She'd imagined it so many times. Her body left where she fell. He would let the wood grow over her and bury her so nobody would find her, and there she would rot away and be forgotten. No one would think of her anymore.

The trees were so densely packed that it was hard to see where she was running. She almost twisted her ankle but saved herself, her hand grabbing at a trunk as she fell, and she carried on running just as she'd run in Wales, the boys coming after her with their sticks. *Stop! Lydia! Wait!*

She glanced over her shoulder and saw a glimpse of him through the trees, gaining on her. She was drawing nearer to the coastal lagoons and mudflats and she could see the silvery sheen of the marshes ahead. And then she burst out of the wood into the openness, and abruptly stopped. The reed beds, the salt marshes, and the boggy grasslands were all gone. She wiped the rain from her eyes. Everything was water. Half a mile away on the shore she could see the tips of the concrete blocks, the fencing, the Martello tower to the south. Hanging over the coastline, hundreds of feet in the air, was a barrage balloon tethered with ropes. An explosion boomed along the beach and there was thick smoke. Between her and the soldiers though was nothing but a huge unbreachable expanse of water being pummeled by the rain.

She looked along the perimeter of the wood but there was

no easier way across. Scattered around in the water were raised islands of grass and occasionally the sagging, broken lines of fencing disappearing beneath the surface. She could hear him coming, almost upon her; she couldn't turn back. She stood for a moment and then waded in. Her feet disappeared into the soft sludge at the bottom, each step sinking deeper until it was almost impossible to pull out. The water came up to her knees and then rose higher with every step so that she struggled to keep her balance. She took another couple of steps forward, hauling her feet out of the mud and keeping her arms high above her. She heard him splashing into the water behind her.

"Wait! Lydia! Stop!"

She tried to carry on, hurrying more than ever, but it was such a struggle, and then he was behind her and grabbing at her wrist. She felt an arm around her and they both fell in. He shouted something in German, choking as he went under and resurfaced; and then he lifted her up, and she didn't kick, she didn't fight—she wrapped herself around him and cried, sobbing into the wet warmth of his neck as he slopped back through the water with her.

"I had to do it," he said, panting. "It was to protect us; to protect you."

"But Mr. Howe..." She cried.

"It wasn't him. It wasn't anyone," he said.

"But it was his bike. I saw it. I saw him."

He wiped the rain and mud from his face. "Look at me," he said. "I don't know who this Mr. Howe is, but, I promise you, it wasn't him."

He carried her all the way back through the woods, out into the garden and across the lawn to the house, where he set her down, dripping, on the drive. The body of the man lay half-twisted in the gravel. Heiden crouched down next to it and gently rolled it over. The man was wearing Old Mr. Howe's clothes, but she saw now that he was much younger, the face solemn and rugged, with eyes of such a dark brown color that they seemed almost black. She felt her stomach turn and a sour sick taste rising up into her throat. She didn't want to look at him but she couldn't help herself. His mouth was partially open and she saw he had a chipped tooth, almost broken into a fang. She could still smell his sweat.

Heiden unfastened Old Mr. Howe's jacket. Beneath it the man wore another. It was little wonder that he had been panting, particularly in the muggy heat. She recognized the Essex Regiment shoulder flash on the khaki blouse, the same that her German soldier had been wearing when he'd first appeared at Greyfriars and the same as the man they'd found in the woods. She watched as he rifled through the man's pockets, taking out a knife, pistol, bullets wrapped in a white handkerchief, and a tin that had a tiny compass inside.

He walked over to the bicycle and opened up the panniers on either side of the rear wheel, pulling out undelivered letters and dropping some of them there on the drive. When he was done he came back and searched again inside the man's clothes.

"He had a pack," he said. "He must have hidden it somewhere."

She nodded. "What was his name?"

He told her. Diederich.

"Was he German?"

"Mm," he said.

"But what was his real name?"

He was still rummaging around, undoing the man's belt and feeling around the waistband of his trousers. He pulled out three more bullets.

"His Christian name," she said.

"I don't know," he said. "It doesn't matter." He looked at her. "Lydia, listen, I had no choice. You do understand that, don't you?"

She said nothing as he hauled the man up so that he could feel around the back of him.

"What happened to the marshes?" she said. "All that water..."

"Flooded," he said. "They've done it to stop gliders and tanks from landing."

"They did it on purpose?"

He did not answer but let the body slump back into the gravel. He slipped the bullets into his pocket. Then he unbuttoned the man's shirt and pulled out a dog tag from around his neck. He took it in both hands and snapped it in two; then replaced the chain inside the man's shirt and did the buttons back up. He tucked the half tag he'd removed into his pocket; then he glanced at her over his shoulder.

"You need to change your clothes. You're wet through," he said.

She sat on the edge of the bath, the door locked and a chair wedged beneath the handle. The rain was easing off, pattering at the window, and inside the bathroom was gloomy. She was covered in fresh cuts and grazes; everything seemed to sting.

For a while she cried silently to herself. She couldn't do this anymore. She couldn't be on her own. She thought about Alfie and whether he was lying under clods of earth in France somewhere or maybe scattered into pieces or maybe nothing but dust blowing across an empty field. She prayed for him and for her father because if there was a God and he was a good God, he would send her father back to her. He wouldn't take her father and mother as well as Alfie. No God could be that cruel.

Eventually she went downstairs in clean clothes and stepped out onto the soggy doormat. The last drops of rain were being wrung from the sky, plopping with a dull *putt putt* into the tin can in the gravel. The sky was gray and miserable but the air felt fresh at last.

He had dragged the body across the lawn and under the trees, and now he was digging out a hole with her father's old shovel. His clothes were soaked and darkened by the rain, and his face, hands, and arms were covered in mud. He looked more like a creature than a man. He turned his head and glanced at her; then he dug the shovel in deep and levered out some soil. She wondered if she should help him. There should be some sort of ceremony. They should say a prayer at least, make a cross, ask God for forgiveness; but she knew that Heiden wouldn't and that she couldn't either, and only when the hole was deep enough and she'd watched him push the body in with his foot did she step back into the house.

Now she sat within the dark folds of the wardrobe and reached her hand out into the darkness in the hope that Button was there. The truth was this: if the boys hadn't hurt Button they would have hurt her. That was what she had told herself and made herself believe. It was the reason why she'd let them do it sometimes, and why she had abandoned him. And now it was her that was abandoned; this was her punishment. *What goes around comes around,* her father had said.

She sobbed quietly into her knees. She could hear the soldier in the bathroom and clamped her hands over her ears. She didn't want him in her thoughts. She didn't want him in the house. She didn't care for him anymore. She wanted him to disappear—not die but to never have existed—and take all the bad things that he'd done away with him.

After a while she came out of the wardrobe and stared blankly about the room, the space made for men who she wished would hurry up and come. And yet one man *had* come and Heiden had shot him. A German. A Nazi. One of his own. She slumped face down on her mother's bed and tried to make herself cry again, but she couldn't even do that. She clamped her mouth to the mattress and tried not to breathe, but even suffocation was impossible.

She could hear him, his feet heavy on the floorboards. Cupboards banging shut. Footsteps in and out of the house, hurrying. Things being thumped into the wall. After a while she could bear it no longer and had to get up and see what he was doing, but the house was quiet and dark again, all the blackout boards put back into place, shutting the light back out as if it had never been allowed in at all.

She found him in the kitchen, where he had lit two oil lamps. Handing one to her, he started off down the hall. She hurried after him up the stairs, and by the time she had caught up with him he was in the bathroom, his shirt draped over the side of the bath. He was studying the wound in his shoulder as if he had only just noticed it. He glanced at her and then turned his attention back to the wound.

"We're leaving," he said. "So pack what you need."

She stared at him. "Where are we going?"

"Come on," he said. "It's time."

He had woken with a jolt. The concrete floor of the annex room was frozen beneath him. He felt the grit and dust under his hand. He had been dreaming of Eva, of lying next to her, stroking her; his fingers still tingled with the memory of her skin.

He listened for the gale outside but heard nothing and looked up from the floor. The window above him cast a trapezoid of light on the wall. He sat up, listening to the silence—the storm now gone—and shook out the coat he had been lying on. He was stiff and cold and aching. Through the window the sky was bright and everything was smothered in snow. In the distance the Ofoten Railway line slowly etched its way round the mountains. He scanned the track but there was no sign of any life.

He found Harris laid out on the floor. Pendell too was wedged in the corner of the dynamite room, asleep. Gruber sat against the wall, picking a peach slice out of a tin with his grubby fingers.

He offered Heiden the slice as if it were a slippery fish. The juice dripped down his hand, leaving sticky trails through the dirty skin. When Heiden declined, he poked it into his mouth and swallowed it, then lifted the tin and drained the juice down his throat, shaking out the last drops.

Where's Bürckel?

Gruber shrugged. *That Englishman's dead as well,* he said, motioning to the man Harris with his foot. *Lucky bastard.*

Heiden squatted beside the body. The man's eyes were glassy and his face was so white as to be almost translucent, a short beard prickling through the skin. He fastened the button on the man's jacket.

We should shoot the other one too and get out of here, Gruber said, *while the storm has stopped.*

Heiden took his Luger from his holster and pulled out the magazine. Three bullets left.

Yes. I'll do it, he said.

As he shaved, his eyes felt puffy and swollen. The shovel he had used to dig the grave had given him splinters; he could see them like niggling little pellets of guilt tucked beneath the skin. He tried not to think about Diederich or the others. Diederich had been the last he needed to dispose of, but now at last they could leave. What was done was done.

He rinsed the knife in the sink—the water brought in from the pump in a bowl—then opened his mouth and dragged the blade down beneath his nostrils. Then he scooped water up to splash on his eyes and held his hands there for a moment, bathing his skin in the coolness and letting it trickle through his fingers and down his arms to the tips of his elbows. He took a breath— *God help us*—and dried his face with a towel.

He would put all of it behind him. Berlin, Poland, Norway, Normandy. The orchestra. The parks and picnics. Sitting on the bench in the institute garden waiting for Eva. He would box it up and bury it; he would turn and walk away.

If there was no God then what was it, he wondered, that had made him who he was? Who had cast him as German when he could have been a Pole, a Jew, or a Bolshevik, English even? This could have been his house, his home, his clothes, this girl could have been his daughter. This life here—and why not?—could have been his.

He turned his shoulder and looked at the wound, less raw and inflamed than it had been, and yet when he gently touched the skin around the edge he still flinched at its soreness. It looked like a toothless mouth and inside the wound was red and tender. In time it would heal and leave a scar. An overzealous new recruit on training. We got it out in the end, he would tell people, but it's left a bit of a hole. He put on a clean dressing, smoothed down his hair, and studied himself, straining his head to stare over his shoulder in the cabinet mirror this way and that.

He smiled, and then tried again, not raising the lips quite as far. All of these things he needed to perfect, if only just for the hours to come. Nothing—not a single thing—should be left to chance.

From the wardrobe he pulled out the last clean white shirt and a pair of mustard-colored tweed trousers and jacket. The shirt fitted as it should, as did the trousers (if slightly long). He found a brown knitted tie that was odd but he rather liked it. He tied it, tightening the knot and straightening it so that it was just so. Yes—everything would be put right. He was not Heiden anymore.

At the dressing table, he trimmed the sides of his hair with a pair of scissors, pushing the damp hair down with his fingers so that he had a better chance of cutting it in a straight line. He carefully combed it into place, giving himself a parting that in time his hair would get used to but at the moment it fought against. He picked up the photograph frame, unclipped the back, and took out the picture. Pendell and his wife on their wedding day, standing outside a church. He looked at himself and at the image; then he carved the same slightly startled expression out of his face, and then readjusted it.

"My son thinks war is an adventure," he said, mimicking the man. "Is that what this is? This generation's great adventure?"

The likeness was better than he could have hoped. The man called Harris had mistaken him after all, so too had Gruber. Even the girl had said how much he reminded her of her father. People were being changed everywhere: identities, religions, politics, beliefs, opinions, loves—everything in a state of flux. A great and global redistribution of everything that they had known. Every man came back from the front different; it was the reason why half had signed up in the first place. They wanted the war to forge them into new men.

Eva. He allowed himself to think about her one last time: lying in the park, her head in his lap, her eyes shiny with sunlight, sparkling bright. That smile, that bubble of laughter. How she'd wrapped her arm around his neck and pulled him gently down, rising up from his lap so that their lips met, so that they would spark and fuse together.

But they didn't. Not when he thought about it now, not even when he tried to force it. She leaned forward but blurred away, and instead it was the face of George Arthur Pendell that he saw in the reflection—side by side at the window as they had been that day.

You want my knife? Heiden said.

Yes. Don't you trust me?

And so he had given the man the knife and watched as he made the three incisions in the match, one up from the base to form two legs, one on either side for arms beneath the blackened head. Pendell had handed the knife back and prized open the bits of match until the figure was formed, then he propped him there against the glass. *A memento,* he had said.

He sat on the bed sorting through the documents. Two piles now. One pertaining to George Arthur Pendell: all the various naval certificates and documents he'd gathered, the letters and photographs, the Royal Navy certificate of service he'd taken from the man—all the evidence he'd need to get him across the line. The other pile related to Jack Henry Bayliss. A name, and nothing more than that, stitched into a dead Englishman's uniform. Fictional letters from a fictional family, identity cards, a soldier's service and pay book, an autographed photograph of a girl he'd never met but who was supposed to be his love, all the bits and pieces of a life created for him. He would need Pendell's identity to get him to the cottage, and there he would transform himself again, this time into Jack Henry Bayliss. And then later into someone else, and then someone else, and then someone else, using all the stories he'd gathered—the week's holiday in Southwold, the wedding in the New Forest, the Torquay Saloon bought from a dealer in Stowmarket—to make each new identity real, until Heiden was long left behind and forgotten, stubbed out almost as completely as Eva had been.

He took a match from one of his pockets and put it in his mouth to suck on; then rummaging around in his kit bag he pulled out his torch, a penknife, and the dog tags and distributed them into the pockets of his new clothes. He flicked through Pendell's certificate of service, seeing the entry where someone had written under distinguishing marks: *Bullet wound, left shoulder.*

They had set off down the slope through the trees and across the snowy clearing. There was no sign of the dead boy called Lewis. His body was completely buried. They crunched through the cold, Pendell gathering his coat around him and Heiden following, his gun trained on him. The air was crisp. The world smelled clean and new.

At the other side of the clearing Heiden motioned him on into the trees. They pushed through the birch and the spruce, dislodging snow from the frosted branches until he told the man to stop and Pendell turned to look at him. He didn't seem afraid, but stood tall, letting his coat hang open, defiant even to the cold.

Was it foresight or divine intervention that had made him say it to the man? *Empty your pockets. Throw it all into the snow.*

The man did—a Royal Navy certificate of service, some letters, a bullet, some coins—and then stood there with the insides of his pockets hanging out to prove he had nothing left.

They stood for a moment—a moment's indecision; then Heiden tossed him the remains of the chocolate. *Take this,* he said. *Now go on. Go!*

There was a slight flicker in the man's eyes.

Did you hear me? I said, go! Run!

The man glanced behind him, at the forest that was endless and silent and empty. He turned back, his eyes still uncertain.

I can shoot you if you would prefer, said Heiden.

He held up the pistol, straightening his arm.

But . . . said the man, then nothing more.

Heiden's finger found the trigger and started to slowly squeeze.

Wait, he said. *Your daughter. Who sits and waits for you. What's her name?*

Lydia, said the man. *It's Lydia. Why do you want to know?*

Heiden didn't reply. He just felt that he needed to know. He held still, waiting, clenching his teeth against the bite of the cold as he held the man steady in his line of fire. Then, just when he thought he would have to shoot, the man turned and slowly began to walk, his boots pushing deep into the snow.

He thought now of the man called Pendell disappearing into the trees, of the darkness slowly taking him until he was little more than a shadow and then nothing at all. Only then, when he had been sure that Pendell was gone, had he fired a single shot up into the branches.

He gathered the various documents, certificates, and papers up into his bag and fastened it, and then went to the window.

Bürckel had been shot as he stood outside the store, still fastening his trousers. He had found Gruber inside.

Oh. You. I almost put a bullet through you. It's not very smart, looking like the enemy, you know.

Gruber laughed and turned back to his packing, stuffing the two remaining tins of food into his bag.

You actually did it then?

Yes. Didn't you hear the shot?

That was when Heiden fired his last bullet directly into the man's back and watched as Gruber's body tipped into the wall, then slumped to the floor. He remembered the sudden flush of silence, all sound suddenly gone, and he had stood there alone in the store for a moment before he finally turned Gruber's body over, the man's dead glassy eyes still registering his last moment of surprise.

Had it been a cowardice in him that had sent the man out into the snow? A moment's weakness? Or had he seen something in the man's eyes, had he recognized so much of himself in him that he couldn't bring himself to kill him, as if putting a bullet into the man's heart would have been like putting a bullet into his own? Sometimes he had fleeting moments of fear that the man might suddenly reappear, as if in his quiet defiance, he wouldn't even die. But he knew that was impossible. By the time he himself got back to Narvik, even wrapped in several coats, he'd been on the verge of hypothermia. It plagued him: the fact that he had not been able to shoot Pendell; and now, it seemed, he couldn't shoot his daughter either.

What had the girl taught him? That magic could be seen in the simplest things: the matchstick was a wooden man, the voice of the sea lived within the curls of a shell, the halls of the house were filled with angel dust that glittered in the sunlight. The house, Greyfriars, had been a sanctuary of sorts for them both; but now it was time to go.

He looked at his reflection in the mirror—the transformation was complete. He could not love another woman—that would be a betrayal—but perhaps he could love a child as if she had been their own. In that, there might be some happiness, even if it didn't last long, even if he had to leave her behind soon. For now, he would take her with him and love her as his own. He'd change her into someone different, and make her love him too.

✶ ✶ ✶

She stood to one side as he hauled the stone cherub out of the way, then dug out the dead cauliflowers, flipping their shrunken heads onto the lawn with her father's shovel before digging the hole. She had heard people talk of treachery, and now that she had showed him where the petrol can was buried, she felt sick to her stomach about it. He was intent on them leaving though, and she had no choice but to help. She didn't want to give him any reason to abandon her there, and she didn't want to be left behind—she needed him to help her find her mother.

All the color of the day was fading, while out to sea rain clouds were brewing again, another storm on its way.

The shovel clanged against something metal and he got down on his knees to scuff the dirt away. The can was heavy and he struggled to pull it out of the hole by its handle, the petrol slopping around inside. Then with a spurt of laughter he held it up and said, "Your mother is a very resourceful lady. You know, I rather wish I'd met her."

Lydia said nothing and stared at the hole. *I'm not helping him,* she told herself. *I'm doing this for me.*

He threw the shovel in among the vegetables and set off towards the garage. She looked up at the house and was suddenly filled with a fear that she might never see it again.

She hurriedly collected her identity card, the maps, and her stories from beneath the broken floorboard under the piano, along with the crumpled and dusty documents—various marriage certificates and birth certificates—that had already been there. She packed them into her suitcase, along with some clothes; then she changed her mind and took the maps back out and, folding them, wedged them into her gas mask box, next to her mother's letters.

She watched him from the window tipping the broken radio into the hole in the garden where the petrol canister had been. He shoveled the soil back in and patted it down, and hauled the cherub back into place, straightening the boy until he was just so.

He tossed the dead vegetables that he'd pulled up into the hedgerow at the back of the garden and raked through the sooty remnants of the bonfire, picking out one or two small discs that might have been buttons and pocketing them.

Inside the house they set the rooms straight, turning everything back to how it was as if the last few days had been a dress rehearsal, and now that they had somehow muddled through, they could do it all for real. Beds were pushed back into place, the dining room straightened, candles and trinkets put back on the dresser; everything was just how her mother had left it. The blackout frames were pushed back into the windows, the nails pulled out of the back door so that it could be opened once more. He filled one of her mother's cases with tins from the larder and a box of Weetabix and lugged it out to the car.

She found the figure resting on the windowsill of her parents' bedroom. A tiny matchstick figure propped against the glass, just like her father used to make. She picked him up and studied him, hardly believing what she was holding. Was it possible that he had come home, that he was there in the house with her, that he would take her in his arms and hold her? *Don't cry, missy. Don't cry.*

She sat on her brother's bed with his toy wooden soldier in her hands and shut her eyes. She could feel the warmth of his light behind her, the tingling of it across her skin. She could feel it glowing in her bones. Alfie. Dear Alfie.

"I'm scared," she whispered. "Come with me, Alfie. I need you to come with me."

She tried to feel a difference in the room, to feel him behind her, to feel that slight warmth, that glow, get stronger. Against the back of her eyelids she imagined him sitting on the ledge, just as he had been that night, his wings and his cricket whites and his bright blue eyes. She opened her eyes and turned to see him—hoping one last time—but the bedroom remained stubbornly empty.

When it finally got dark, she was bundled into the car, her suitcase placed in the boot next to his kit bag and the suitcase of food. He handed her the picnic blanket so that she could wrap it over her knees when she got cold. Mr. Tabernacle was sitting in the back, his single gem of an eye so black that it looked like a finger hole in the darkness.

She waited while he locked the door of the house and returned the key to beneath the stone cherub, then shut the double garage doors, scraping them through the gravel. He opened the driver's side and climbed in. For a few moments he studied the switches around the instrument board and felt at the gear lever, and then he started the engine. It coughed and choked, rumbling into life with a clanking sound from somewhere beneath them. He undid the button on her father's jacket and ran his fingers around the inside of the collar, then took a map from the pocket of his door and handed it to her.

She looked at him. "Where are we going?" But he was concentrating on putting the car into gear. There was a grating sound and it jerked forward. He fumbled at the gear stick, and the car lurched again before setting off down the drive. She turned back to look at the house as they passed through the gateway and turned into the lane.

As they made their way along the road she kept glancing behind her to see if she could see Greyfriars, if only its two chimney pots helplessly poking up from behind the trees, but eventually even they were gone. Her father had been made to remove one of the car lights. The one that still remained was screened so that only narrow slits of light could break through creating barely more than a haze. Heiden drove slowly but steadily, both hands on the wheel. His eyes were focused on the murky darkness ahead. She looked over the silhouetted hedgerows. In the far distance along the coastline, something was burning—a seething orange glow spreading up into the sky. Germans laying waste to the land. The smoke stained the night an even darker gray and then thinned out along a smudged line as if the sky was teasing it out into something soft and fine. A muffled boom echoed across the field and shuddered through the car. She wondered where he was taking her. A camp somewhere? Some military headquarters? Perhaps a field filled with tents. Or a field with nothing in it, that he would walk her out across until there was nothing and no one around, and then he would shoot her dead.

They made their way along the lane, the engine rickety, and every joint and nut and bolt in the car seemed to judder and quake. The road was still slippery with rain, and littered with stones and twigs and chomped-up bits of concrete.

Rain began to clatter at the windscreen. She looked about for Germans, but it would be the towns and cities that they would be after, he had told her; they would hardly bother capturing the fields. She wondered where her mother was, and Mr. Morton too, and Archie Chittock and Tommy Sparrow and the rest of the Local Defence Volunteers, and even Button—poor Button, she wished he was with her. There was another boom along the coast and the car swerved. He glanced at her, reassuring, and leaned further forward in his seat. She wrapped the picnic blanket around her legs. She could see the ridges of his knuckles gripping hard at the wheel.

★ ★ ★

They stopped to drag a rusting bedstead out of the way and a broken handcart that had been set out as a vain attempt to block the road. When they reached the village the streets were deserted. Glass from the broken windows of Pringle's shop was blown across the street, and it crinkled and crunched under the tires as they drove through. The unlit streetlights stood sorry headed. The blacked-out windows were dead and lifeless. Some of the front doors were broken through, and she glanced around for shadows moving—any sign of life. They swerved around a blown-out oil canister that looked as if something dreadful had erupted from it. There were coils of wire across the side streets and numbers painted large and white on front doors. And then the village was gone and the road took them through the blackened fields. As she realized how hopeless everything was, she thought she might be sick.

They skirted the edge of Rendlesham Forest and drove out onto the open heath.

Eventually he slowed and without warning pulled into a gateway. With the flick of a switch the car fell silent, and the vague light against the tangle of gorse was gone. He didn't look at her but stared out of the window at the darkness around them. He would kill her now, out on the heath. He would drag her body away from the road and leave it under the gorse and nobody would find her for days or weeks or years. She could feel herself tightening so much that she might crack or burst or scream. She pressed herself into the seat and fumbled for the door handle.

"Don't," he said without turning.

She could see his heavy form next to her but his face was in shadow. She heard his breath, the trawl of it like the sea. His hands slowly released the steering wheel.

"There are things I want to discuss with you, Lydia."

"Things?" she said.

"Yes."

"Are you going to kill me?"

He turned to look at her. "No. No, I'm not going to kill you."

"Then will you let me go?"

"No. I can't do that. You know I can't."

"Why not? I won't tell anyone that I've seen you. I won't say anything, I promise."

"We need to be together now, Lydia. We need to help each other."

"But . . . where are we going?"

"We are going to the Cotswolds," he said. "Have you been? I think you're going to like it. It's ever so pretty. I know a little cottage there that we can live in. It used to belong to a friend of mine, a professor I once knew. No one is living there now. We can make it ours for a while."

"Ours?" She didn't understand.

"Yes. While we decide what to do."

What about the Germans, the invasion? She had been quite sure that he was going to take her to a camp.

"Have you ever wanted to change your name, Lydia—to call yourself something else?"

She looked at her reflection in the side window, the rain pummeling down her face in watery rivulets. The storm battered at the roof of the car. She turned back to him.

"I can't go with you," she said. "Wherever you're going . . . We have to find my mother. You promised."

"Yes, yes," he said. "And all in good time. I think we are going to be very happy."

He seemed suddenly uncertain. What had they stopped for? Was he sick? She had heard about soldiers that had seen dreadful things turning crazy, mad.

"This is what I wanted to talk to you about. We need to make an agreement," he told her. "When we reach the checkpoint, we will have to show them some identification, proof of who we are, where we live . . . and I am going to be your father."

"My—what?"

"I have his papers, his clothes, everything I need."

She stared at him.

"Do you understand? Do you understand what I'm saying, Lydia?"

Yes. Slowly she *was* understanding—everything that he had done. The jacket, shirt, braces, shoes, the side parting in his hair, the slight change in the way he moved, the way he talked, him practicing words that were new to him like *tapioca* and *cauliflower cheese*. All his snooping around, his collecting information.

She stared harder and tried to think of her father's face, but all she could see was the man sitting next to her, a man who wasn't her father, who was quite mad—she understood that now.

He clicked his finger and thumb at her.

"Are you listening? You have to pay attention, Lydia. Listen. We are going to a house that we are renting in the Cotswolds. That is what we are going to say. We are meeting your mother there, and I am your father. You tell them that, if they ask. If they ask you anything else, you agree with whatever I say. Otherwise, you say nothing. Do you understand?"

She looked at him. "Do you understand?" he said. "We need to get this right."

"What happens when my father comes back?"

He stared through the windscreen as the rain swept across it in currents.

"My real father," she said.

"And what if he's dead?" he said. "What if he doesn't come back, Lydia? Have you thought about that? You see, we find ourselves here in a bit of a situation, you and me. I mean, look at me, here in his clothes, in his car, with his documents, with his daughter, and looking just like him. Right now, no one but you would know. So, if they ask you, you tell them that I'm him, your father. Otherwise we won't get through. It's as simple as that. We just need to get through, and then we'll sort it out."

She stared at him. She couldn't believe what she was hearing. She shook her head.

"Do you want any chance of seeing your mother again?" he said. "If you don't arouse their suspicions they'll let us pass and there will be no reason to be afraid. I promise. Or do you want me to kill you? Because I will have to do that if you don't do what I say."

She began to cry. She didn't believe any of his promises anymore. How could she believe anything that he said? She looked at the windscreen and saw her father's face in it, a face that looked so much like hers, so much like his. She had the vague notion of someone talking, someone speaking right beside her.

"Listen to me. What I am telling you is the truth. Your father is gone."

"He's not gone. He's on a ship."

"But I can take his place. You can come with me and I can love you, I can look after you, I promise. I can be him in every way, any way you want—"

"No," she said. "No."

It was all she could manage.

"What if your mother is dead too? Think about that, Lydia. What if there is no one left? Who will look after you? Where will you go? What will you do? Have you thought about that? Have you? Who will feed you? Who will clothe you, Lydia? Who is going to care?"

Her tears streamed now thick and heavy.

"I can look after you," he said. "I can help you, I promise, with whatever you want. You just have to say it. You just have to tell them I'm your father, and come with me to the Cotswolds and to the cottage. We'll hide away there for a while. We'll be safe. And then we can do whatever we like. We can go anywhere. Be anyone we want."

She shut her eyes and felt the heat of the tears burning lines down her face.

"Please," he said. "Please."

As the car drove on she felt strangely numb to everything. The storm clouds pulled back across the sky and the rain eased. The car smelled damp and muggy. She stared at herself in the window. She didn't know what to do.

They passed a blown-up pillbox behind a hedge. She could hear the low drone of aircraft somewhere above them. She looked at the map in her lap but it was too dark to make anything out of it other than a tangle of roads and rivers. She had no idea of how to get them to the Cotswolds, or even where they were now that all the signposts had been taken down. He slowly maneuvered the car around logs in the road and an old railway sleeper. Further on, they had to drive up onto the verge to get around an old Morris Eight dumped in the middle of the road and completely filled with earth. It reminded her of the house on the beach that she had imagined filled to the roof with shingle, and the people who had lived inside, their throats filled with sand and grit and tiny crabs. She remembered the line of shells laid out down to the shore for the sea nymphs to follow. She would follow it now if she were there, all the way in.

The roadblock was simple enough, made of the trunk of a pine tree coiled with barbed wire and balanced between the joints of two smaller trunks that had been dug into the ground and acted as a gate. Three uniformed men manned it. One stood in the road and stopped each vehicle; another waited at the makeshift gate; and a third, younger than the others, ferried back and forth, helping first the man who was interrogating each driver and then running back to help his colleague lift the gate so that the vehicle could pass through. On one side of the road was a hexagonal pillbox, outside of which was a lit stove nestled in the grass. The makeshift gate was hauled up again and a truck passed through. Between the roadblock and the Crossley were two other cars, both black. Heiden mumbled something and slowed the car down to a crawl. Her heart was beating fast.

"Okay. If you remember what we talked about," he said, "everything will be all right." He lightly touched the back of her hand with his. "Yes?"

She felt the tingle in her skin where the tips of his fingers had made contact with her, and she nodded. It was as if, in that one touch, he had made her his.

"Now wipe your tears," he said.

They pulled up behind the car in front, the dim light of their headlight washing over its boot and bumper. It was a black, muddy Hillman Minx, a single man inside with his arm hanging out of the window. The jacket was tweed and dirty. Ahead of the Hillman was a larger car, and the two soldiers were questioning the driver and his passengers. Both soldiers stooped to speak through the window.

She looked through the side window at the woods beyond.

My father, she said to herself. *He's my father.*

If she did not mean it perhaps it would not matter.

The car up front pulled away under the makeshift barrier, and Heiden put their own car into gear and edged them forward.

As the two soldiers came to the window of the Hillman Minx

just in front of them, she saw their uniforms more clearly. It was unmistakable—the armbands had the letters LDV.

"They're Local Defence Volunteers," she said. "They're English!"

"Yes," he said.

"But the invasion...We heard it on the radio! The announcement!"

He turned and looked at her, but he said nothing.

"But..."

She desperately tried to remember the announcer she had heard on the radio. He had said something about London. She was sure of it. The name. But what else? Was it only that? The word *London?* It was Heiden who had said that it had fallen, and she had believed him, not questioned it. So, what had they prepared the house for? Who had they been waiting for? One man— Diederich—now dead? Had it all been a lie? And was this why he was pretending to be English? He wouldn't have wanted to take on a British identity if the Nazis had already invaded, but he would if he was the only German here, if there had been no German landing and England was still England and not overrun at all.

"Did you take my mother's money?" she said.

"What are you talking about?"

"My mother's money, under the floor."

"We don't have time for this. You have to remember what I told you. I'll help you find your mother," he said, "but only if you do what I told you to do and say what I tell—"

"Did you take my mother's money? From under the floor. There was a floorboard."

"No. I don't know what you're talking about."

She stared at him, hard.

"You've got to do what we agreed," he said. "I need you to listen to me."

She could see it in his face. She could tell from his eyes that he didn't know what she was talking about. If he had found the money he would have taken the documents as well. She wondered if they were what he had been turning the house upside down for—a handful of marriage certificates and birth certificates that were now hiding in her gas mask box.

She turned back to the window. If he hadn't taken the money from under the floorboard then her mother must have done so herself, and if her mother had taken it that might mean she was still alive—that she had gone from the house of her own accord.

"Lydia, this is serious. If they ask, you tell them I'm your father. You understand? We're in a defense zone. We have to get through."

The young soldier ran to help lift the gate, whilst the other stood back from the Hillman Minx as it drove under the raised trunk. It was only as its exhaust pipe dragged and clattered along the road that she remembered meeting it on the lane no more than four or five days ago. It was the man who had scared her with his pockmarked face. He had told her that she wasn't supposed to be there, that everyone was gone, and that she would get herself shot. She wished now that she'd gone with him, that none of this had happened.

Heiden edged the car forward to where the soldiers were and wound down the window. Spats of rain blew in and a head appeared. The man had red rugged cheeks and his hair dripped from under his cap. His shoulders were sodden through, his nose slightly puckered as if he were about to sneeze. She could barely look at him.

"Dreadful night," said Heiden.

"It's only supposed to be authorized personnel in here, sir," the man said. "I need to see your papers."

"Papers?"

"Yes. Your clearance permit, sir. You're not supposed to be in here without a clearance permit."

"Oh, I see. Well, I'm afraid they didn't give me one."

Something changed in the other man's voice. "Right. Well then, can I see your identity card please, sir?"

"I don't have it, I'm afraid. I've misplaced it."

"'Misplaced it'?"

"Yes, but I've got my certificate of service, various other documents and bits and pieces...I'm in the navy..." He took a small selection of papers from his pocket and handed them to the soldier who rifled through them, shining his torch over a photograph and then into Heiden's face. "You still need a permit, Lieutenant Commander..." He looked at the document in his hand. "...Pendell."

He shone the torch into the car and swept its beam over Lydia.

"Hello, what have we here? Under no circumstances, sir, are children allowed into the testing area. No members of the public, and no children, under any circumstances. It's extremely dangerous." It sounded like he was spouting from received instructions.

He held the torchlight into her face and then swung it so it glared at Heiden.

She squirmed in her seat. She couldn't breathe and it was too hot, even with the window open and the rain coming in.

Heiden moved his hand across his stomach as if to scratch then laid it there, resting. The soldier flicked through the various certificates and bits of paper again and then handed them back. "I think perhaps you ought to get out of the car, sir."

"Yes, yes. Of course."

Heiden opened the door and got out. The rain splashed off the door frame and into the car. She was suddenly cold and shaking. She needed to pee.

The man left at the gate watched. She glanced over her shoulder to see if any other cars were coming, but the road behind was empty and dark.

Outside, Heiden said something about Lydia running away and having to be fetched from the house. He kept calling her his daughter. She stared at her knees, her hands pushed between them. There was something about an escort. It was the escort that had the permit but he'd been called out somewhere else, an emergency.

"Ahh, that will be Shingle Street," said the second guard. "We found a German soldier on the beach there this afternoon."

"Good Lord. Dead, I hope," said Heiden. He laughed. But the guardsman didn't find it funny.

"And where are you going?"

"The Cotswolds. We have a house there. Nice and quiet. That's where my wife is."

"I see." He paused. "No permit. A misplaced identity card." He sucked air in through his teeth. "Who did you say your escort was?"

"I'm sorry, I can't remember the chap's name. Barnes or Burns or something."

"Bridges?"

"Yes, that's it. Bridges."

Judging by the soldier's grunt he didn't think much of the man.

"Right," he said. "Well...I better just have a look at your daughter's identity card as well. You have got *that,* I suppose?"

"Lydia has. Yes." He smiled.

The soldier leaned into the car, resting one hand on the driver's seat so he could lean across to her. She bit her teeth together.

"I need to see your card, miss," he said. "No need to be afraid. Won't take a moment and then you and your pa can be on your way."

She took her card from her gas mask box and handed it to the man. Her hands were trembling but he didn't seem to notice. While he was studying it he spoke to Heiden.

"You're in the navy then?"

"Yes. I've just come back from Norway." He leaned casually against the side of the car.

The soldier snorted. "A ruddy fiasco that was, I 'eard."

"Yes, rather."

The soldier returned the card to her and pulled back out, one hand holding the top of the door rim, his head still leaning in.

"You've almost got your father into a whole pile of trouble," he said. "Running away like that...And you've quite a drive to the Cotswolds. That's my wife's neck of the woods. Where in the Cotswolds is it?"

She looked at him. She couldn't think. She opened her mouth to try to form a word, a name, anything, but there was nothing there.

"Not sure? Bourton-on-the-Water, is it?" said the soldier. "Moreton-in-Marsh? Chipping Norton...? Stow-on-the-Wold?"

She shook her head.

"Your house then, is it?" said the soldier.

"Yes," she said.

"You been before?"

"Yes, lots of times. Lots."

"But you don't know where it is?"

She didn't know what to say. She glanced desperately at Heiden, her cheeks burning, but the soldier caught their eyes.

He stared at her, then leaned in closer so that his voice was almost a whisper. "Is everything all right, missy?"

She clamped her teeth together and nodded but her eyes were already filling—she couldn't help it. His smile slipped and for what seemed like an age he looked at her and she saw he was frightened too, and then, slowly, he lifted his hand from the driver's seat, the heel of his palm still down but his fingers raised to her in secret reassurance.

He carefully pulled out from inside the car. "Sorry, sir, but can I see your papers agai—"

There was a sudden shot and Lydia shrieked. Behind the door the man slumped heavily to the ground. She threw herself forward and pressed her head into her knees, wrapping her arms over herself. Shots came suddenly, fast and hard, and there was shouting; flashes of light played against the back of her eyes. Bullets panged off the metal, and the windscreen shattered, glass coming down over her. Bent double, she fumbled for the door handle as the shards of glass fell from her, and she pushed it open, tumbling out onto the side of the road. She scrambled onto the verge and into the ditch, and then, running as fast as she could, she stumbled down a bank and ran away into the woods and the dark mass of the night.

She ran on, hugging at her stomach, half breaths and sobs bursting out from between her clenched teeth. Her clothes were heavy and sodden to her skin. Her feet dragged like iron, and when she could run no more and walk no more, when every muscle was worn out, she fell to her knees and felt the dirt beneath her hands and the rain still pummeling against the back of her head.

The edge of the road that she had found herself on was wet and hard. She was sweating and panting. She had no idea how long she'd been running. Nor did she know quite where she was—just that she was out on the heath somewhere where Alfie had caught butterflies. The heath was sodden through and scented, the broom and heather rolling out into the dark and beyond, while above her the sky was black and cavernous, stuffed from end to end with cloud. The gunshots were the only sound she could hear now, still echoing in her head and making it hurt as if the echoes alone were striking holes into her skull. She pulled herself back up onto her feet and tried to stumble on.

TUESDAY

AT SOME POINT during that long night, with the road spanning out endlessly in front of her, she had found herself unable to go any further and had collapsed on the edge of the verge, taking breathless lungfuls of air. She had stared, she didn't know how long for, out into the empty blackness, her arms wrapped tightly around her knees, gently rocking herself, and the night clinging to her, dark and cold and wet. Not a single light could be seen. No sound could be heard but her breath. There had just been the gray fields rolling on like carpets of ash and the occasional scattering of trees standing like cloaked figures waiting for her to struggle up onto her feet again.

Through the village, down the middle of the road, past the blown-out petrol can and over the window glass blasted from Pringle's shop . . . She gave little thought as to what might have happened there. Gun practice. Bomb practice. A whole village cleared to become a testing ground. Trainee soldiers rushing through. She herself walked through the empty streets as if she were passing through a dream, her feet barely touching the ground, heart barely beating. Everything was desolate. Deserted. The front doors were sandbagged. Gardens were given to weeds. Vegetables going to seed. If there was gas, let it take her. Let it get into her mouth, her throat, her stomach and lungs, and let it sparkle there. Let her know nothing of what was to come until her whole body was succumbed to it and everything turned black.

She left the village behind, and the lane rolled on ahead of her. From above came the drone of a plane. She was going home. She had always been going home. Even in the silent nights in Wales when she'd lain in bed she had imagined walking home along the lane, the sound of tractors churning in the fields, cars cheerily tooting their horns as they passed, great tits and jenny wrens zipping along the hedgerows. When she got back everything would be different. She was quite certain of that. Alfie would be asleep in his room. Mother and Father would be in theirs. She could slip into Alfie's bed unnoticed and sleep for a hundred years; his breath washing over her skin, an arm around her, his heart beating into her back. She'd sit on her father's lap like she used to, or walk out into the snow with him. She'd take him by the hand. And everything would be warm and light. The sun would glow from deep within her and shine out of her wings.

She crunched up the drive, past the tin can now filled to the brim with water, and then stopped outside the house and looked up at the closed shutters and the patches of moss on the roof. Moonshine washed out from behind the clouds, giving silver lines to the house, to the edges of the walls, the guttering and windowsills. She stood on the steps and tried the door. Locked. She walked across the drive and onto the lawn, now wet and soggy beneath her feet. The stone cherub was heavy, and she struggled to edge it this way and that until she could see the key hidden beneath. She picked it up and cleaned it against her dress, then walked back across the lawn, feeling as if she were in a dream.

The key was stiff and reluctant, and it kept slipping in her hand. After a few tries though the mechanism clicked and she pushed open the door and, with relief, locked it again behind her. The house was black inside, and she crept silently into each room. The dining room. The study. The sitting room. Everything was dark and empty, the silhouettes of furniture looking barely there at all.

In the kitchen the back door stood ajar, the wood around the handle splintered and wrenched apart. She froze in the doorway and listened. Her eyes hurriedly scanned the ceiling as if she might see someone through the plaster and rafters. She could hear no sound but the soft stirring of the trees. She paused, hesitating, then slowly reached forward, opened a drawer, and pulled a torch from it. She was not afraid, not anymore; she would no longer be afraid.

She moved cautiously out of the kitchen, shining the torch through the hall, and then she crept her way up the staircase, feeling each wooden step give a little and groan as if she were slowly waking the house from its slumber. On two of the steps were spatters of blood, and there was a stain on the wall as if something bleeding had fallen against it. "Hello?" she called. "Hello?"

She moved along the creaking corridor, the darkness giving way in front of her as she walked with the torch and then closing up again after her. When she reached Alfie's door at the end she carefully opened it and shone the torchlight in, but the room was empty. She slowly made her way back, listening to the soft sound of her sandals along the wooden floor. Something skittered along a pipe and there was the judder of a shutter somewhere. For a moment she thought she saw a battered and bruised Button standing at the end of the hall with the tethered, gas-masked lamb on its wheels, but it was just shapes and shadows. The corridor was empty.

She stopped at the bottom of the attic stairs and looked up

into the darkness where the hatch had been lowered into place. She took a few steps up, tentatively shining the light against the heavy square lid.

"Hello!" she called again. "Are you there?"

She put the torch down and reached up to push at the hatch, but it wouldn't move.

"Are you in there? It's me!"

"Go away." His voice was weary and sounded muffled.

"No. Let me in."

"You have to leave."

"I don't want to. Let me in."

She pushed at the hatch again but it still wouldn't budge. She banged on it with the palm of her hand.

"Please. Heiden. I'm sorry."

She took a step back down the narrow stairs and waited. After a while she heard the heavy scrape of the ottoman being pulled back, and then the hatch was lifted. A torch shone down into her eyes, blinding her, and his voice came again.

"What do you want?"

He watched her climb up through the opening and he closed the hatch after her, then pushed the ottoman back across with his left hand, the other limp and bloody at his side.

"You're hurt."

"Yes."

He'd taken a shot through the palm of his hand. It had been stupid of him to raise it, as if a raised hand, a *stop*, could have halted a bullet. Now the bones were shattered, tendons ripped, a bloody mess that he couldn't even bring himself to look at. The pain, however, had numbed everything else, even his exhaustion. He shouldn't have come back to the house. And now she was here as well, and he was oddly thankful.

"You're covered in blood," she said. "You need something around your hand. Sit down."

He did, among a nest of jackets and coats on the floor, their damp smell, old and festering, lifting into the air. She left him there while she got a couple of tea towels from the kitchen, antiseptic from the bathroom, and a glass of water filled from the pump.

"Give me your hand," she said when she returned. He held it out for her, raising it a little to try to stem the blood that was still running down his arm.

He felt light-headed, exhausted now that he had sat down and the girl was with him.

She squatted next to him and rested his hand in her lap, and studied it. For a moment he thought she might be sick but she wasn't.

"It's a bit of a mess," he said.

"Sorry," she mumbled.

"Don't worry. I'll live."

"It's all right," she said. "It's just..."

The bullet had blown through everything and out the other side, so that even where the wound had swollen and closed up again, the torchlight still shone through and made the open flesh a translucent salmon pink, now awash with blood. His fingers were too painful to touch but he knew they had no life in them now, no longer his at all but just something he would lug around with him, dead and useless.

She wrapped one of the tea towels around his hand as a dressing and tied it firm. He gritted his teeth, clenching his jaw, and snorting breath. He sobbed a little as she did it and then breathed hard and furious again. She said nothing to him.

Once she was done, he wiped at his eyes and slumped back against the wall. Above him daylight was beginning to press at the window. If he couldn't sleep, then let him die. He thought about his grandfather, about standing as a child between his grandfather's legs, the old man showing Heiden how to hold the saw, bending it into an *S,* then pulling the bow across. *This is called the sweet spot,* his grandfather says. *Where the saw is straight. This is where you play the note.* With his grandfather guiding him he pulls the bow across and slowly bends and flexes the saw so that its note quivers in the air.

When he woke again, she was still there watching him. He had no idea how long he had slept, or if he had slept at all. The morning sun had moved around the house and now bathed the attic in a warm, fuggy light. The air was full of dust and glitter. He had no feeling in his hand but the pulsing throb of pain. He saw how dirty she was, covered in blood. She had grazed her knees and the heel of her hand. Her eyes were red and bloodshot. Beneath the dirt and grime, she looked so pale it was as if she were barely there at all. She was vanishing in the sunlight, fading into the wall behind her, and as his eyelids lowered again she completely disappeared.

He was swimming now and the sea glistened and prickled through his uniform, catching at his breath. Around him were Lehmann, Kappel, Diederich, Pfeiffer, and Theissen, their breaststrokes barely etching a ripple, their rucksacks clamped to their chests like limpets, their British ammunition boots tied and hanging from their necks, dragging beneath them through the water. They fanned out through the mist, their blacked-out faces half-submerged. Their breaths were taut and clipped as they pulled out a slow rhythm of strokes and passed through the scatterings of a torpedoed tug: torn scraps, empty oil cans, blasted bits of crate, and the body of a seaman, face down and bumping gently against the debris. He was hanging back, letting the others get further ahead. An occasional searchlight skated out across the sea, and one by one they slipped beneath the water as it passed over. Every time it happened, he swam off to the left, suddenly pulling fast and furious beneath the surface, edging closer and closer to one of them. Only when he came up the second or third time could he tell that it was Kappel who was nearest. He hung back some way behind him so as not to attract attention. Each of them had their eyes on the sky and the dark charcoal-lined coast: the lighthouse of Orford Ness in blackout, pointed skywards like a finger. Kappel let out a water-logged cough beneath the drone of a single plane flying over—one of "their boys," pregnant and sluggish with its load. Then the searchlight combed the sea again and Heiden ducked under and swam furiously. He caught hold of the man's ankle and Kappel turned, surprised, but Heiden's grip was tight. Beneath the water he pulled him down and got him in a lock. The man struggled, arms and legs thrashing, air bubbles foaming from his mouth. The jerk of an arm. The glint of a knife, dug in, and again, and again, blood gushing out in threads and coils and spiraling clouds that seemed to leave his body in trailing puffs. Heiden tugged the knife free from the man's stomach, air and bubbles and blood washing out with it, then he drove it into his windpipe and Kappel went limp. He hurriedly untangled himself from the man's arms and, leaving the body to sink down into the cold darkness under the weight of the man's rucksack, clothes, and waterlogged boots, he furiously kicked and swam his way up to—

His eyes opened and he gasped. The girl was staring at him. He felt at his throat and fumbled furiously in his pocket. They were still there, the seven tags. He rummaged through them, picking out Kappel's—yanked from the man's neck as he drifted down into the dark.

When he closed his eyes he could still see the body, looking down at it through the bloody water. Moored contact mines hung beneath them like strange sticklebacked moons.

They emerged from the water along the beach. Only he had glanced back but the boat and any sign of Kappel were gone. The others were already moving on. They did not speak or signal to each other. If any of them were bothered about Kappel's disappearance they didn't make it known. They would lose men on a mission like this; it would be a miracle if later the S-boat picked up any of them alive.

They spread out, silently, as they headed for the radar masts at Bawdsey Manor, and one by one he hunted them down as they made their way across the marsh and into the woods. Lehmann was stabbed through the back of his heart. Theissen through the windpipe. Only Pfeiffer had struggled, grabbing Heiden's wrist and smacking it against a tree so that the knife was dropped and then pulling out his gun, but not quick enough—Heiden had already fired.

He buried their bodies in the woods. Only with all of them dead could he walk out of the house a different man and no one would question his disappearance. If any of them had made it back to the S-boat or were captured and interrogated, Heiden would be hunted down. That was why he had waited for Diederich. He had purposely left the youngest in the group till last, as he knew that on his own he wouldn't carry out the Bawdsey Manor mission and, being a stickler for rules, would show at the rendezvous—Greyfriars—if Heiden waited long enough.

He had taken the dog tags from each of them before he buried them. He looked at them now in his hand. Seven dog tags, including those of Gruber and Bürckel. He had never meant them to mean anything to him, but now he held them tight.

★   ★   ★

You hunt or you are hunted, his grandfather said. But now he couldn't shake the image of Kappel's body falling away through the water, his blood seeping out of him as he went, like threads gently lowering him down. Or the surprise and fear in Pfeiffer's eyes as they had struggled in the wood, Pfeiffer trying to smash the knife out of his hand. And then Diederich, shot in the drive-way at Greyfriars, dressed as another man, but the same solemn and rugged face from the boat and the blown-out café at La Chapelle: brown eyes that were almost black, the chipped tooth shaped into a fang—a wolfman shot to the ground before he could make it to the door.

What had he done?

He held out his hand and offered them to her.

"You need to take these," he said.

"Are they all dead?"

He nodded. "They have families. They need to be told. You give them to someone in authority. Do you understand? Tell them that I killed them."

Gruber had been the easiest because he would have killed them if Heiden hadn't shot him. Bürckel—just because by that point what did it matter? Gruber had been right: Bürckel was a liability; he would have made mistakes. In the heat of war it boiled down to such trivialities. When all sense was gone and there was no reason-ing with oneself or even reason to reason, what did another bullet matter, what was another death? He had thought that in Norway almost every single day: if someone had shot him, he wouldn't have felt it; he felt quite sure that he was dead already.

He had broken into the work shed that first night, his flashlight sweeping hurriedly around the tools, looking for something with the smallest blade, something clean and precise. Hiding in the wood, within sight of Greyfriars, he had removed his jacket and his shirt and had heated the small hooked point of the carving knife in the flames of matches, dropping the used ones into his pockets. Stuffing his mouth with his handkerchief, he had driven the blade into his shoulder twice at right angles, so that the wound would heal puckered, like a bullet hole.

It was unlikely that an S-boat had been sent back to look for them. With the radar at Bawdsey Point still working they would assume the mission a failure, the six men lost. Over the following days they would scan the British reports for news about spies being caught or a possible beach landing, and hearing nothing they would be pleased, relieved. Hitler would lose no sleep over it and no one would play bells for them, yet there were bells ringing.

He opened his eyes. "They don't usually ring," said the girl. She was standing on tiptoes at the window. "Not even on Sundays anymore. It's because of the war. It must be a mistake."

"They're coming for me," he said.

"Who are?"

"Men," he said. "Your rescuers."

"From the roadblock?"

"No, not them. They're dead," he said.

She came down off her toes and looked at him. "You came on your own," she said. "You and these men." She opened her hand to the collection of tags. "There was never going to be an invasion, was there?"

"No . . . I don't know."

"Why did you lie? All the things you said and did . . ."

"I couldn't let you run away and tell anyone that I was here," he said. "I needed to keep you in the house. I needed you to need me and be scared enough not to try to run."

They had received intelligence that the British were clearing out a defense zone. A ten-mile stretch of the coast would be empty but for the army. They would evacuate the area, use some of it for testing, and with the area deserted it would provide Heiden with the time to prepare for his journey inland unhindered. He just needed to ensure that he got rid of the rest of the men on the mission. The house, Greyfriars, would be abandoned, as they all were, and here he would transform himself into George Pendell, a man who lived in the defense area and who they would need to let through. From there he would change himself again and again, until in the turmoil of war all trace of who he had once been was gone. He would escape the memories of Eva and Germany. He would rub his old self out and start anew.

But then there was the girl...standing here now in her torn dress, her grazed legs and muddied skin. She had grown so much in these last five days. He hadn't planned for her to be here, he said. "No one was supposed to be here."

"But I was," she said. "Why didn't you kill me?"

"I don't know," he said. "I should have."

"Then why didn't you? Aren't you brave enough?"

She stood over him now. She didn't seem at all scared.

"Did you do this?"

She held out her hand. Held between her finger and thumb was a matchstick man.

"Did you?"

He said nothing.

"You've seen him, haven't you," she said. "That's why you're here. That's why you think you can take his place. That's how you knew my name, isn't it? You've seen him. Where? Is he all right?"

"He was in Norway," he said.

"Norway? But how? Where is he now?"

"He's not coming back, Lydia. I'm sorry."

"How do you know? How do you know that?"

"He was one of the men in the store with me, hiding from the storm that I told you about. We took them hostage. A necessary part of war, I'm afraid. We were stuck with them for five days. He told me a little about you and your brother, about your mother, and the house. Greyfriars. He made it sound so beautiful, so...peaceful. War opens up so many new chances, opportunities to change yourself, be something different, better. We have to take them when they come. It's the only way to survive sometimes."

"But what happened to him?"

"The two men he was with died. I shot two others, my compatriots—two of the tags I gave you—but I couldn't shoot him. We were too similar, so similar, your father and I—and not just in how we look. We understood each other. I couldn't kill him, Lydia," he said. "So I sent him out into the snow. I'm sorry."

"Why? You let him go. Why are you sorry?"

He shook his head. "A man can't survive alone in that kind of cold. We were miles above the Arctic Circle. I sent him out to die, because I couldn't bring myself to shoot him. I'm a traitor, Lydia; a coward. I wasn't being compassionate to him. I was being weak."

She stared at him and then shook her head.

"No." She would not believe him, and yet tears welled in her eyes and ran down her cheeks.

"I am telling you the truth," he said. "Your father is gone."

"But you let him go?"

"He would not have survived a day out there in the cold on his own."

"But you spoke to him. You spoke to him?"

"Yes."

She stood there looking at him, her frame so small, so delicate. He suddenly wanted it not to be true, to somehow erase it all: Norway, France, the whole damn war, to take it all back to a moment with Eva, a moment in the park, her kiss on his lips, to hold it there forever, but he couldn't. Everything was decimated. Everything that he had been was in ruins.

"Yes," he said again. "I spoke to him. All he wanted was to go home, to you, to his family. And...perhaps that is why I let him go. I don't know. War is the most ridiculous thing." He laughed. "I don't even know what we were doing there, in Norway. We were there so you English couldn't be." Then he laughed again. "How ridiculous."

Outside, the bells were still ringing.

He had always wanted to see more of England. He had thought, foolishly perhaps, that he could take the girl and make her his: love her as if she were theirs, his and Eva's. They would drive along the country lanes in the Crossley Torquay Saloon with its sliding roof which they would stop to put down in the summer when the weather was warm. Up and down the Cotswold Hills they'd go. A dog called Baxter or thereabouts bouncing around in the back and barking at the cows. She would sit by him, the girl, and not be afraid. She would laugh at his jokes, the map in her lap, her fingers following the road; and they would stop in villages for tea, or a light lunch if they could find somewhere that served. *Tapioca pudding. Cauliflower cheese.* No one would think twice about him. How nice, a father and daughter out together on a summer's day.

"I could have been a good father," he said.

"But you're not my father. You never will be," she told him. "Whatever happens."

"I know that," he said. "I know."

He could feel hot tears welling in his eyes and before he knew how to stop it, he was sobbing. "I'm sorry," he said. "But I can't go back. I can't be part of that Germany. It is not *my* Germany anymore." He tried to swallow his sobs. "I had a love there..." he said. "I had a love... Wherever you go, you're always there waiting for yourself to arrive. You think you can let it all go but you can't. It clings. No matter what you do, how far you go, how many strips of skin you tear from yourself." He pounded at his head with his fist. "It's in there. In your head. Inside. And you can't get rid of it. Do you understand?" he said.

He looked at the girl. He could hear the bells tolling their urgency; men coming with dogs.

"I am at the end," he said. "I have to go."

"Go?" she said. "But go where?"

"I shall be caught now. They'll come through the trees, across the fields, along the roads. They'll find me and catch me... They'll hunt me like one of your foxes."

"So what do we do?" she said.

"What do we do?" he said. "Lydia, it's over. This... Don't you see?"

"But what about me? What shall *I* do?"

She turned her head and stepped away. She felt the tears running hot down her face.

"Come on," he said. "You're braver than that."

"I'm not!" she sobbed.

"You are. You need to find your mother, Lydia. Do you hear me?"

"Yes." She nodded. "I know."

She watched him take a deep breath. He was in pain. The blood from his hand had soaked through the dressing and she saw how badly she had put it on. It was already unraveling.

"You're bleeding again."

"It doesn't matter."

His shirt was drenched through with blood. There were stains down his trousers and pale, drying lines of it down his arms and over his face.

He was right. There would be men at Greyfriars soon, coming through the trees, just like she had known they would, although now it was him they were hunting. Was it his wail that she had heard that first night, before he came—the wail of a wounded beast, his cry in the night? Like a man turned into a bear. Like Bearskin, she thought.

His smile widened and she saw the pain in his eyes. A sharp intake of air as the twinge passed through him.

He said something but it was lost in the sound of vehicles pulling in through the gate, car doors opening and feet on the gravel. He closed his eyes for a moment, and when he opened them again, she saw for the first time that he was afraid.

He took the pistol from its holster around his waist. His hand was shaking, tremors quaking through his arm.

"I'm sorry about your father. I won't ask you to forgive me because you can't and you shouldn't. I shouldn't have left him. There is so much that I wish I could change."

She turned her back on him.

The men outside broke into the house. She heard the front door being rammed open. There was shouting; boots running across floorboards; doors being thrown open and barged through. Voices. *Lydia! Lydia!*

"I can't let them catch me," he said. "You know that, don't you?"

But what could they do to stop it? Even if they barricaded themselves in, they would have to come down from the attic at some point.

"When they see me with you they will kill me, they will think the worst," he said. "Men with faulty guns that don't fire properly. It won't be clean. It will be slow and painful. I'm a coward, Lydia. I couldn't bear it. And I don't want you to see that."

Already there were dogs barking. Men pounding up the stairs. Heavy boots and shouting, and someone yelling down the landing, *Lydia! Are you here?*

She didn't know whether to call out, to shout, *I'm here! I'm here!*

She looked at him. He wasn't moving. He still had the gun in his hand. She wanted to take it from him.

Lydia! Lydia Pendell!

She could hear them downstairs, going in and out of the bedrooms.

"You are a very brave and admirable young lady," he said. "Thank you for your company, for giving me some hope—no matter how short lived." There were tears streaming down his face now and she tried to get down on the floor with him, to wrap her arms around him, and bury her head in his chest, but he wouldn't let her.

"No. Get back," he said. "Stay back."

There was thumping at the attic hatch, men shouting, someone calling, *Lydia! Are you in there? Open the hatch!*

She tried to call out to them but something was stopping her.

"I'm sorry," he said under his breath.

"Why? What are you doing?"

"Will you open the hatch now and let them in?"

"No," she said. "I don't want to."

"Please, Lydia," he said. "Open the hatch."

She shook her head. She couldn't do it. She wouldn't.

He lifted the gun and pointed it at her just as he had that first night.

"Turn around, Lydia, and open the hatch."

She didn't move. She shook her head again.

"I can't."

"Please. Please, Lydia. That's an order, God damn it. Just do it." He released the safety lock.

She nodded. Then she turned her back on him, knowing in that moment that the shot would fire. And it did—the sudden concussion of a blast and a thrumming in her ears as if the world had been sucked from around her. She turned and shouted. He slumped slowly onto his side. A rush of sound flooded back, a deluge of voices—*Lydia! Lydia!*—banging and yelling from beneath the hatch. His body found an awkward resting place among her mother's fur coats, his eyes bright and wide and blue in the sunlight, empty but still fixed on her. His name was there on her lips but she couldn't say it; and then the room tipped her from it and she slipped into darkness.

THE DAY IS beautiful: fresh and sunny. After the rain every-thing looks invigorated, somehow brought back to life. She sits in Alfie's room looking down onto the garden. Butterflies flutter about the buddleia. The air is filled with the scent of damp grass and the smell of sun-dried corn washes in from across the fields.

She imagines her father walking out into the snow-bound forests of Norway, stepping through the snow and not once look-ing back. He would disappear into the trees and snow would fall from the branches, covering his tracks. She never thinks of him dying out there, just slowly, peacefully fading away until there is nothing left of him but mist. Perhaps that way, one day, he would be found. They would stand on the railway platform and, just as she had envisaged him vanishing into the fog of Norway, so, on his return, would he reappear out of the smoke and steam of a train engine as if from nothing more than a conjuror's trick.

In truth though her father would never return to her. But Alfie often did. She felt him with her sometimes, as if he was holding her safe in his smile. She'd found a tiny white feather that morning blowing down the hallway.

She hears a car pulling up outside and her mother going out to meet it.

"Come on, then!" her mother shouts. "The car's here! Let's go!"

Someone from the army was driving them to Wickham Market, where a friend of Bea's was putting them up.

She takes a matchbox from her pocket and slowly pushes it open. Inside lies the matchstick man with his charred and blackened head. She rests him against the window; a memento that she has been there, or a sign if her father comes back while they are gone, even in his spirit—that he should wait for them. She puts the dog tags Heiden had given her into the box, counting them in one by one. She'll have to hand them to someone official, but not yet.

In time, of course, there would be school again, games, squabbling, laughter. They'd get new chickens, grow new vegetables, perhaps get another rabbit from Heathcote Farm, just like Jeremiah. They would open up Shingle Street and she would walk along it, remembering the line of shells leading down to the shore and the house filled with pebbles, Alfie standing on the slope watching out for boats on the horizon or maybe the back of a submarine surfacing like a whale. Her mother would tell her to pull her socks up, or do up the buckles on her sandals. There would be a normality of sorts, order restored; the days would come and go. She would think about the man called Heiden less and less until he became nothing but a story that was told, if not by her then someone else: the day the German came.

Across the lawn, she spots something she's never seen in the garden before: a white parakeet. It sits on the branch of a tree preening itself, and only when the car engine starts and her mother calls—*Lydia, we're waiting*—does it open its wings and lift up into the sky.

She gets up off the bed and, taking a final glance around the room—at the wooden soldier, the cricket bat and ball, the butterflies trapped in their frame—she leaves and quietly closes Alfie's door behind her. Her hand guides her down the banisters as she makes her way down the stairs, the matchbox held safe in her other hand. The house is dark but peaceful; a cool breeze passing through it, its breath blowing around her ankles. Through the door she sees Button looking back through the car window for her and her mother standing by the open door. She stops for a moment in the doorway to watch the bird passing overhead, and the afternoon is warm and bright as Lydia steps out into the sun.

ACKNOWLEDGMENTS

I'd like to take the opportunity to acknowledge a few people without whom you would not be reading this and who have given me invaluable help, advice, and support in the production of this book and my journey to this point.

Firstly, I would like to thank my editor, Sarah Murphy, for her boundless enthusiasm and, in particular, for taking such a big gamble on such a little me. Also, the rest of the team at Little, Brown, who have welcomed me into their publishing family, as well as Catherine Cooker, my copyeditor, for her eagle eyes and for teaching me the difference between "fringe" and "bangs," and everyone else involved in the production of this book (in particular Ben Allen for guiding the book so painlessly through to publication, and Lauren Harms for the fabulous cover design). I'd also like to thank everyone at Simon & Schuster UK—most importantly my UK editor, Jessica Leeke—and my US and UK agents, PJ Mark and Will Francis, both at Janklow & Nesbit. Terry Chapman, author and senior historian at the Imperial War Museum, London, and Adam Dighton at the University of Salford for hunting out my factual blunders and setting me straight on a few things! Also Sophie Hardach for generously reading it through with her enthusiastic German eye. Thanks also to the staff of the British Library and the Imperial War Museum for providing access to unpublished documents and countless fascinating books. My dedicated Bath Spa alumni workshop group—Sam, Jenni, Karen, Becky, Pam, and Anthea—need special mention for never ceasing to push me, and whose advice, support, encouragement, and valuable criticism helped shape the story into what it has become. The end result? Not only a better novel than I ever could have produced without them, but also a tougher skin. Thanks also to the staff at Bath Spa University for their prior guidance whilst I studied for my master's there. The most special and heartfelt thanks, of course, go to my parents for their unwavering love, belief, and patience, and for never doubting me, even when I doubted myself. My brother, Jonathan, too, and sister-in-law, Helen, for their endless support and enthusiasm, for being my get-out-of-London retreat, and for giving me the two most adorable nephews a writer could want, William and Henry, who bring me joy every minute I see them and keep my feet firmly on the ground. Finally, to everyone else—friends and family too many to mention—who have supported, loved, enthused, challenged, and occasionally propped me up over the years. Thank you.

I should also like to take this opportunity to point out that whilst some of the minor characters who appear in this book are based on historical figures, and many of the locations described exist, it is important to stress that the story is a fiction and that the portraits of the characters that appear in it are fictional, as are some of the events and places, including the village of Willemsley. Any factual inconsistences are my own, but some may be deliberate wanderings from the truth put into play for the benefit of the story.

ABOUT THE AUTHOR

Jason Hewitt was born in Oxford and lives in London. He has a bachelor of arts degree in history and English from the University of Winchester and a master of arts with distinction in creative writing from Bath Spa University. Between his degrees he spent a number of years working in a bookshop in Oxford before moving into the publishing industry, where he worked primarily as a marketing manager for a number of professional and academic publishers. He is also a playwright and actor. *The Dynamite Room* is his first novel.